BRAVE
LIGHTNING

A K ROBBINS

Author's photo by Brent Darnell
Front Cover design by Sapizol
Back Cover Design by Tudor Maier

Reviews

**Read what people are saying about
Brave Lightning**

Brava! I have a movie of her playing in my head. More, more please. Brava!

Carla Fraser DeVries

"WOW!" Best seller for sure. Brava is a very lucky lady to have you on her side!

Boo Newell

Totally hooked on Brava. Don't want to see my appointments.

Karen Ellis, DVM

Dedicated to

My husband, Brent Darnell. I'd done it again; gotten in over my head when Brent leaned in close and whispered, "You can do more than you think you can." Thanks for being right about that, Babe.

My mom, who is the inspiration for Eugenia. Thanks for the laughs Mom.

The members of my tribe, both family and friends, who think I'm weird and love me anyway.

In Memory of

My dad who made everyone's day brighter even when his were difficult.

Sheila and Sifu. I hope you like the way I let you live. Thanks for staying close.

My J and G. Thanks for the protection and guidance. I'll remember you on my tattoo.

Chapter 1

We were departing for Turkey in an hour when I got the call. My husband was going on a business trip, but it was much more personal for me. As a kid, I had learned that Istanbul was a "city on two continents" and visiting that exotic place intrigued me. I hadn't even purchased trip insurance because I'd told myself "nothing in the world would keep me from going on this trip." Famous last words.

While in the Atlanta airport I got a call from our daughter Sahara, who was twenty-one weeks pregnant with her second child. She'd gone into labor and was in danger of losing the baby. So I kissed Kevin goodbye at our gate and changed concourses right in the middle of the airport. When I switched my flight from Istanbul, Turkey to Orange County, California, I had the most ridiculous thought—"do I have the right clothes?" Like that mattered. Little did I know that was just the beginning.

I'd gone directly to the hospital from the airport, and when I saw my son-in-law's face, I knew. Sahara had lost the baby as well as a lot of blood, so they were keeping her for a few days. I hadn't heard from Kevin to see if he'd arrived safely and had tried calling him a dozen times but had only gotten voice mail. While in the hospital,

I experienced that herky-jerky sense of time where five minutes seemed like five hours, and then an entire day had elapsed in a moment.

We were finally able to take Sahara home on Thursday around noon and had just pulled up at the kids' apartment. Irvin was carrying our bags and I was supporting Sahara, who was still weak from physical trauma and grief. I heard a hawk screech overhead and looked up but couldn't see it.

Of course, I'd held myself together for the kids, but now all I wanted was to get in a hot shower and cry. The stink of fear and travel and the hospital clung to my hair and clothes. I was a bundle of emotions; relief that Sahara was OK, sadness at our loss, worry over Kevin, and bitterness about losing the trip of a lifetime.

Amidst the swirling emotions, I was aware of my phone ringing. Digging through my purse I grabbed it and saw that it was Kevin. I only now realized that it had been three full days since I'd left him in the Atlanta airport.

My feelings had alternated between fury that he hadn't called and worry that he'd been kidnapped by Muslim extremists. But Sahara's needs were more immediate, so I hadn't dwelt on it.

"Are you OK?" The conflicting mix of anger and fear added an edge to my voice I couldn't disguise.

We got inside the door and Irvin took hold of Sahara's arm and led her toward the living room. I hung back in the foyer and realized I was shaking from nerves, so I leaned against the doorjamb to steady myself.

"Of course," he said sounding annoyed. "The job is brutal, that's all. It's taking a lot out of me. I'm working eighteen hour days and –"

Hurt that he hadn't asked about our daughter, I interrupted, "Sahara is going to be fine but she lost a lot of blood. She's devastated. The baby was another little girl."

"Oh God, Brava I'm sorry. I meant to ask about her right away but my work has been so demanding, and the jet lag horrible. I feel so disoriented."

I could relate to the disorientation, but for different reasons. Annoyance turned to regret that I wasn't with him. "What's it like there?" I asked.

"The culture is unimaginable, and I've never seen people so dedicated. There are hundreds of mosques here; one on every corner it seems, and each one has a balcony where a crier calls out to the Muslims five times each day. They all stop their worldly tasks and kneel down to pray."

It sounds like he's quoting from some tour brochure extolling the beguiling sights and sounds of exotic Istanbul.

"It's surreal being here," he continued, "As much as I can't imagine stopping everything five times a day when I am in the US, I admit I'm drawn to it and have been secretly praying with them. I guess this all sounds a little strange, but Brava, the truth is for the first time in my life, I feel so … peaceful."

I can't even get him to take a break for a quickie if I dance around him naked, and now he's taking prayer breaks? Anger flared in me.

"I've got to go, Sahara needs me," I lied. I hung up so fast I forgot to ask when we'd talk again. With the added time difference on the west coast, I was having trouble figuring when I could reach him.

"Mom, how's Dad?" Sahara questioned. I was certain she noticed the brevity of the call.

"He asked about you, and he's just overworked." It wasn't exactly a lie. "You know how it is when he's on these projects. They want to suck every bit of knowledge out of him. He's working eighteen-hour days but seems to be settling into the culture just fine."

A little too fine if you ask me.

I quickly changed the subject. "I'm going to stay with you until Saturday and then your Aunt Olivia will come out for a while if you'd like."

Sahara smiled. It was the first time I'd seen her smile in three days. She has ebony hair like her dad, and got the blue eyes and ivory skin from my red-headed side of the family. Her lips are naturally a deep rose and the contrast between her hair, skin and lips make her beauty unique. When she smiles, it's as if I can see the face of God.

"Oh, LaLa will make me feel better. I'd love for her to come."

LaLa is my sister. When Sahara was little, she couldn't say "Aunt Olivia," so it came out LaLa. By the time my second daughter came along, it had just become Liv's name. There was never a more fitting nickname. Olivia is like a melody. I felt a little jealous at my daughter's delight in my sister's visit, but it was understandable. Olivia has a sunny disposition and sense of fun that everyone loves.

She was even a delightful child. I, on the other hand, was the "peculiar" one. I could always sense when something was "off," as if I felt vibrations in the airwaves or something. It seemed obvious to me, but no one else could feel it. They called me "too serious and too sensitive". I was especially sensitive to animals; but not so much with people. I once beat up a neighbor boy because he slapped his dog in the face. When my dad made me apologize to the brat's mom, I spit out, "I'm not sorry. I think it's only fair he got as good as he gave."

I watched as Irvin got Sahara a cup of tea and a blanket and settled her on the sofa. He kissed the top of her head and whispered something I couldn't hear, but I saw the look that passed between them. I felt like an intruder on their intimacy, and I missed Kevin with a physical ache. We had that same ability to communicate volumes with a look or a touch. Sometimes, he'd walk out of the room and return with a cup of coffee or a glass of wine for me, and I'd ask "Did I say that out loud?"

Now I was sorry I had hung up prematurely. I stepped out of the room and called him back. I got voice mail again and was instantly pissed. We'd just spoken a moment ago so how could he be unavailable now? He always answered his phone when he was out of the country. It kept us connected, and I'd have thought he'd be even more diligent given the circumstances with our daughter. Doubt and fear began to boil up in my gut, and I needed a good strong drink to squelch it.

Irvin left to pick up Riley, their two-year-old, who had been staying with a friend. I showered and screamed into my washcloth as I finally had the meltdown that I so badly needed. I washed my hair with the apple-scented shampoo that smelled of my daughter and pictured the stink of these last few days swirling down the drain with the suds. I wasn't sure how much the shower and meltdown helped, but at least I smelled good. I left my red hair wet and it curled up naturally in the dry air. I poured myself a whiskey and felt it burn in my belly as I took deep breaths to relax.

When Riley got home, she squealed in sheer delight to see her mom and me and was blissfully unaware of the devastation of her lost sibling. It was impossible to brood with her beauty and energy filling up the space. She looked so much like Sahara did as a child. We went for walks and collected leaves. I heard the hawk again but still couldn't see it. It was disconcerting. I remembered playing with my girls in this way and felt a sense of awe at the cycle of life.

I stayed a week, bouncing back and forth between emotions like a tennis ball. On the one hand, I felt delight in my granddaughter. And on the other, I felt escalating panic over my AWOL husband. I tried calling dozens of times, but I always got his voicemail. I emailed over and over and continually checked my phone for messages from him.

As the time for my departure neared, I was genuinely relieved to be going home. It's fitting that young people have two-year-olds. They have the energy for it. And the turmoil of mixed emotions had wrung me out completely. I was grateful to have seen Irvin treat Sahara so well. I suspected that their love ran deep and during this painful time I saw a side of him that touched me. He cared for her so tenderly, I knew he'd be there for my girl.

But I was getting more and more upset about the distance that had grown between Kevin and me. I didn't understand what was happening, but I knew in my heart that something was very wrong. In the past when he was on these trips, he was just as busy but we always found time to talk; if even for a quick "I love you." We'd not spoken at all in over a week, and his apparent unconcern about Sahara was causing a rift.

On the flight back to Atlanta, I was thinking about the fact that my children were on the opposite side of the continent and my husband on the other side of the world. Yet I was relieved to be going home. I was desperate to devote my energy to finding Kevin and oddly looking forward to the rhythm of my days.

I love my job and most of all I love my time with my nephew, Gene. In fact, I am closer to him than I am even to my own girls, much to my regret regarding the girls, and much to my delight regarding Gene. He is more like me than Olivia. She frequently says, "He should have been yours." Our biggest similarity is that Gene and I are both introverted; something Liv thinks is a character defect that we should go to therapy to "get over."

Also, we share a common passion. I've been studying martial arts for years, and Gene is taking Kung Fu with me. Even our instructor who we call "Sifu" remarks that he can't believe Gene isn't my son.

"He even makes some of the exact same mistakes you did."

My girls are girly girls and despite my efforts to coerce them into martial arts, they never took an interest. Sahara quit Kung Fu because she said the uniforms, "make me look poochy." I thought Sifu's head was going to pop off his shoulders when she told him that.

I wondered what home meant to me these days. I had grown up in Pennsylvania. Olivia first moved to Atlanta with her doctor husband, Brian. When Kevin had trouble finding work as an engineer up north, we followed, and Brian recommended me for my job.

Almost immediately, Atlanta felt like home. Even now as I flew into the city and saw the beautiful gold dome of the capitol building I felt tears prick my eyelids. Scotland is the only other place that feels that way. The first time I went there with Kevin, I felt at home. I remember saying to him "They look like me." He smiled at me with a twinkle in his eye and answered, "I think you look like them."

Then he sang The Beach Boys, Good Vibrations to me. It was our song. He always sang the part "I love the colorful clothes she wears, and the way the sunlight plays upon her hair." Together we'd sing, "I'm picking up good vibrations. She's giving me excitations." He said he carried that song in his heart whenever he was away from me. When we put our girls to bed, we wished them "good vibrations" like other people said "sleep tight."

Chapter 2

My worry over Kevin became near hysteria once I'd arrived home and was undistracted by the kids, I was frantic to reach him and called and emailed dozens of times. I was wondering how to contact the embassy in Istanbul when it occurred to me to call Joan, his secretary and see what she knew. Joan had been Kevin's assistant for many years, and he trusted her completely so I knew I could too.

I was on hold for a long time, and as I waited for her to answer, I stood in front of the bookshelf that was jammed with well-worn travel guides and family photos. My gaze wandered to a wedding photo of Kevin and me, and I felt sick. My favorite was a photo of Riley hugging a stuffed Beagle that I had sent her.

I smiled despite my mood and thought, "After I figure out what's up with Kevin, I'll call to check on Sahara."

Sahara and Irvin had moved to California a few years ago to further their careers. About a year ago, to my great regret, my youngest daughter, Louise Marie, or Louma as she called herself, had abruptly quit college and followed her sister to California.

I was especially sad that I hadn't gotten to see Louma, who was on vacation in Mexico with friends. Louma is the funnier one of my girls. I never realized how she lightened any situation with her humor. Oh, I could certainly have used some of that in California. The girls were close, and she'd called often to check on Sahara who reassured her that she'd need her more after Olivia and I had left.

When Joan finally came on the line, I began babbling about my not being able to reach Kevin, calling his mobile, his being kidnapped, or left dead in a ditch. I heard my voice rising with each new disaster until I realized she was utterly silent.

"Oh God, Joan you know something and you're not telling me. Is Kevin hurt?" I was nearly screaming now.

"No," she interrupted, and then stopped, silent again.

"Joan, just tell me what's wrong. Nothing could be worse than what I am making up in my head. How long has it been since you heard from him?"

"Uh, Brava, uh that's just it, I heard from him an hour ago. I've been talking to him regularly."

Silence.

"I see. I guess it's just me he doesn't want to talk to," I said.

Joan answered weakly. "Brava, I'm sure there's some explanation." Her words trailed off, and I'm not sure who wanted off the phone more.

"Yea, I'm sure there is. I'm just not sure I like it."

In the coming weeks, I told no one about the distance between Kevin and me, not even the girls. When people asked about him, I gave vague answers like, "His trip has been extended", or "I'm not sure when he'll be back." After some time, it stopped their questions, but I'm certain it did little to assuage their suspicions. Gene probably figured it all out but didn't say anything. In fact, Gene probably had an app that tracked Kevin's movements with a GPS. I found myself constantly anxious, worried about money, uncertain about my future, and gaining weight at an alarming rate.

When I was presented with the divorce papers a few months later, I wasn't shocked. I had gotten into a routine without him. It wasn't comfortable, but it had grown familiar. Kevin had stayed in Istanbul, converted to Islam and quietly divorced me through the mail.

Seriously, who does that happen to?

His lawyer included a letter with the papers and suggested I get an attorney of my own. When I read them over, I saw that Kevin had cashed only a small amount from his retirement and had signed over everything else to me. I didn't cry, I didn't get an attorney, and I didn't allow myself to feel anything. I signed the papers with my maiden name Brava Falcone, dropping the hyphenated Glenn I'd used for twenty-six years. I took care of all the legalities that very day, and it was done. The therapy came later.

Chapter 3

Waltzing up to the clinic with Gene in tow, I saw Mom dressed in turquoise shorts and a pink and yellow T-shirt. Mom is eighty-something, cute, petite, dark-haired and looks like she's about sixty-something. But she has a terrible sense of fashion. Liv inherited Mom's cute size four body and I, unfortunately, inherited her fashion sense. Gene towers over Mom. He looked so grown up; almost like a man and nearly six feet tall in his cargo shorts and T-shirt with his size thirteen feet. We tease him about his shoes. He even laughs as he admits, "Oh, I'm a girl about my shoes." Today they were Vann's. It's that, or Nike or a few other brands he favors.

I've worked for twenty years as a receptionist for two doctors. Dr. Milton Jackson is an old-fashioned medical doctor who's a dinosaur in this age of specialists. He truly cares for his patients and their families. Dr. Sheila Berry is a gifted psychologist and my best friend. Mom has been a patient of Dr. Jack's for all the years since she and Dad moved to Atlanta. I've always loved my job, but even more so lately. It's easier to avoid my own problems when I have other people's as a comparison. That way I can convince myself I don't have it so bad.

Mom uses the clinic in much the same way Liv goes to the country club. They both get their social needs met, but Mom's venue is cheaper. Her visits are more frequent lately, and I suspect it's to check on me. I think she's had a harder time dealing with my divorce than I did. On a recent trip to Sicily to cheer me up, Mom told our extended family that Kevin was dead. I was having a hard time understanding Mom's Sicilian dialect, but Liv got it. I recalled the conversation.

"What did she say?" I'd asked Liv. "Tell me."

She'd paused, took a deep breath and answered. "She said you were married to a "brutta," for twenty-six years but wouldn't leave him because you didn't believe in divorce and then he died."

"Are you kidding me? She told them Kevin was a brute, and now he's dead?"

"Yea, Brava. I guess the fact that he went to Turkey, became a Muslim and divorced you through the mail just doesn't translate."

"Hey Mom, what are you doing here?" I smiled. I went around the desk and hugged them both. Mom smelled good as usual. On a vacation to the Bahamas a million years ago she had gone to one of those places where you can create your own personal fragrance. Every piece of her clothing is permeated with the aroma. It has some lavender, vanilla and something very spicy. It suits her.

She began pulling baskets of cherries out of a ragged green grocery bag and laying them in a line on top of my desk. For a moment, I wondered if the sack was like a clown car and cherries were going to keep on coming and coming.

"Publix had cherries buy one get one free so I bought one for you, Sheila and Dr. Jackson. Now put them in the refrigerator and write a note so you don't forget to give them to them," Mom continued.

"OK, I will. Thanks, Mom."

"Write a note right now while I'm watching you. I don't want those doctors going home without their cherries."

"That would be a tragedy, the doctors leaving without their cherries," I said as I wrote the note while she watched. Gene rolled his eyes and grinned.

Missing the sexual innuendo she hefted her bag back onto the counter digging inside for something else. Mom's bags are epic. She has a method unbeknownst to us of choosing them. It isn't based on fashion, color or chronology. She hauls around the fabric sacks despite the fact that my dad buys her designer purses for every special occasion. Each time she gets one she "oohs" and "aaahs" and puts it in her closet saying, "I don't want that to get ruined. I'm keeping it for good."

This one was lime green with white letters that said, "Do your bowels a favor. Get a colonoscopy."

"Nice bag Mom; where'd you get it?" She missed the sarcasm.

"At the senior extravaganza. I went back twice and got two. I tried to give one to your sister, but she said she wouldn't use it even to carry her groceries."

Gene said, "I wouldn't go with her if she did carry it."

"But you're with Grammy and she has it," I replied.

""It's Grammy. She cracks me up. What can I say?"

"Well, no matter," she said rummaging through her bag. "Here is an educational, informative article that I want you to show Dr. Jack."

Dr. Milton Jackson is a big man with dark skin and a booming voice. He has huge hands and a resonant laugh. He is the gentlest man I've ever met and is a practicing Buddhist. Mom thinks he's achieved sainthood. I wonder if Buddhists have saints but that's of no importance to Mom.

"Ask him if he thinks it will help the arthritis in my fingers."

Finally finding what she was looking for, she pulled out one of those scandal rags you see at grocery store checkout counters; the ones that have true stories of alien abductions and Sasquatch sightings.

She continued talking. "It's a remedy from South America or India or somewhere foreign. It's the Goni fruit, and it's supposed to work miracles on everything. Mrs. Leighton, three trailers down can get me a good deal on it. You know, her son is the world traveler that married that Columbian girl. She was cute when they got married, but now that she's got four kids to him, she has a fat ass."

That stung. I thought of my ever-widening ass. Mom and Liv eat like lumberjacks and remain a size four. Lately, I'd noticed that my pants had become capris, so either my pants had gotten shorter or my ass had gotten wider.

She handed me the magazine. In addition to the fact that it was a scandal rag, the "article" was actually a paid advertisement. I pointed that out and asked her if she had confused it with the PDR (physician's desk reference).

Handing it back to her, I said, "I believe I'll skip showing this to Dr. Jack." I could just hear his laugh. It sounds like cello music. He loves my mom and seems amused by her antics.

"Perhaps I'll show it to him after all," I said grabbing for the magazine. She laughed, and I did too.

"Where are you two off to now?" I asked.

"I'm helping Grammy with a computer problem."

Mom interjected. "When I try to get on my computer that little blue circle keeps going around and around and around."

Gene grinned behind her back. As they left, she reminded me to tell the doctors about their cherries.

They were hardly out the door before I called Olivia.

"So Miss Hoity Toit you wouldn't carry the lime green colonoscopy bag?"

I told her about the cherries and the educational, informative article, and we got to laughing so hard I was afraid I was going to pee my pants at the front desk. The Falcone girls aren't known for their strong bladders.

"I gotta go. I'm gonna pee." And I rang off already running to the bathroom. Sheila just laughed as she viewed my race to the bathroom.

Chapter 4

My muscles ached with fatigue after such a long day at work. Driving home at 7:30, I could barely focus enough to stay between the lines when I suddenly found myself in the grip of a terrible spring thunderstorm. It had been sunny and clear when I left the office and it seemed weird that the storm arose so abruptly.

Shit. I just want to get home. I was exhausted and overwhelmed that I had to be back at work so soon. *If I can just make it home to my bed and close my eyes for a few hours, I'll be OK.*

The torrential rain made the patch of road increasingly treacherous, and it rendered my wipers nearly useless. My instincts told me to pull under a bridge and wait it out, but my desire to get home won out. A clap of thunder resounded and a brilliant flash of lightning hit the road directly in front of me. It shook the ground so violently I was sure it would crack the asphalt. I felt the electricity raise the hairs on the back of my neck and arms. The air smelled oddly like sulphur. I heard myself screaming, "I'm hurt! I'm hurt! I'm hurt!" over and over until I realized that there was no one to hear me, and I was still driving.

"So I must be OK." I thought.

Shaking from the experience, I pulled over to get my wits. I checked my body scanning all my limbs and decided that I wasn't in fact hurt, just shook up so I pulled back onto the road and continued with a racing heart.

Almost as soon as it had begun, it stopped. I drove out of the rain and thunder into cloudy skies painted pink and orange. I drove more slowly to watch as the orange globe of the sun dipped behind the darkened hillside. A hawk, silhouetted by the sun dove into a field and came up clutching a squirrel, still squealing, in its talons. I crossed myself.

I was grateful to be home safe and sound, but I was still feeling a little rattled. I grabbed for a glass of wine to settle my nerves and gulped rather than sipped it. Realizing that it had quickly gone to my head because I hadn't eaten since noon, I looked in the fridge for something to throw together. The coffers were low. I found the remains of a loaf of bread with a slice and the crust and made a tomato sandwich. I wolfed it greedily and collapsed into bed already dreading my encounter with Cow Patty tomorrow.

Cow Patty's real name is Camilla Patti, and she has a therapy appointment with Sheila ever Friday. She wears so much make-up that the first time I saw her I asked if she was in "The Atlanta Debs." It's a play about rich girls in Atlanta and done at a theater down the street. I guess that started us out on the wrong foot. She always wears a scowl on her face like she smells a bad odor. And, in fact, I think she does; her perfume. She must take a bath in it. It's one of those old-fashioned Estee Lauder perfumes that old women think are elegant.

She has more money than God but holds her clothes together with safety pins. She is the most distasteful person I have ever known. I can't see that she is improving with therapy either. She takes a jab at me every single week, and each week when she leaves, I ask Sheila, "What did she talk about? She's as mean as ever. Do you know what she said to me today?"

Sheila is about my age (*fifty-something is all I'll own up to*) with silver hair cut in a stylish A- line. She wears brightly colored clothes in shades of red, turquoise and orange. She used to be a nun, Sister Mary Gervace, and I think she wants to dress as differently from that as possible. She wears big stone cabochon rings, jangling bracelets and dangling earrings. But as different as she looks from a nun, she still has a beatific smile and the most integrity of anyone I've ever known.

So each time I rant about Cow Patty, Sheila smiles that nun smile. We both know she'll never tell me anything. But it is a routine we have, practiced and perfect in its familiarity. Something to be counted on in a world where too many things change.

I pictured Cow Patty lying in bed beside her ancient Bassett Hound with her hair in curlers and a green mask smeared on her face. I just knew she was planning her meanness for the next day. I hate that she comes on Friday. Everyone else loves Fridays for the obvious reason and that bitch robs my joy.

Last week she came in complaining about her bad complexion. It really is bad. She has old acne scars, and I think that's the reason she wears so much make-up, but it only accentuates her new pimples. I really wanted to ignore her, but I didn't want to appear rude. So I said, "Yea, who thought we'd be dealing with breakouts after puberty?"

She responded with, "Yeah, I felt really bad about my face 'til I saw that pimple on your chin." I was so stunned I put my nose back in my charts and fumed.

Why can I never come up with a witty little quip like a character in a Dean Koontz novel? They do it when their life is in danger, and I can't manage a retort even after I've practiced in the mirror.

I slept poorly and dreamed that a hawk was standing over my bed screeching at me over and over. It stretched out its wings and flapped them until a great wind blew.

Chapter 5

I was startled awake by the sound of the alarm. I reached and slapped but missed the snooze button. The alarm was screaming so I flung my arm again to silence the shrieking, and I heard the lamp crash to the floor with a clang of metal on hardwood.

I can't deal with this before coffee. Hell, I can't even make coffee before coffee.

I seriously considered hitting the snooze and going back to sleep, or leaving the lamp on the floor until I'd had at least two cups of coffee, but I couldn't let it lie, so I dragged myself out of bed.

At least it's not ceramic.

When I reached for it, I missed.

I really must still be asleep.

I reached again. Again my hand came up empty. Feeling a little disoriented, I tried a third time to get hold of the lamp. This time, I watched in horror as it clearly slid out of my reach, skittered across the floor and wedged in the corner. Nausea welled up inside of me. I turned my back to it, desperately trying to convince myself that it was pre-coffee hallucinations.

I went to the bathroom and everything seemed okay until I tried to flush. I reached to press the lever and the toilet flushed while my hand was still hovering over it. I'd kept the light off, but I heard the toilet flushing over and over and could picture the water circling the bowl. The toilet paper began unrolling at a furious pace. I felt dizzy.

I slinked to the kitchen to get my coffee. I got hold of my favorite cup without incident until I put it on the coffeemaker. The coffeemaker jumped around on the counter like a bucking bronco. I was really freaking out now and desperately needed coffee, so after shoving my cup into place I lunged and pushed the button. Fortunately, that worked so I snatched my cup, inhaling the aroma, and took my coffee back to bed. I silently thanked Kevin for the extravagant coffeemaker that only required a button push.

Averting my eyes from the lamp in the corner I thought, "If I don't look at it, it isn't there." I had a dog as a child that thought if he got his head under a blanket we couldn't see him.

Same logic applied here.

After finishing my coffee, I had nearly convinced myself that nothing weird had happened. I went for the second cup, and the dining table did a little dance as I passed. Picture frames jiggled as I walked by them. It was as if my furniture had come alive in the night. I thought of the play, "Beauty and The Beast," that Liv and I had taken all the kids to. I recalled the dancing, talking teacup and wondered what awaited me in the kitchen.

The coffeemaker tried to get away from me again. I repeated the button lunge and seriously considered adding some whiskey to my coffee. I took it back to bed and crawled under the covers with my knees hugged to my chest and the cup held tightly between both hands as I sipped; too afraid to move very much.

After the second cup, I'd had sufficient coffee that I could no longer convince myself that this was a hallucination. I gingerly got out of bed and poked it. Nothing happened.

One more cup, I just need one more cup and everything will be OK, I lied to myself. I reached for my cell phone to check the weather and it hopped away from me and fell between the nightstand and the side of the bed, beyond where I could reach it easily.

So much for that.

Drinking my third cup in the kitchen, I attempted to unload the dishwasher and each time I grabbed for the silverware it jumped away from me. I reached for a plate and it rolled from my hand. Tears leaked, then flowed from my eyes as I grabbed for items. The more I snatched and grabbed, the more things flew out of my reach. Glasses and plates fell to the floor and smashed. The bottle of wine from last night crashed onto the floor spilling its red liquid like a puddle of blood at my feet. Its sweet smell made me nauseous, and I gagged.

I was sobbing at this point. I don't know what made me think of rubber gloves, but I grabbed them from under the sink. I was more desperate than hopeful, but they seemed to help.

I stood very still amidst the mess crying to myself. I didn't know what was happening. I felt overwhelming anxiety and a dizzy, nauseating feeling in my stomach. I didn't know what to do next, but I knew I couldn't go to work.

I had to call the doctors, but how would I explain my reason for missing work?

Hi Dr. Jack, I can't come into work today because I woke up this morning and lo and behold I've turned into a tornado.

I never, ever call in sick and even if I were sick, I'd go see Dr. Jack. I was frantic to let the docs know I couldn't be at work, but I'm not a good liar. And the truth would never do. It finally came to me. I'd tell them I broke a crown and needed to see the dentist before the weekend. I made that call first, leaving the message on the machine. I had momentary concern for Dr. Jack and Sheila and worried how they would get through a busy day without me, but shoved the thought away. I had more urgent things to handle.

I was afraid to move, and so I remained frozen in the center of the kitchen, looking at the devastation, thinking. I decided I needed to call Gene. Gene is absolutely brilliant. And I don't think that just because I'm his aunt. He is. He's been tested.

I thought, "If anyone can figure this out, it's Gene."

Wearing my rubber gloves, I was able to get my phone from between the bed and nightstand without incident. Texting was another matter. *Who knew you couldn't text wearing rubber gloves?* I managed to find my stylus in the desk drawer and used it.

I texted him, fumbling with the stylus and gloves. "Any tests you can't miss today?"

"No why?"

I knew Gene would worry about me if I didn't reassure him, especially when I told him that I was getting him out of school.

"I'm OK. Need your help. You're the only one that can help. Coming to get you."

"Should I worry? Are you sure you are ok?"

"No worries just something very weird. Be there in ten minutes."

When I got to the school, Gene was waiting by the curb. It seemed like just yesterday he was so little that when I hugged him I tucked his head under my chin and smelled his hair. Until recently, he still smelled of baby shampoo and little boy. But since the growth spurt he smells of dandruff shampoo, shaving cream and some manly cologne. As I pulled up to the curb, I alternated between wishing he were still that little boy and feeling incredibly glad he wasn't, because today I hoped he'd be my savior.

Despite my reassurances to the contrary, I could tell he was worried when he got in the car. And when he saw the heavy rubber gloves up to my elbows, his face went from worried to puzzled and back to worried again.

"Brava, you're scaring me. What's going on? I don't think you're wearing rubber gloves as a cute accessory. I pray this is a plumbing problem."

"Not plumbing Gene. I have no idea what is going on, but when we get home, you'll see. Then you'll figure it out. But for these few minutes just talk to me about something mundane."

We rode home in silence.

I followed Gene into my kitchen. He braked hard, and I smacked into his back. "What the fuck?"

I didn't correct his language because this situation called for "What the fuck?" Besides, my niece and nephew never censor with me. They know that different rules apply with me than with their parents.

"Did someone break in? Who did this?"

"I did Gene, and that's the problem."

He peppered me with questions. "Are you OK? You never even make a mess, what happened?" He was really getting anxious now.

I pulled off a rubber glove and wrapped it around my hand leaving just one finger exposed. I pointed my index finger at a spoon lying on the floor. It skittered away, banging into the wall and bouncing off. I shoved my hand back in the glove and looked at Gene.

His face was so screwed up that it would have been funny in different circumstances.

I asked, "Do you know what could have caused this?"

"Not exactly." He dragged out the words, looking worried, and more confused than before.

Then his face went from worried to something else I couldn't read. "Actually, it's kinda cool. Do it again."

I glared.

I replayed my morning, event by event while we stood in the midst of silverware, pots, pans, and broken glassware.

"I don't know what's happening, Gene. I hope you can figure it out. If anyone can, it's you." I was trying to hold it together, but tears stung my eyelids.

"Come here," I commanded. "There's more."

He sidestepped the puddle of wine, and we walked past furniture askew, picture frames at odd angles, a couple books and magazines on the floor. In the bedroom, I pointed out my bedside lamp shoved into the corner on the floor.

He demanded, "So you just woke up this morning and things started flying around? What? Were you visited by aliens in your sleep or something?"

"Don't be a wiseass Gene. My heart is pounding so hard I think I'm gonna have a heart attack. You're going to have to call 911."

"So yesterday was normal and then you went to bed and woke up to this?"

"Yea, I worked 'til seven and came home, had a glass of wine and a tomato sandwich and went to bed."

"You had a glass of wine with a tomato sandwich? Disgusting."

"Eugene, do you really want to criticize my food choices? At this moment, my life is hell."

"Sorry. What else happened yesterday, Brava? Something had to happen to cause this."

"Nothing Gene. It was a usu–. Wait. Something did happen on the way home."

I excitedly explained about the odd storm and lightning striking near me, sure now that that's what caused this.

"If that's it Gene, can you make it go away?"

He hesitated. "Brava let me do some research on lightning strikes. Did your computer survive this?"

"Let me check," I said.

"No. You sit down with your rubber gloves on and let me check."

"I need a martini," I said. Too rattled to make a martini, I dumped a shot of gin in a coffee cup. I sat on the sofa sipping my gin and brooding while Gene went into the office and worked on the computer.

I thought, "What am I going to do if it won't stop? I can't wear rubber gloves all my life."

My mind began racing with thoughts; none of them positive. I could never go to a restaurant, or eat off silverware, or cook a meal. I had a horrifying notion that I'd have to get my arms amputated and get rubber prosthetic hands. I was thinking crazy at this point.

I speak some Italian because of mom's side of the family. I recalled a phrase in Italian for when thoughts go around and around in your head. It's "giri in la testa." It translates literally to "a tour inside your head." There was a whole tour company of thoughts inside my head.

The best thing about this whole day is that I won't have to see Cow Patty – that bitch.

I yelled to Gene. "What will I tell them at work if I can never go back?"

"What did you tell them today?" Gene hollered from the other room.

"I said I broke a crown. Other people can call in sick, but if I were sick, I'd go see Dr. Jack."

I thought of the wonderful doctors I work for and wondered if I'd ever get to go back there; Dr. Jack with his booming voice and gentle ways. My heart broke most of all at the thought of not seeing Sheila every day.

I hollered back to Gene. "I had to come up with something the docs can't fix so I chose my teeth."

Thinking of my teeth gave me another horrifying circumstance to dwell on.

"Oh God, what if I touch my mouth and pull all my fillings out? I haven't even brushed my teeth this morning," I mumbled, but Gene heard me.

"You're drinking at 9 a.m. before you even brushed your teeth?"

"Focus Gene, I am drinking at 9 a.m. because I am a freak!"

"Maybe you're a superhero Brava, not a freak."

A brief thrill of excitement went through me at the thought but quickly turned to more panic. I'd fantasized about being a superhero, but in my fantasies it didn't feel like this. As a child, I'd even fantasized about being a princess, but I'd have made an awful princess. I wondered if I'd make an awful superhero, too.

"I feel like a freak. I called you to figure out a way to make it stop."

"Working on it."

Chapter 6

Shortly after Kevin divorced me, I boarded a plane bound for Pittsburgh, telling no one where I was going. St. Julian's, the only place I long for in Pennsylvania, is the quaint stone church next to Bear Creek that we attended as kids. The church is rescued from feeling cold by the sunlight streaming through the stained glass windows. Prisms of light glitter over the pews in colors of emerald, sapphire, rose and amber. The sun rises on Sunday mornings behind the altar and illuminates Jesus and the apostles at the Last Supper. Huge copper and steel chandeliers handcrafted from a refinery in nearby Pittsburgh add more golden light to warm the pews. On my coffee table, I contemplated a bowl of river stones that I had collected over the years from my beloved Julian's.

When we were little and got bored with the service, Mom and Dad let Liv and I go outside to play. The sunshine on the creek made golden splashes as we played in the water. We had our favorite trees where fairies lived and made houses and toys for them while Mom and Dad prayed inside. Olivia and I came home each week with our pockets lined with quartz stones that we believed to be diamonds. As a child, it seemed a magical, mystical place. It still did.

The day of my solitary sojourn, I arrived at Julian's in the morning while the sun illuminated the last supper window. I sat in the church and let the multicolored prisms of light fall on my skin. I didn't even pray. I just sat. Around noon when the sun was overhead, I went outside and marveled at the diamonds in the rushing water. I visited the fairy trees that had grown large and shaded parts of the creek. I touched the rough, gnarled roots where Olivia's and my fairies lived. I lined my pockets with pebbles. I still remember that moving visit to Julian's when I'm in need of comfort. I remembered it today.

"How's it coming Gene?" I called out to him.

"Give me a little more time. I'm getting there," he called back.

"What are you looking for? I want to help."

"Aunt Brava, I think it's best you sit still. I promise I'll fill you in as soon as I figure out what I'm looking for."

Still wearing my rubber gloves, I got another shot of gin and dumped it in my coffee cup and continued my musings. We joked that we were raised half Catholic, half Episcopalian. We went to the Episcopal Church but still revered Mary and the saints. We had the blue Mary statue in the yard where we planted begonias in the summer, and I'm ashamed to admit put plastic roses in the winter.

I considered praying on the prayer beads tossed beside the river stones on my coffee table. Then I worried that the prayers wouldn't count because I was wearing rubber gloves to hold the beads. Then I laughed at that. Out loud.

Gene hollered from the other room "Are you drunk? What's so funny?"

"Not funny; ironic. Like my life. Are you done yet?"

"A little more time."

Three hours of internet searching and two shots of gin later, Gene sat down beside me on the sofa and asked, "Have you ever seen those shows on TV about the pyramids, ancient civilizations and aliens?"

"Oh God, if that's the best that you can do I'm going to have to amputate my arms and use rubber prosthetics."

"Hunh?"

"Never mind. You know how my thoughts run away with me on a good day. Imagine the scary place my mind is today. Go on." I urged Gene.

"Okay, just answer me if you've ever seen those shows speculating on how ancient civilizations did things like build the pyramids."

"Yea, I've seen them, but that's all they do is speculate. They appeal more to someone with about a sixth-grade education".

"They do Brava. It's TV. It's written for the public and that includes Cathy and her family."

I smiled despite myself. Cathy is Kevin's sister from his adopted family. Kevin's biological family must've been really smart because Kevin's brilliant, but I always thought the gene pool was a little shallow on the adopted side. Then Cathy married a redneck from Alabama named Bubba.

No shit, his given name is Bubba. They further diluted the already shallow gene pool. When Kevin and I were still together, I kept my mouth shut.

Some months after Kevin left, Cathy called and blamed me for her brother becoming a Muslim and staying in Istanbul. I'd had enough therapy at that point that I didn't believe her, but not enough to keep quiet. We've never spoken since, and it suits me. Since then "Cathy stories" have become a source of much amusement. I felt a heart tug for Gene because he knew the Cathy reference would make me smile.

He continued, "In all seriousness, Brava, there's a group of world-renowned physicists who believe that ancient humans had the power to teleport, to levitate, to move objects with telekinesis. Their evidence lies in the unexplainable monuments and comes from ancient writings and drawings. There are even some biblical references for it."

I listened with rapt attention.

"Obviously modern humans have lost the abilities. These guys are doing research to see if we can regain these powers. It's top secret, and it's staying in the scholarly community because you can imagine what might happen if governments found out about it."

"Well, if it's so top secret, how do you know about it?"

He gave me "that look."

"All right. I don't want to know."

Gene grinned. "If I told ya, I'd have to kill ya."

I rolled my eyes.

Gene continued. "They believe the powers were manifested in humans by changing our vibrational frequency. They're experimenting with methods like cold, heat, electricity, and martial arts and yogic practices. The physical methods are showing some promise."

"Great Gene, what does this have to do with me?"

"I think the lightning changed your vibrational frequency and now your frequency is reacting with the frequencies of everything around you."

He paused and I thought back on the events of the morning.

"But it isn't everything Gene. The bed, the cup, they didn't react."

To emphasize my point, I removed one glove and poked the seat of the chair. "See."

"Brava, let me explain. Frequency is the number of times a vibrating structure moves back and forth during one second. It's measured in Hertz. The field is call–"

I interrupted. "Gene, skip the science lecture. I called you because you're brilliant, but I'm not. How does this relate?"

"OK, sorry. Give me a minute, and I'll explain it." He paused, thinking quietly.

"Think about it like this Brava. You're familiar with sound and vibration, right?

I nodded.

"They are inseparably linked. Sound is always caused by vibration. Some structure or object must be vibrating for sound to occur. Are you getting this?"

I nodded again.

"You are structure number one vibrating at a really, really rapid rate. Since the lightning, the number of times your structure moves back and forth against a second structure is extremely high. The things you touch have a frequency of their own, so they are moving back and forth against you. Some of them react more violently than others. The rubber gloves, which was a brilliant idea, by the way, stop the travel of your vibration."

"Have you figured out a way to make it stop?" I asked impatiently. "That's all I wanna know."

"Not yet. Listen. I wanna ask some questions to these researchers. I need their help."

"No!" I screamed. "No, Gene. Those researchers aren't any better than the government. They'll use me as a scientific experiment for their own gain. Swear you won't ask any questions. Promise me, Gene."

"All right, all right. Then I need to hack further into their research, and I can't do it from here. I need my computer. Dad's working and Mom's at the club. Here's what I think we should do. Get some rubber soled shoes, and keep your gloves on. Take me home and drop me off. Then you come back here and start cleaning up. It'll keep your mind off things and make you feel better. I'll call you when I have the information."

"Promise me they won't know. No one can know."

"Brava, trust me. I can get in their research, and I swear to God no one will ever know."

I grabbed my yellow rain boots and pulled them on over my pj's and headed for the car. I looked over my shoulder to see if Gene was coming only to see him holding his hands over his mouth to stifle a laugh.

"What?" I scowled.

"If you could only see yourself."

"Get in the car."

Chapter 7

After I dropped Gene off and returned home, I tried to remain hopeful and positive, but I am hardwired for negativity so I felt overwhelming fear and despair. Without Gene, I didn't feel the need to filter my feelings or hold them in, so I let the tears flow. I stomped and cried and cussed as I picked up all the broken glassware and plates and loose silverware. I whimpered while I sopped up the wine. I cried myself dry and straightened my house. In a short time, it looked so normal that it was deceptive. It almost seemed as if nothing had ever happened. I took off a glove to check. Sure enough, the fork flew across the counter and went behind the refrigerator.

Shit.

I texted Olivia, again fumbling with my rubber gloves, and told her that Gene was spending the weekend with me. Gene had always been difficult for Olivia but was better understood by his dad. Brian is a pediatrician and a quiet man; as unlike Liv as one can be. Theirs is the perfect match. But Gene's teenage rebellions caused big problems between him and his dad. I suspected they both were relieved when Gene spent time with me.

When I picked up Gene later, I asked, "What did you learn?"

"Let's get home first and sit down, and I'll tell you everything." It was the second drive that day we took in silence.

When we got to my kitchen, he said, "It looks better than this morning. I've got good news and bad news; which do you want first?"

"Always bad news first. Get it over with."

Gene paused and said, "No. Good news first. I'm overruling you."

Fear clenched my gut. *The bad news must be really bad.* My mind raced down some scary roads. But in an effort to hide my fear from Gene, I quipped, "So why did you give me the choice?"

He didn't even engage in the banter, further intensifying my fear.

"Listen Brava. I think you were right about not letting those researchers know about you. I believe at least two people have died ..." He continued talking, but all I heard was "died la la la la."

I wished that if I were going to die anyway, I'd have died last night from the lightning. I was feeling faint and Gene must have noticed.

"Are you OK, Aunt Brava?"

"Gene, am I going to die?" I whispered the question.

"No Brava," he nearly yelled it. "The bad news isn't that bad. I'm sorry, I'm not doing a good job getting this out. I'm mixing it all up. Let me start over. I really believe you're going to be OK. Better than OK."

"Do I need a drink?"

"Probably, but wait 'til after. Take a deep breath, and let me start over. This may take a while. Have you eaten anything today?"

"Yea, a few bites. I'm OK."

"All right. Let's go sit down."

He threw those words over his shoulder as he headed for the living room and I followed. "I think you can control this thing that happened."

That meant he didn't think it would go away. I took a deep breath and composed myself. We walked into my cozy living room, and I snuggled up on the couch, curling my legs beneath me, pulling the fleece blanket over my knees and hugging myself tightly around the middle. I felt like I would break apart. Gene sat in Kevin's recliner facing me.

He began with, "The researchers worked with young men who had no families, because they had nothing to lose and were willing subjects. They covered up their deaths."

I interrupted. "But if they were young and healthy that would make them stronger than me, and you said some died."

The phone rang and to my horror I reflexively answered it.

"It's your mom. Butter is on sale at Publix. It's $2.29 a pound. And it's usually $2.99. Do you need some?"

I can't fucking believe my mother is discussing the price of butter at the same I'm discussing deadly scientific experiments with Gene.

I looked at Gene with wide eyes and tipped my head like a dog.

Thinking I could get off the phone quick, I said, "Yea I think I'm low on butter. Thanks, Mom."

Then I panicked that she'd want to bring it over.

Mom continued, "I'm picking some up for me and for Mrs. Cohen too."

"I don't think I know her." I instantly regretted saying that because it opened the door for one of Mom's stories.

What in heaven's name was I doing?

"Yes you do, she's the one that lives five doors down on the left. The Catholic that married the Jew. It's her third husband. The first two died. His kids hate her. They think she's a gold digger."

"A gold digger? Seriously? She lives in a trailer!"

"All I know is I'm glad I still have your dad. I don't know how these women keep finding husbands. I'm sure I couldn't do it. They must give off vibes."

"Ah, Mom, I don't mean to cut you off, but I'm in a bit of a mess. Can you call me later before you come over?"

I hung up and screwed my face.

"Gene this is insane. I'm afraid I'm going to die, and my mom found butter on sale. Do you have anything to offer me that will help? Those boys died."

"Bear with me. I think I can explain some things that will help you. Those researchers were either arrogant or evil. I'm not sure which."

I responded, "When you've lived as long as I have, you may come to the conclusion that they are one and the same."

"In this case, I believe you're right."

"Anyway, their premise was to get healthy strong kids to try experiments on to increase their vibrational energy and see if they could develop powers of telekinesis and telepathy. From the research, I think the powers got out of control and killed the subjects before they could harness it."

I cut him off with, "Shit, Gene."

He continued as if I hadn't spoken. "I think it's *because* they were so young and strong and male that their own bodies' energies fought against them. Like I told you about opposing vibrational frequencies, it backfired. I think the researchers missed some critical points. And I think I found them. If I'm right, Brava, I think you were destined to this because I think you are one of the few people in the world who have the ability to harness this power."

Silence. *This was not going the way I had supposed.*

"I don't want it, Gene. I want you to make it go away," I begged.

"You may not be able to do that. Bear with me Brava, please." His voice was pleading. "I have to give you some history first. Do you know much about Grandpa's heritage?"

"We're Scottish. We never talked much about that. We had more to do with the crazy Italian side of the family. When Dad talked about his family, it was mostly about religious tyranny."

Gene asked, "What religion were they?"

"It's a puritanical sect called Holy Calgarists; lots of hellfire and brimstone preaching.

That's why were raised half Catholic, half Episcopalian. All my cousins wear long dresses, no makeup or jewelry, and never cut their hair."

"So they dress like the Amish?" Gene asked.

"Sort of, except they can wear any clothes just so they're long. The girls wore denim jumpers one time to swim in our pool. I thought they'd drown from the weight."

Gene asked, "I wonder why they strayed so far from their roots?"

"What do you know about our roots?" I questioned.

"I've been doing genealogical research for years, Brava. It makes Mom crazy. She wonders how I could be more interested in a bunch of dead ancestors than in playing football and dating cheerleaders."

"Sounds just like Olivia," I mused.

"From my research, I'm certain that we're descended from what is now Scotland; most likely the Isle of Grier."

"I guess that explains the red hair, huh?" I asked.

"And the temper."

I glared at Gene.

He continued, weaving a tale that took me away from my problems.

"Anyway, I've gone back with online research as far as I can. The next step would be actually digging through church records. Even so, we'll never have definitive proof. Originally there was a group of Celtic people who lived on Grier. The Celts were elusive and had no written language so they were completely assimilated into the Roman Empire before the time of Christ. Almost all we know about them comes from the brackish place where facts and legends mix."

I was mesmerized.

"The Celtic creator of the universe was female, and women were both the spiritual and martial leaders of Celtic society. Legends tell of men coming to the isles to train under the women who were fierce warriors. Yet the Celts had a strong sense of the sacredness in all life, especially of animals. Many of their gods were birds, and they're considered to be bearers of divine intervention."

I realized that my arms had relaxed, and I was intent on the story. I had almost forgotten my troubles, but I remembered them with a physical jolt that sickened me again. I kept quiet, however, nodding to urge Gene to continue.

"Anyway Brava, there's more, a lot more, and I'll tell you all of it later. For now, here's it in a nutshell. I think you were destined to become a warrior with special powers and there's a legend that supports it. I'm afraid that you won't be able to get rid of what happened to you. I think you are meant to use it."

I was stunned. This was definitely not how it was supposed to go. I felt sick. And sorry for myself. I used to have a normal life with a husband that I thought I'd grow old with. That got turned upside down with the divorce, but now I was supposed to imagine myself as a superhero righting wrongs and leaping tall buildings, or shooting fire from my wrists. Actually shooting fire sounded like fun, and I wanted to start with Cow Patti. I said as much to Gene.

"Shooting fire from your wrists is incredibly unimaginative, Aunt Brava. It's been done. In a comic book."

I managed a weak smile.

"Gene," I began weakly, but my voice rose with each word until I was screaming. "I know you think this is cool and have an image of me like a cartoon character superhero, but I'm a fifty-something-year-old grandmother who works as a receptionist at a doctor's office. I look like Weezy in Steel Magnolias only fatter. I have no fashion sense, and I'm too serious. Do I look like, sound like, or act like a fucking warrior who can save the world? Goddammit just make this shit go away."

"Weezy in what?" Gene look stupefied.

I realized he was too young to get the movie reference. And the wrong sex.

"Never mind," I said.

Gene changed tacks.

"OK Brava, let's start with managing this in the moment. In nearly every legend I've read, there is a talisman. You need a talisman."

"If you mean like King Arthur's sword, I'm screwed. All I have are our martial arts weapons, and you do know that they are mass produced from some factory in China, don't you? The workers probably make fun of Americans trying to act Chinese. They are not imbued with magic powers."

"No Brava. They are not what I mean."

"Then I'm missing it Gene. What do I have that could possibly be construed to be a talisman?"

"A talisman can be a weapon, but it can also be something used for protection. That's what you need."

"OK, even better; tell me what on earth can protect me except for rubber gloves. That would be just my luck. I'm a superhero, and my talisman is a pair of rubber gloves. That fits my life perfectly. "

"It has a ring to it, but I'm serious, Brava. I've thought a lot about it. I really think the stones right there are sacred talismans for your protection." He pointed to the Julian stones that I'd been pondering what seemed like days ago, but was only this morning.

"Oh God, I'm doomed. Those are stones I picked up from the Julian's Church creek. They're not talismans."

"Or," he dragged the word out. "You can keep the rubber gloves. Your choice." Gene stopped talking and looked away from me.

"But I …" I stopped. The silence loomed.

I relented because I had no other options and tried to hope that the rocks from Blessed Julian's were indeed talismans, so I chose my favorite. I had found it in an eddy in the creek. It had a hole in the center and looked like the water I'd found it in. I always left it on top of my bowl no matter how many other stones I brought home. I put a cord of leather through it and tied it around my neck. I had to admit that it did make me feel more solid somehow. Or safer, perhaps. So my hope blossomed into belief.

All at once, exhaustion overcame me like a wave. I could hardly hold my head up. The day had caught up to me. No matter how much I wanted to explore this with Gene, I simply had to lay my head down.

Gene saw it in me.

"Aunt Brava, you haven't eaten hardly anything today. Won't you let me fix you a bite of something?"

"I can't eat anything and besides I'm way more tired than hungry. I need to sleep. Maybe it will be better tomorrow."

Gene assured me we would continue our work tomorrow. So, after getting into bed, I gingerly removed my rubber gloves and thankfully fell into an exhausted slumber.

I awoke early Saturday morning while it was still dark. In that wonderful moment between sleep and wake, I nestled deeper under the covers hoping to fall back asleep. Then I remembered Friday and went into freefall.

It had happened a lot after Kevin left. For twenty-six years, I'd awakened and reached for him. For months after he was gone, when I felt the empty place beside me, I had this same terrible feeling. It was as if the ground beneath me rocked. I've felt it on stairs when I thought I was at the bottom but had another stair left; that terrible disorienting moment as my foot reached out to touch the floor that wasn't there.

I'd endured months of panic attacks and terrible, gripping anxiety but with lots of therapy, faith, as well as a truckload of Xanax I'd managed. I'd only recently begun to look forward to the familiar comfort of my days, and even to the future. I'd given some thought to taking a cruise and even trying internet dating. But here I was again.

"Maybe it's OK." I thought. "What if I get up and I'm normal again? Maybe the lightning wore off, and I'll be fine."

"Dear God," I prayed, "if you make this go away, I promise I'll never complain about anything again."

After Kevin left, I'd prayed every day for God to bring him back. I promised that if He did I'd say a rosary every day for life, I'd never swear again, and I'd be nice to Cow Patty. I made many other promises I was unlikely to keep. But God didn't answer that prayer and depending on how I looked at it, thankfully or regretfully, I didn't have to keep the promises.

I dreaded getting up, but I had to pee, so I took a deep breath and reached for the lamp. It nearly fell off the night table. It looked like I wouldn't have to keep this promise either. It seemed God only answered other people's prayers. Despair washed over me. It left me as wrung out as the time Kevin and I were at the beach, and I almost drowned. A huge wave rolled and tumbled me over and over and finally deposited me on the sand, scraped and bruised and gasping for breath. This morning I could almost smell the salt and seaweed as I lay in my bed reeling and mired in self-pity.

I got up, put on my rubber gloves, peed, and went to the kitchen for coffee and to see if Gene was up. The kitchen was trashed, and I could smell that Gene had made something containing lots of garlic and onions. From the detritus, I figured it was spaghetti. I saw him from the kitchen window in my backyard. He had two bails of pine straw that I had been intending to spread this weekend. Somehow I knew he wasn't gardening.

What's he up to? I wondered as I watched and sipped my coffee.

I thought about how different today looked than I had pictured it when I got the pine straw. Funny how we make plans thinking we know what the future will look like only to have it be unrecognizable in a moment. I imagined some fictitious woman getting the phone call that her husband was killed in an accident. Maybe my fate wasn't as bad as hers, but it sure felt awful to me, and then I felt guilty for feeling sorry for myself.

I had two cups of coffee as I watched Gene, who hadn't realized I was awake yet. He set up what looked like a shooting range. He was setting cans and bottles from my recycling bin on the straw bales.

I knew I couldn't go to Kung Fu in my condition. I loved the peace and serenity of Kung Fu on Saturday mornings. I especially loved it when the weather was nice and we practiced outdoors. The sun would rise over the buildings and set my hair and our weapons on fire. But I could just picture myself this morning doing the beautiful slow form and having swords and weapons fly off the wall or out of people's hands. So the lies continued. I knew Gene wouldn't go to Kung Fu either, so I texted our teacher that we had a family crisis.

He texted back with uncharacteristic understanding. "OK, take care, and I'll see you Tuesday. Sifu."

I was puzzling over his niceness when Gene came in.

"You're up. Look at the superhero shooting gallery I set up for you. Come on, let's see if you can knock off the cans and bottles without knocking over the bales."

I followed Gene outside. I was still wearing my rubber gloves, but despite my protective gear, I felt mounting anxiety. If the bedside lamp was any indication, I feared flying cans and bottles. As I walked under the pergola, the wind chimes began to clang. I tried to tell myself it was the breeze, but it was hot and humid, and the air was perfectly still.

Gene asked me to take off the gloves and "shoot" the cans with my fingers. I didn't want to shoot cans. I wanted this to go away. Hell, I even wanted to do my gardening. But I had to know either way, so I slowly and deliberately removed one glove. For some reason, I was still thinking of Cow Patty and how she'd made fun of my face. I pictured her ugly face and pointed my index finger like a gun and "shot" the can. To my shock, the can flew off the bale, hit the wall behind and ricocheted near Gene's head. He ducked and whooped and laughed uproariously.

"Way to go Brava, Superhero! You wanted to shoot fire out of your wrists, but look at that! You've got a loaded gun in your finger!"

I wavered between feeling horrified and thrilled at the surge of power I felt.

I put the glove back on and had a dancing, wiggling little fit while Gene tried to high five my gloved hands. We were dancing around each other like ancient Druids in a springtime ritual. I confess I got caught up in it.

I needed to catch my breath and re-think everything. "Coffee, need more coffee."

"One more time Brava, shoot another can."

Still a little giddy, I shouted "take cover." I wiggled my fingers from the rubber glove and aimed it away from Gene. Like the first one, this can flew off the bale and hit the rock wall behind it. It ricocheted in a different direction.

"Now more coffee." And we headed to the kitchen.

"This is amazing, Brava. See I told you, you were a superhero. Think what you can do with this!" Gene was babbling a hundred miles an hour. I confess I was a bit thrilled with the feeling of power, but worried about its implications also. It felt different from yesterday somehow.

I got another cup of coffee and stood sipping it in the kitchen while Gene scrambled eggs. I tried to go inside my head to figure out a way to get my old life back, but Gene made up scenes with me righting imaginary wrongs and causing chaos in his high school. I had to laugh in spite of myself.

"Aunt Brava, do you think you could make the principal drop his pants in assembly in front of the whole school? That would be hilarious. And I'd love to get back at Miss 'I think I'm sooo hot' cheerleader Christy, who dissed me at Homecoming. Can you bounce her boobs out of her top during a cheer on the basketball court? At halftime?"

"Really?" I asked. "That's what you're thinking right now?"

"This is the coolest thing that's ever happened in the history of the world, Aunt Brava. Think what we can do with this."

"We?" I asked with one eyebrow raised.

"Yea, Brava, You need my help with this. It's you and me against the world. Righting wrongs, correcting injustices–"

I interrupted. "Like dropping the principal's pants in front of the school?"

"Well," he dragged the word out into two syllables. "Maybe. Would you?"

"Maybe not, my nephew. After we eat, will you help me get me rid of this lightning problem?"

"Maybe not, my aunt. This is way too cool to get rid of."

Chapter 8

Gene was undaunted in his efforts to make me into a superhero, and I was equally undaunted in my efforts to get my normal life back. But it worked to take the same steps to get to different ends. If I could work at knocking the cans and bottles off the bales, I could learn to control the lightning and *not* send things flying. However, by the end of the day, I was no further ahead when I wasn't wearing my rubber gloves. The talisman helped, but not enough.

Saturday evening I had my talisman around my neck, and I was sitting on the couch sipping a glass of wine that I held in gloved hands. Gene asked, "So do you want to hear the rest of the story?" He sounded just like Paul Harvey, and I wondered how he even knew of him.

Gene began by telling me about his research and the legend that he'd found repeated over and over in Celtic lore. I sat sipping my wine and listening quietly.

"There is a goddess in Celtic legend that is the goddess of lightning. She's called Dealan. In the legend, a man murdered his own daughter by cutting off her head because she lost her virginity to her young lover. He escaped justice by reasons lost in the intervening years, but Dealan abhors injustice. So during a festival in the center of the village, Dealan created a giant thunderstorm and struck the man with lightning while all the townspeople watched him writhe and seize and die horribly.

"Dealan favors a particular clan called the Seaghdha clan. I don't know if I'm pronouncing it right, but it means hawk or falcon. Every ten generations she favors a female from that clan who she touches gently with lightning and gives them special powers. In return, Dealan expects her to correct miscarriages of justice.

"Aunt Brava, I want you to open your mind because the legend I've told you has been passed down for generations, and I really believe it's being fulfilled in you."

Now that was a turn of events I hadn't expected. I was incredulous. "Gene, that's a fairy tale. I can't believe you think that's real. I was driving down the highway when lightning happened to strike near me. And I didn't see any Celtic goddess around when it happened. I think Olivia may be right. You're living too much in fantasy games on your computer. Maybe you should date a cheerleader."

"I tried and she dissed me, remember? Brava, I want you to give some consideration to your heritage through Grandpa's line and to your name for that matter. Will you open your mind for a minute and listen? Please?"

I sighed a huge sigh and answered weakly, "OK. I'll listen." I was too tired to do otherwise.

"You are likely descended from the clan in the legend. You're most definitely descended from a Scottish Isle and your name means Brave Falcon. The Celtic people saw the sacredness in all animals, especially birds. Brava, who else do you know who makes the sign of the cross over road kill and has a bird cemetery in their yard?"

I got defensive. "I feel so sorry for those animals. They have no instincts to protect them from cars. Besides, I didn't think anyone noticed that I prayed over them."

"They all notice and make fun of you behind your back, present company excluded, of course. And I don't think anyone else but me knows about the bird graveyard."

I had a moment when I felt badly that my family made fun of me, even though I knew they thought I was weird, but then I remembered I had bigger problems.

"How do you know about the graveyard?" I asked.

"I've spent a lot of time here with you, Brava. I've seen you pick up a dead bird and bury it by the pine tree and cross yourself. I love that about you. Just don't tell anyone. It spoils my hard-ass image. But all this is beside the point. What do you think of the legend?"

"Gene, I really don't believe it, so let's just work on getting my real life back and then we'll see about the rest." I had no intention of seeing about the rest, but it worked to placate him for the moment. "I'm going to bed. I'm so tired, I can't see straight. I love you."

I curled up in my bed, turned off the light and removed my rubber gloves. I thought I'd fall asleep in a moment but had too many thoughts running through my mind. This was dragging on. I figured the energy would dissipate after a day or so. But it wasn't lessening at all. The only thing that worked was wearing rubber gloves. I kept picturing myself at my job, cooking, sewing, reading, driving, all while wearing rubber gloves. How would I ever live a normal life? It was a rough night. I finally fell asleep a little after one a.m. and awoke at three and again at five. I finally got up at seven. I reached for the gloves first and got coffee to take back to bed. Only after two cups did I remove the gloves and reach for the lamp.

Nope, it's not getting any better. What am I going to do?

Evidently, Gene had been up working on the computer last night. I found him crashed on the sofa with his laptop. He was still wearing his shorts and shirt from yesterday and his hair was mussed over his eyes. He looked so big and yet so like the little boy he was just yesterday. My heart swelled with love for him, and I relished the moment I could just watch him sleep. A big greasy bowl was sitting on the coffee table and the house smelled like popcorn. I realized that we hadn't eaten dinner again last night. In fact, I couldn't remember when I'd last eaten.

Gene awoke and shot off the sofa like he had a rocket up his ass. That shattered the moment. I needed to ease into my day gently but thankfully I'd had two cups of coffee so I could better handle his enthusiasm.

"Brava, I've got this figured out. I've been up most of the night working on it."

"By your wild enthusiasm, can I assume you're not going to tell me how to make it go away?"

"That would be a fair assumption. But, wipe that look off your face, Brava. I do think we can work on controlling it *while* we work on using it."

"It's a start," I sighed. "Before we go any further, I need food. Will you make some scrambled eggs?"

"Sure. Follow me into the kitchen so I can talk while I cook."

Gene began chopping onions, and I took over while he got the eggs in the pan. I was crying from the onions, and Gene was laughing at me.

"What's your plan?" I sniffed and asked with little enthusiasm.

"Remember when I told you the researchers were using martial arts techniques with those boys?"

I nodded as Gene finished cooking the eggs and put the plate in front of me on the counter. I wolfed my eggs and toast standing in the kitchen and without tasting them as Gene continued.

"Well, the martial arts showed some promise. Some of the boys were able to move objects telekinetically before things went bad. I think they were misguided by false martial arts techniques. They hadn't developed their chi over a long period of time. They were just doing the physical moves without the internal conditioning."

I thought of all the work I'd done with Sifu to develop my chi. I had cussed him under my breath when he made me hold a pose for twenty minutes while I did deep breathing. I struggled when we worked on incorporating the five emotions into the Beautiful Crane form. We did them over and over and over. I recalled the time he told me he could read my mind as I did the form. "You're "thinking" the moves not being the movements."

Maybe I should be grateful to Sifu, I thought. He made me hold each Crane movement while "being" fear, joy and the others. He'd watch me and say "You're thinking joy, not being it. The only one you can materialize is 'fear.' Let fear go, Brava and be joy."

I had tried to do the form while remembering events in my life that made me joyful or angry, and he stopped me each time. "You're thinking, not being. Let it be in your body and move through you. You know the form. Trust it."

When I finally "got it" one day, I thought Sifu would jump for joy, but Sifu didn't ever jump for joy. I got a "not bad, Brava," and a wide grin. When Sifu really smiles a big smile, he almost looks Chinese. He squints his eyes up so that you can't see them. That was the only clue that he was proud of me. He squinted his eyes.

Gene said, "I know what Sifu does with me to control the chi and my breath, and I know you've been working on this for twenty years. You can control the chi the way that the subjects of those experiments couldn't."

I dwelled on this for a time in silence. Gene waited. I thought some more.

"Let's go out back," I said. "I'll try."

"You'll do it. Don't try." He quoted Sifu.

We spent the whole weekend working to control the objects flying all around me. It seemed that if I could quiet my mind, things flew around less. Gene developed a phone app to help me calm myself. It was really ingenious. He made an image of a gauzy golden flag that floated toward me and away from me as if it were moving with my breath. I took a deep inhale as it came toward me and then exhaled as it moved away. It calmed my breathing and stilled my mind. After working on it for several hours, I was able to remove the gloves and walk through the house without furniture dancing around. Silverware remained a problem.

By Sunday evening, it was apparent I wasn't going to be able to go to work the next day.

Gene said, "Brava, you're screwed if you go to work tomorrow, so you better start planning your lie now to call in sick."

"I'm a terrible liar Gene, you know that."

"Leave it to me. I can weave a very believable lie. I'm actually quite good at it." Gene grinned.

"I don't want to know more about that, do I?"

He ignored that comment and said we needed to stick to the original lie about the broken tooth.

"Call Dr. Jack tonight and tell him that it was a front tooth and the temporary fell off. That way you're toothless in the front. Tell him you're in great pain."

He hesitated and rushed on, "Oh, and you had a reaction to the antibiotics so your face swelled up like a baseball, and you couldn't possibly come into work like that."

"Gene, I don't think I can do it and sound convincing."

"I could punch you and swell your face and knock out your tooth if ya prefer, but I think we've got enough on our plate for the moment. Come here and put a few of these pebbles in your mouth and practice."

He palmed a few of the smaller Julian stones and shoved them toward my mouth saying in a leering, sinister voice, "Open wide, or I'll have to hurt you."

 Before I knew it, I had complied and had a mouth full of dirty river stones.

He had already picked up the phone and was dialing Dr. Jack. I had no choice but to talk when he answered.

"Dr. Jack," I mumbled around the stones filling my mouth.

"Brava is that you? I can't understand you."

Gene grabbed the phone from my hand and said, "Dr. Jack, this is Gene. I'm here with Aunt Brava and she's a sight! The temporary crown fell off! She has no front tooth and a face like a baseball. She won't be able to come in tomorrow. And you wouldn't want her to. She'd scare your patients away."

Dr. Jack said something I couldn't hear. Gene nodded and nodded, saying "unh hunh," and I was going crazy wondering what Dr. Jack was saying. I glared at Gene.

 Gene answered. "She's done Epsom salts and ice all weekend, but she's no better. I feel so sorry for her that I've given up going on spring break next week to stay with her. She's going to the dentist tomorrow, so I'll call ya back after. Brava says she is sorry to let you down."

Dr. Jack said something else I couldn't hear, and Gene answered, "Thank you so much, Dr. Jack. I'll pass your concerns to Aunt Brava. Don't worry about her though, I'm here for her."

"You are way too good at that Gene, and that takes practice. I don't even want to know just how much."

"Never fear Aunt Brava, I wouldn't admit to anything if ya did." He laughed.

"Now about spring break. I've been so self-absorbed that I completely forgot about next week being spring break. Weren't you going to go to Panama City with your friends?"

"Yea, I was supposed to, but I'd spend the week getting drunk and trying to pick up chicks. I'm no chick magnet, so trying is the operative word here. I figured the time here with you becoming a superhero would be way more fun."

"I've no intention of becoming a superhero. Our goal is to get these to S-T-O-P." I spelled it out. "And I don't want you to give up spring break for me."

"If I thought I'd get lucky with any chicks this week, it would be no contest. But you're stuck with me now because they left yesterday. Don't worry, I won't hold it against ya."

Chapter 9

I never made it to work that week. Monday Gene and I worked with the breathing app and the cans and bottles without success. I think I was more agitated rather than less, so at one point it was as if a tornado had come through my back yard. We both had to duck for cover from flying cans. That day Gene again called Dr. Jack.

"You'll never believe what happened Dr. Jack. I was at the dentist's office with her, and I heard a really loud bang and a yell. So I ran back to the room. I expected to see Aunt Brava on the floor, but instead found Dr. Floss on the floor flat on his back with Brava leaning over him. He was out cold and if that weren't bad enough, he'd dropped the temporary and broke it."

Gene listened and then said, "I know, right? What bad luck. They almost had to call the EMTs for Dr. Floss because we couldn't get him to wake up. But finally he did. We left a little while after that, and he assured us he'd take care of Brava tomorrow."

I alternated between being amused by the story, and appalled that Gene had crafted such an outrageous lie.

Gene's response was, "Would you prefer to tell him the truth?"

Tuesday was even worse than Monday. I woke up in a mood. I was pissed off at nothing in particular save for the state of affairs in which I found myself. Even the rubber gloves weren't enough; I had to wear my rubber gardening boots too. Gene got me my coffee, and I used two gloved hands to get it safely to my lips.

I was scrolling down my Facebook page hoping to get in a better mood. That backfired. My cousin in Pennsylvania posted one of those damn posts with a graphic picture of a tiny puppy that had been viciously abused. It said, "Hit like if you're against animal abuse."

I went on a rant! "According to Facebook, Gene, I don't like Jesus, and I'm in favor of animal and child abuse." I hate that shit. I get on Facebook to read everyone's lies that their life is like a Norman Rockwell painting. I don't believe the lies. I just like to read them. And then they post this shit. I've got a knot in my gut the size of Montana."

I continued, "Are they so stupid that they think I'm "for" animal abuse because I didn't hit the "like" button? Or worse, do they have child and animal abusers as friends on Facebook? Maybe I'll post that on their wall. 'Do you have Facebook friends who abuse animals that you're reaching out to?'"

   Gene got me my second cup of coffee, and I suspected he spiked it. I didn't care if he did. In fact, all the better. I felt like getting ripping drunk. I continued, "I don't watch CNN for a reason. Or Fox News. Or any damn news. I sure as hell don't go on Facebook for violence. I wish they'd leave the horrors of abuse to CNN."

I kept on and on. Gene evidently knew better than to interrupt me. After a lengthy rant that ran the gamut from Facebook posts to religion, I ran out of steam. Gene just looked at me and asked, "Would you like to work on controlling the lightning?"

I noticed that he didn't ask me to work on becoming a superhero, and I was grateful. I took a big, deep breath and nodded. The day did not go well. I was no further ahead than I was Friday morning when I awoke with the lightning in me. I couldn't control it to become a superhero if I wanted to. And I didn't want to. I wanted it to go away. I wanted to go to work and talk with patients about hemorrhoids and PMS and vomit. In fact, I longed to discuss poop or vomit as long as it was someone else's. Anything was better than being the tornado I had become. I was a danger to myself and anyone in close proximity.

The lies grew to ridiculousness, and if I hadn't had such a long history of trust with the docs, they'd have no doubt called me a liar and fired me. On Tuesday, I got a friend of mine that had retired as a receptionist for a surgeon to fill in for me and that helped. When I went back the following Monday, Dr. Jackson asked to see the dental work. I had no choice but to open my mouth.

I said, "He did such an amazing job, you'd never even know I had anything done."

He just gave me a look and said, "I don't know what's going on with you Brava, but you know you can trust me with anything, don't you?"

"Yea right," I thought. "Anything rational."

I just smiled and thanked him for his support.

I was a nervous wreck that the lightning was going to escape from me and start objects flying. I had taped Julian pebbles around both my ankles and wrists, and around my waist. It was hot, and I was wearing pants and a long sleeved top to hide the talismans. I wore rubber soled shoes and had my phone in my pocket in case I needed my app. I was sweating from heat and nerves. I'd tucked a couple stones in my bra, and I feared they were going to slide out on a rivulet of sweat, so I sneaked to the bathroom the minute I had a chance and scotch taped the stones to my chest. They barely held for the sheen of sweat.

I was in front of the sink tapping baby powder under my pits when Sheila walked in the bathroom. I yanked my shirt down too hurriedly and Sheila noticed.

Seeing my flushed face on top of the odd behavior, she asked worriedly, "Brava, are you OK?"

"Just a hot flash," I answered, fanning my face. "I guess I need an appointment with Seishin."

Seishin is our friend, and an herbalist who I've seen while going through menopause to avoid moments like this one. Of course, this was not a real hot flash. I'd made up my mind to never be like those women I'd seen fanning their faces and talking about their brains becoming mush since menopause. Whoever started that shit? In ancient times, older women were revered for their wisdom. I was going to be one of the wise.

Sheila, like Dr. Jack, cocked one eyebrow and looked at me like she knew I was lying. I was so pissed. My life had turned into some comedy skit. I reviewed all that happened the past week with the lies, the legends, the shooting range, the rubber gloves and the stones taped all over my body. Even under the circumstances, I managed a sardonic smile in the mirror before returning to the front desk.

I made it through the next hour without incident, but as lunchtime approached, I felt a burning around my ankles, wrists and belly. I was scared to death that I was like those young men who died from the increased vibrations. The more I worried, the worse it got. I was hot, and burning everywhere I had taped the talismans. Maybe I would have been better off to have rubber gloves for talismans. At least they wouldn't kill me as I was sure the stones were doing. If I lived until lunch, I was going back to rubber gloves. I'd wear rubber gloves and boots and put on a rubber hat if need be. In fact, I could make whole outfits from rubber. Maybe I'd even wear a rubber burka to protect me so only my eyes showed through. The whole thought of me in a rubber burka after Kevin left me to become a Muslim seemed perfect for this ridiculous irony that was now my life.

I was on fire and couldn't get out of the office fast enough. I left before my usual lunchtime without saying anything to the doctors. I feared that if I didn't get the stones off, they would kill me. I was certain I'd be just like those young men in the studies. I drove home like a maniac and raced in the front door ripping off my clothes as I ran to the bathroom mirror. I snatched and grabbed at the tape, tearing it off and flinging it with stones still attached into the sink. Everywhere the tape had touched had red, oozing, itchy, weeping sores. I was praying to God to let me live and praying to Him to let me die painlessly when it occurred to me that the sores were from the tape. I am allergic to adhesive but had totally forgotten about it in an effort to get as many talismans on as possible. I examined the sores, and once I was certain that it was the tape and not a dreaded side-effect of the lightning, I felt faint with relief. I jumped into a cool shower and rubbed and scratched until I was bloody.

On Tuesday, Gene and I showed up at Kung Fu with a lot of trepidation after having missed last week. Sifu generally had a harsh punishment in store. Class went on as usual and as it went on I alternated between relief that he wasn't going to punish us and anxiety that he was only postponing the inevitable. It turned out to be the latter.

As soon as everyone had bowed out, I grabbed for my sword and was heading for the door when Sifu yelled. "Brava and Gene stop."

To Gene, he said, "Twenty minutes on the heavy bag, and if you stop to rest, you'll go twenty minutes with me. You decide."

To me, he said, "Hold horse stance for twenty minutes. If you rise up to give your legs a break, I'll start the timer over again at zero. I have no social life so I can stay all night. Maybe next time you'll think twice about having a family situation during Kung Fu."

I made it through the first ten minutes by picturing how pissed I was at Sifu and thinking of what I'd do to him if I let the lightning loose. But I was afraid it would get loose. So, for the next ten minutes, I pictured my breathing app and tried to relax into the posture. I could hear Gene banging on the heavy bag and listened to the staccato rhythm of his punches. I felt the sweat bead up on my forehead from the effort. When Sifu stopped us, I didn't even look at him. I grabbed my sword and barely bowed toward him and the ancestors. It was really disrespectful and not like me at all.

Chapter 10

I was finally getting the hang of living with the lightning. I wore the stone talisman around my neck and wore rubber soled soles. A little pouch to tuck a pebble or two in my bra helped. Hypoallergenic tape affixed some stones around my wrists and ankles, and I kept my relaxing app close, making frequent trips to the bathroom to calm myself. I'd lock myself in the stall and whip out my phone, breathing in and out with the golden fabric.

Objects flew around me less often lately, but I still used plastic table utensils as silverware gave me the biggest problems. I just avoided fancier establishments that used real silverware, and cooking proved a challenge. Sandwich joints worked the best. I existed by eating finger food and my ass was showing it.

Sitting at my desk contemplating my life, I looked up to see Terry and Doris. Terry brought his wife Doris for therapy every week and sat in the waiting room like he was doing her a big favor; like the therapy was for her, and he didn't need it. I suspected that he beat her and it upset me so. I repeatedly asked Sheila about it, but she would never tell me anything.

One day when Sheila was travelling, I did an awful thing. She called from Chicago and asked me to retrieve something from her desk. She needed some information for her lecture, so she walked me through finding the hidden key to her office and the needed material. While there, I noticed the keys to her filing cabinet in her top desk drawer. I completed the task for her and assured her I'd lock her office and keep the key at my desk so she could find a new hiding place on her return.

That's when I did something I still feel guilty about. I dug in her file cabinet and read Doris's file. It even contained photos of the bruises Terry inflicted on her body where no one would see them. I knew I was right about him, but the knowledge pained me. I was critical of Doris for staying with him, and mad at Sheila for not doing more. I was conflicted about their situation and my guilt in knowing about it. In the end, I was glad that my job didn't require me to routinely live with information like that. I learned a lesson about secrets that day.

I ramped up my efforts to get Sheila to convince Doris to leave, but couldn't tip my hand about what I knew. Sheila wouldn't even acknowledge that he beat Doris but said that as long as she kept coming for therapy there was hope.

Terry is particularly good looking in that black Irish way. He has dark curly hair, the bluest eyes I've ever seen and a dimple in his cheek. Someone told me that a dimple is a place where an angel kissed. I couldn't believe an angel ever kissed this guy. And on top of the good looks, he has such a charming manner that despite my hatred for him, I often found myself starting to smile and chat with him. Then I'd remember that I hated him and turn my back on him.

It was infuriating, and in those moments I understood Doris a little better. It was as if he could weave a spell over people. Today, he was sitting there wearing his stupid baseball cap trying to chat me up about the Braves. Again I found myself smiling and chatting with him and then feeling angry at myself and furious with him. I was even furious with the angel that caused his dimple.

To avoid being caught up in his spell, I pictured smashing his face into the water fountain and seeing blood splatter. I was really getting into the vision when I felt this nauseating butterfly feeling in my stomach; a surge of it. I had a feeling of vertigo, the room began to rotate around me, and I was quite still right in the center of it. It felt just like a terrible hangover.

Just when I thought I was going to vomit in the trash can right in front of him, Terry seemed to jump off the sofa and hurl himself into the drinking fountain, smashing his nose. I heard the loud crack of bone as his nose broke, sending blood splattering onto the floor, walls, and the fountain. I smelled the metallic scent of his blood and watched in horror as it seeped into the carpet, spreading out and growing pink at the edges. He was screaming, "Call 911, call 911" and holding his hands to his face to catch the blood spewing from his nose.

Doors flew open in the treatment hallway, and people poured out of the rooms. I looked up to see Sheila running down the hallway, but it seemed as if it was in slow motion. I fixated on the swinging of her earrings. Today, they were red metal circles with a turquoise stone dangling inside. The circle was going around and around and around the stone. I noticed the scene getting really small like I was looking at it through a telescope. I realized I was holding my breath and tried to gasp in air. I couldn't breathe. I'd had plenty of panic attacks before, but this was the worst.

I was sure I was going to black out. I was croaking out the words, "I can't breathe," but it was barely audible. I gasped a few more times and then finally got my words to be heard. By then, I was yelling "I can't breathe, I can't breathe." Someone finally shouted above the chaos, "If you can talk, you can breathe."

Terry was still yelling to call 911. Someone was yelling "Put ice on it. Where's the ice?" It was pandemonium.

Sheila helped me regain my breath while Dr. Jack and Doris tended to Terry. They applied towels and ice packs, and I think everyone just assumed I had called 911. By the time someone realized no one had called, the situation was under control.

Dr. Jack took Terry to a treatment room and mended the broken nose. Terry came out with cotton cords hanging out of each nostril and eyes that were already starting to blacken. Doris was crying and supporting him and cooing soothing words like he was an injured child. The whole scene sickened me, and the thought that perhaps I'd caused it, sickened me worse than anything.

When Doris and Terry finally left, Dr. Jack looked to me for an explanation, and I said I didn't see anything until he hit the fountain and blood spattered.

"He must have tripped," Dr. Jack said, scanning the floor for trip hazards. I readily agreed.

I was worse than horrified. I had "thought" that scene into reality. It was as if I had written a screenplay and Terry had acted it out like he was reading from the script. I wished it had been a movie. At least the blood wouldn't have been real. I could still smell it. Just when I thought I was getting used to the lightning in me this had to happen. I knew I'd caused it but was still trying to find another explanation. I needed to talk to Gene. I hated to rely on him so much. I didn't want to burden him with this, but he was the only person I had told, as well as the smartest person I'd ever known. He was the obvious choice.

I texted him yet again, "Anything too important to get out of?"

"O shit, what happened?"

"Something really bad at work. I caused an accident. I'm OK though." I'd tell him about Terry later. He only needed to be reassured about me and knowing Gene he'd say Terry deserved it.

"If I leave before six too many questions, I have Kung Fu. Can it wait 'til then?"

Gene took additional Kung Fu classes to learn the fighting arts. My fighting days were long over.

"Yea. I'll pick you up at the school at six."

I wore rubber gloves, both for hygiene and to trap the lightning as I scrubbed the blood off the walls and drinking fountain, I had caused enough trouble today. As I scrubbed, I recalled a time shortly after moving to Georgia that I studied meditation under a woman that had once lived in an ashram, whatever that is. I had thought of her as some combination of spiritual leader, guru and nut.

She had done her darndest to teach me about karma. She explained that I shouldn't do something mean to someone even if they had done something mean to me. Tell that to a half Sicilian, half Scottish gal and see if she gets it. Furthermore, she told me that I couldn't even wish for mean things to happen to someone or that counted against your karma as much as if you'd actually done them. I explained to her that that's called a curse, and when you're half Sicilian and half Scottish, curses are in your DNA. I didn't understand karma, and I really couldn't see how it could get in my head and know what I was thinking.

I explained to her, "I just want to be a pretty good person. I don't want to be a saint. Look at the lives of the saints. Things didn't turn out so good for them."

That was her last straw with me, and we didn't work together anymore after that. I took up Kung Fu. I loved knowing I was learning multiple ways to kill someone. It appealed to me more.

Scrubbing the carpet and inhaling the iron scent of Terry's blood, I wished I *had* learned to control my thoughts back then. Now all I had to do was think something mean and it really happened. How was that going to affect my karma? I was screwed for sure.

When I told Gene what had happened at work with Terry, I told him what I knew about him beating Doris from searching Sheila's office. I expected him to say Terry deserved it, but I didn't expect him to say what he did.

"Aunt Brava, I think that was Dealan meting out justice and using you to do it. I told you I thought you were meant to use these powers. Resisting them caused Dealan to get upset so she took it into her own hands or yours, depending on how you look at it. It sounds like Terry got a taste of his own medicine. That's justice in my book."

I was taken aback and wondered to myself, "Could that possibly be true?" Up until that moment, I had disregarded all of Gene's theories as a bunch of teenage fantasies. But I had a moment of indecision regarding it, and then got a hold of myself.

"Gene, it's just that the lightning in me hasn't gone away; and it will. It must. I don't think for a minute it's Dealan or your superhero fantasies. There's a physical explanation. The lightning got into me and now I'm vibrating like you told me in the first place. But my thoughts must have raised the vibrations. It was as if he responded to my very thoughts. That part is so disturbing, I can't tell you. I had the stones on as usual and was feeling calm until he came in."

Gene, ever the scientist, said, "If it's true it will work again. I left the bales out. Grab a can and let's go out back to the range."

We did. I pointed at the can like I had previously done. Nothing much happened. I thought about the can jumping like a jumping bean. It jiggled but didn't jump. I thought about it flying in a figure eight. I jumped up and down while I thought about the can jumping and down. It barely wiggled. I pointed my fingers and flapped like a bird at the can. The most I got was a wobble. I removed the talismans that were taped and tucked and tied to me. I took off my rubber soled shoes. I pictured the can doing a back flip and it only tipped over. I pointed and waved and wiggled, and it rolled about a bit on the hay bale.

"Brava?" He left the rest of the question hang in the air like a stink.

"Gene, I am burning an image in my brain of what I want that can to do. It's not working. But today it was absolutely, exactly what I was thinking. There is no other explanation than that Terry somehow responded to my very thoughts. It's just not working because I'm exhausted."

"There is another explanation, Brava and I already gave it to you."

The sun was low in the sky, and it was shining on my face. A breeze blew a lock of hair in front of my eyes, and I noticed how red it was in the sun. As a kid, I hated my red hair, but now I am quite vain about it. Today it looked almost like fire in the sunlight. I heard the gong of the chime that Kevin and I had gotten at the Great Wall of China. I smelled someone's dinner grilling nearby. Tears slid silently down my face.

"For God's sake Gene, please get over the superhero fantasies and help me," I begged, crying harder and holding my face in my hands to hide the tears.

"Aunt Brava, I'm so sorry this happened to you." He paused, and then continued.

"Not really, I'm only sorry you are so upset. But I *am* trying to help you. You just keep resisting. You want your old life back. And I don't think it's going to happen. The sooner you accept it, the sooner you'll learn to live with it."

I couldn't for the life of me imagine that I was a superhero called up by a Celtic goddess to right injustices. I could sooner believe in alien abductions and Sasquatch sightings. They at least happened to other people. There was no more unlikely person than me to become a superhero. There simply had to be another explanation. I would figure it out somehow, but I realized I was on my own. Gene was brilliant, but his fantasy mindset was clouding his ability to find the explanation to make this stop. If he wouldn't help, I'd figure it out myself.

"Gene I love you, but I cannot accept and will not accept that I am a superhero. I guess I'm on my own to make this go away. Come on, I'll take you home and then I'm going to bed."

I hated being at odds with Gene. We'd never had a disagreement before. I dropped him off at his house and drove the whole way back home with tears clouding my vision. By the time I got home, I was sobbing hard, heaving, wracking, and painful cries. I climbed into bed and literally pulled the covers over my head.

"Hail Mary full of grace," I prayed, preferring a rote prayer to Mary because I couldn't talk to God right then. He had abandoned me again.

I tossed and turned so much the covers twisted around my legs, and I felt like I was burning up. I prayed the Hail Mary in Italian. "Aveo Maria piena di gracie." I slept little. I dreamed that a huge red-tailed hawk was looking in my window.

I awoke to a text from Gene. "Mornin' B. I love you. I'll call ya after school."

I felt a lot better. Of all the ways my life had changed of late, Gene's and my relationship had only deepened. I couldn't bear to have something get in the way of that.

Chapter 11

I was desperate to get home, toward the end of the day I was pulling the charts for tomorrow. The new tape holding the stones was better. It didn't turn my skin into a weeping red, itchy rash, but it was restrictive and a little itchy. I'd worn extra stones to ward off a repeat of the Terry incident. I couldn't wait to hear from Gene and repair the rift.

I looked up to see two of Dr. Jackson's patients heading toward the door. I was really annoyed because I knew they didn't have an appointment, and this had the potential to end in a disagreement. The more likely ending was that I was going to be working late. Dr. Jack would never turn a patient away.

I was so frustrated. I wanted to get out of there and get to Gene. As the Dunners came in the door, the paper clips jiggled and skittered. I knocked over the pen holder to cover it up. As I bent over to retrieve the pens I had scattered on the floor, I took a deep breath and settled myself.

Mr. and Mrs. Dunner were a sixty-something, very proper, southern gentlemen and lady. I watched as he helped her quite solicitously to a chair and then approached the desk. Annoyance had turned to concern as I watched him assist her. She was obviously in distress.

"Mr. Dunner, what's wrong?"

He looked anxiously left and right to check that no one was in earshot and leaned over my desk. He was so close, I could smell his aftershave. He cupped his hands around his mouth like he was going to yell, but instead he whispered, "Something is wrong down there." He pointed towards the floor.

"Down there?" The words had come out of my mouth seconds before my brain registered the fact that "down there" did not mean the floor. In the next moment, I was sorry I had asked.

"You know," he said, "her treasure box. I think it's broken."

I've always believed that my being born a Yankee was a cruel accident of birth. I took to the southern culture, food and especially the climate like a duck takes to water. But one thing I've never understood about southerners is their efforts at being "proper." It ranges from insincere to ridiculous. In the North, I'd heard "down there" referred to as a vagina, a hoohaw, a hootch, a pussy, and even the "c" word. But never a treasure box.

"It's delicate," he continued, and I wondered if he meant the subject or the treasure box, and I was reluctant to know either way.

Cutting him off, I handed him some forms. "You fill out the paperwork referring to the new complaint, and I'll tell Dr. Jack you're here. I'm sure under the circumstances he'll want to see you even without an appointment."

While Dr. Jack saw to Mrs. Dunner's treasure box, I remembered being with my friend Elaine at an art show when we ran into a woman I'd never met before. After some perfunctory introductions, Elaine "oohed" and "aahed" over this gal like they were best of friends. I felt a wave of jealousy and then was embarrassed that I was jealous. Elaine invited the gal over to her house and she reciprocated and they parted company giving each other air kisses.

"How do you know her?"' I asked, trying not to sound jealous.

"That bitch tried to steal my husband," she blurted.

I was incredulous. "I don't get it. I thought she was your long lost best friend. You invited her to your house. Why would you do that?"

"She knows better than to ever show up."

"I don't understand," I said. "Up north we'd have just snubbed each other."

"That wouldn't be nice." She explained in a tone usually reserved for children.

"At least we'd know where we stand," I retorted.

"We do too. We've grown up here. We know the rules. You don't."

After work, I picked Gene up at his house and we went to mine. We hugged and apologized, and I cried until he got uncomfortable with the emotional display and cracked a joke. He again reminded me of the legend of Dealan but told me that there was a part that he'd left out.

"Brava, in the legend, the first girl from the Seagdha clan has a nephew who helps her correct injustices. That's another reason I think you fulfill the legend."

I couldn't believe it. *Was it possible Gene could be right?*

"Seriously Gene?" I asked.

"No, I made that part up. Wishful thinking," he quipped.

We both laughed and all was well.

"But Brava, I have been researching. Lightning strikes 6000 times per minute somewhere on this planet. That's 8,640,000 times per day. I'm trying to figure out a way to get myself struck. If you don't want to be a superhero, I do. Maybe Dealan will pick me and modify the legend!"

"Gene if you get struck by lightning and die, your mother will kill me. Stop!"

"I'll stop trying to become a superhero if you accept you are one. And I can help you!"

"Eugene Malone. That is blackmail."

"Whatever it takes, Aunt Brava, whatever it takes."

We continued working at the shooting gallery in the backyard to no avail. I couldn't will the objects to move using my thoughts. I couldn't imagine what happened the day in the office with Terry. Gene insisted that my failure to move cans in the yard went toward proving that he was right. The cans wouldn't move because there was no injustice. But things sure seemed to wiggle and wobble if I was rattled. There was no injustice there that I could figure out. It remained elusive.

Chapter 12

I left work Friday afternoon a few weeks later, dreaming of a glass of wine and longing to get in my jammies and stay that way 'til Monday. It had been a particularly exhausting week and Cow Patty had been meaner than usual.

She animatedly told me about this obese woman she'd seen at the mall. It was clear that she was disgusted by this lady. When she described her, she said, "You know she was really wide in the ass, kinda like you."

Seriously? That woman was a menace. Only after she walked away did I come up with the perfect retort. *Oh? And like you're Miss Twiggy?*

Cow Patty is far from skinny. If I judged it correctly, those jeans she'd squeezed her ass into were a size 18 or 20. And she probably had to lie on her back and suck her belly in to get the zipper zipped. To top it off, her boobs preceded her through a doorway by a good eighteen inches. There was no way she bought her bras at Victoria Secret. She probably bought them at Frugal Frillies in the maternity section. I had a perverse desire to yank her top up over her head and see if she had nursing flaps on her bra.

I never think of a retort in the moment. But next week I was going to be prepared. I would google "insults" and practice until I could rattle one off. I figured it wasn't quite appropriate in my trusted position with the docs, but it wasn't like she was going to tattle on me.

Holding myself together made me exhausted, and I was constantly anxious that someone would notice the scissors slide out of my reach or see the paper clips bouncing on the desk. Lately I was better able to manage the lightning, but barely, and it wore me out to do it. I was dreaming of that glass of wine and my fleece blanket when I noticed that I had a voicemail. Wondering when the call came in, I listened. It was Lucia.

I'd met Lucia and my other friend Seishin shortly after moving to Atlanta at a "Lose your Inhibitions" seminar. The seminar didn't take, but the friendships did. By fate or divine intervention, I was seated between Lucia on my left and Seishin on my right. It was at the Georgia Dome and there must have been 10,000 people there. The music was blaring when Irene Novilicki came on the stage. She was a huge, black woman and was wearing layers of lime green and purple robes that dragged the floor behind her. She had on ropes of beaded necklaces and bracelets that must have added twenty pounds to her already substantial weight.

We began by standing up and introducing ourselves to our neighbors, which was the only sane part of the seminar. After that, she had us gyrating and hollering all over the place. Tony Robbins had nothing on Irene Novilicki. Before the first break, when I was already planning to bail out, she told us that she had commandeered a hotel pool and the seminar would culminate at midnight with us all getting naked and jumping in the pool. At that exact moment, Lucia turned right and Seishin turned left and they both looked at me and said, "Wanna get out of here?"

We bolted for the door only to be met by an usher who warned us that there was no re-entry to the seminar. Once we left, we were out for good. We all three chimed in unison. "No problem."

We left and went to a small bistro to have lunch and a glass of wine. We ended up having a lot of wine, and I called Kevin to come and get us and drive us all home. He did, graciously enough, and we became fast friends that day. Much like our seating in the seminar, I was really close to each of them and the hub around which our friendship revolved.

The message from Lucia said that she knew I was at work, but she had a moment alone in her car and just wanted to say she hoped I was having a good week. I called her back and got her voicemail. Frustrated because we seemed only to exchange messages since she had the twins, I told her of my plans for jammies and wine.

I'd seen Lucia through a divorce, the wild times after the divorce, a remarriage, and the twins. She'd seen me through my girls leaving home, the divorce from Kevin and becoming a grandmother. I haven't had the wild times post-divorce yet, but I'm not in my thirties with a great body like Lucia. I wished if Kevin were going to leave me anyway he would have done it when I was in my thirties. I'd still have had my girls, but I'd have had a much better body.

Around 4:30, my phone rang and it was Lucia again. "It's me" I hollered into the phone, thankful to finally talk to her in person.

"You mean it's really you, not voicemail?"

'It's really me!"

"Are you in your jammies yet?"

"I wasted no time."

"I'm free. Mark's got the kids 'til seven. I'm coming over."

"Have you eaten?"

"No."

I had a momentary worry about keeping the lightning situation from Lucia but pushed it away as I longed for the normalcy of our friendship. To reassure myself, I did grab a few Julian stones and stash them in my bra. I put on my sneakers to take advantage of the rubber soles; cute with my jammies I was sure. I ran to the kitchen, grabbed a bottle of white wine and stuck it in the freezer. While I was in there, I found some beef ribs and frozen green beans. I opened a bottle of red for me and gulped some down. It relaxed me. I was singing Billy Joel's "bottle of red, bottle of white, it all depends upon your appetite." I threw dinner in the oven.

I got placemats and cloth napkins, and lit the candles wondering when she had last eaten at an uncluttered table, with candles and wine. I worried over plastic or metal silverware but decided to brave the real stuff. It would look ridiculous with candles and cloth napkins and plastic utensils. I just hoped I had enough stones on me. When she arrived, I handed her a glass of chilled white wine and a plate of antipasto. We sat curled up on either end of my sofa sipping wine and chatting and gossiping like the old days.

I talked with her about books I'd read and some garden plans I was working on. I didn't tell her that the garden was intended to calm the lightning in me. She loved hearing about those things she didn't have time for anymore, and never made me feel like she was resentful of my freedom. It had always been an easy friendship that I cherished. Her motherhood had made these times few and far between. I wondered if I was a horrible person because sometimes I felt resentful of her twins, especially since Kevin left. Also, I felt anxious because I hadn't told her about the lightning. Gene still stubbornly held to calling me a superhero. I wondered how I'd work that into a conversation.

Hey Lucia, guess what? I was struck by lightning a few weeks ago by a Celtic goddess, and I'm a superhero who's supposed to right injustices. What's new with you?

"How's Seishin?" she asked, interrupting my mental musings.

"Great. She just got a new puppy, and I've never heard her so happy. She's in love."

"Speaking of love, is she dating anyone?"

"No. But I broached the subject with her. Do you know Evelyn Cutter?"

"Huh unh." Lucia shook her head.

"She's an Atlanta gal, bestselling author that writes grisly crime novels. They're too gruesome for you to read."

"You're so sensitive, how can you read that stuff?" Lucia wondered.

"I'm an enigma. I just can't stand a movie or a book where an animal dies. Kevin used to preview them for me. But people brutalizing each other doesn't bother me. Anyway, Evelyn and I don't run in the same circles, but it seems our circles overlap so I see her around and she knows I'm a fan. I saw her the other day, and she mentioned breaking up with her partner and joked about being back in the dating game. I mentioned it to Seishin and she began to hyperventilate, so I dropped it."

"You think she'll always be alone?" Lucia asked

"I wonder," I mused. "I've never known her to be with anyone."

We ate dinner by candlelight while she caught me up on the kids and Mark.

He'd recently had a cancer scare and had his tonsils out. Her mom, Colleen, had come to stay with the twins while Lucia went to the surgery center with Mark. She knew her mom couldn't manage both kids all day and arranged for the nanny to come, but Colleen had them alone for about an hour and a half. About 45 minutes after leaving, Lucia got a call from an emergency medical technician who was at her house. Apparently, Colleen was helping Colin out of his high chair when she looked around and couldn't find Karin. She screamed and called her name and searched the house. Finally, she became panicky and called 911.

A moment or two later she found the door ajar and Karin crawling backwards down the front steps of the house. She called back to the 911 center and said, "No need to come. I found her."

"That's not how this works," explained the operator. "When we get a call, we have to follow through with it. They are on their way."

"They" turned out to be three police cars, an ambulance, and a fire truck, all with lights and sirens blaring. Lucia was using her hands to describe the emergency vehicles driving through her neighborhood. She looked like a kid with a toy car in her hand, but of course she was minus the toy.

"And to top it off," she continued, "not only did they call me to inform me of the incident," she put her fingers into quote marks around 'the incident', "they questioned Mom like she was abusing Karin. Furthermore, they told my mom that they had to take Karin to the hospital to be checked for hypothermia.

"Thank heaven Mom has a brain in her head though, it's often doing twenty things at once so you might not notice it. She balked and said 'It's 69 degrees and she was only out of the house for about two minutes.'"

I was laughing so hard my belly ached. Enough time had elapsed since the incident that Lucia could laugh a little, but it was a bit less funny to her than me.

I caught her up on the girls and Riley. We didn't mention Kevin. And, of course, I never mentioned the lightning. Thankfully nothing flared it up.

Seven o'clock came too soon.

Chapter 13

A couple weeks later we were at a Malone Family Reunion at Stone Mountain Park. I had always been invited to these reunions though I was technically "family once removed." But Olivia's kids and mine were inseparable when they were little so they chose to include me and it continued. I was especially grateful since I'd lost Kevin's family in the divorce. Everyone was playing bacci ball and watching the little kids run around in the park. We had cooked steaks on the grill and had lots of great side dishes. We'd had a few cases of beer, and the bottles were piling up.

I enjoyed all of the Malones except for Brian's brother, Brad. I breathed a sigh of relief each time he missed a family event, but he was here today and gunning for an argument. He was an arrogant ass. He had the number "24" tattooed on his biceps and when anyone asked what it meant, he answered, "The number of hours in a day that I'm awesome."

He was in a group that included Gene and Venice when I heard his voice rise, and he began to rant on a subject that makes my blood boil.

"Ya want an easy way to clean up your Facebook account?" he swaggered.

"Post this: 'Since Roe vs. Wade was passed; 45 million souls have been aborted. It's my status and my FB page. If you want to disagree, fine. If you are rude, you're deleted.' Ha Ha, I posted it and that got 'em going."

Venice said, "Uncle Brad I saw your post and no one was rude. You just basically deleted all the people you didn't agree with. And then had the last word and wrote "end of thread.""

He sneered at her. "I suppose you call it healthcare and get all invigorated by the right to abort your baby for any reason?"

I could tell Venice was exasperated. "I agree with the girl on Facebook who said, 'I'll save you the hassle and delete myself.' If I weren't your niece and didn't want to play nice with family, I'd delete you too. Besides, I don't value a man's opinion on abortion or anything else you'll never have to face."

He retorted with, "Men are citizens and fathers and have every right to protect innocent life. So, bottom line, you either think it's OK to kill a baby or you think it's wrong."

I was furious. I can't stand him, and I really can't stand any man spouting off on abortion. Whether you are pro-choice or you think abortion is a sin doesn't matter a bit to me. But one thing I know deep in my soul is that not even the most hard-bitten bitch on earth wants to have an abortion. Women who make that choice need compassion, not criticism.

I am also fiercely protective toward my kids and nieces and nephews; Cathy's kids excluded. And Venice didn't deserve that. I felt the lightning rise and felt the now familiar nausea and anxiety. The world began to close in. I nearly panicked. I knew something was about to happen, and it wouldn't be good. I was trying to find a way to get it under control. Then I impulsively changed my mind.

Until that moment, all I had wanted was for the lightning in me to disappear. I had cried and begged and prayed to have my old life back. But in that moment it all changed. Gene was so excited about my "powers" as he called them and had repeatedly encouraged me to use them. Even though I had some doubts, I was mad enough to try. I got his attention and called him away from the group.

"Hold these," I said yanking my pouch of talisman stones off over my head. I pointed toward Brad and Venice. "Keep your eyes on them. I'm taking your advice."

I turned my attention to Brad and focused my already riled up energy at his feet. I pictured angry fire ants biting at his feet and ankles. I noticed him begin to wiggle and move his feet around, so I moved it higher to his calves and knees. Now he was getting more animated and stomping his feet and pulling his shoes and socks off.

Venice was concerned. "Uncle Brad what's wrong with you?"

"I think I stepped in fire ants."

Dear sweet Venice reached down to help him get his shoes and socks off, but I was far less compassionate. I moved the energy higher to his thighs and groin. I was getting off on it now, and Gene was laughing hard, encouraging me.

Brad was really dancing around now, slapping and clawing at his legs and groin and yelping in pain. The rest of the group kind of backed away and looked around as if they wanted advice or help or something. I hated the fact that Venice was upset, but I couldn't stop myself. Re-playing all of his asshole comments through my mind like a litany made me love every minute of his torture. Gene was laughing so hard he was shaking.

At this point Brad totally freaked out and yanked his pants and underwear off, bent his head between his legs to look, and grabbed and slapped his hairy balls and ass. Finding nothing there to brush away, he took off running, naked from the waist down and jumped in the lake.

Poor Venice was the only one who seemed distraught. I think the rest of the family secretly felt that he deserved whatever punishment he got though they knew not from where it came. I stopped the lightning, grabbed my stones from Gene and was reaching for my phone app when I realized I didn't have my phone.

Gene was laughing uproariously now, and I gave him a wide-eyed glare to stop drawing attention to us, but the shock of what I had just done coupled with the screwed up look on Gene's face got me tickled, and I giggled. And then I got to laughing harder and harder until I squinted up my eyes and I was crying and snorting. In short, I was hysterical. And then the inevitable happened. I peed. And I don't mean a little drip in my panties while I crossed my legs and made it to the bathroom. I mean I started peeing and crossing my legs and sucking it in and squeezing, but I peed a river down my light blue pants and into my shoes while I screamed and laughed and cried all at once.

"Oh God, Gene I just peed my pants." I was still laughing and crying. "Walk behind me to the bathroom so no one notices."

"Brava you just did the most amazing thing I've ever seen in my life and you peed? Really? That's how we will remember this most awesome moment? You peeing?"

"Gene just help me get away before anyone notices. Walk behind me to the bathroom."

"And then what? Are you going to take off your pants and come out naked like Uncle Brad?"

I had just a moment to wonder about my next move when Gene picked me up and ran to the lake and threw me in.

Chapter 14

During the months when I was still uncertain of both my marital and financial status, I had started an internet business sewing purses to make some extra money. The bags had become so popular I couldn't keep up with the orders on my own. So I had enlisted the help of the "girls." Kevin's settlement meant that I wasn't desperate for the money, but what I made from the purses helped me afford some extras, and it was so much fun that all of us agreed to continue doing it on the first Friday of every month.

That initial Friday evening prior to the lightning, Sheila followed me home from work. I cranked up the volume on the 60s radio station and we got ready for the other girls, opening wine and setting out prosciutto and cheese and olives.

Mom and Liv showed up next looking like clones from opposite sides of the track. Liv was stunning as usual. She was wearing a royal blue full skirt with white swishes on it. Her impossibly tiny waist was cinched with a wide black belt and a large jeweled clasp. Her shoes were black, strappy sandals that clicked when she walked and the same jeweled clasp as her belt. Her toes were even painted royal blue to match her outfit. Her bag was a small, black Brighton clutch with a silver shoulder strap.

Mom, walking beside her, sported a bright red sweatshirt that said, "Best grammy in the world", pink Capri slacks and green gardening clogs. I couldn't wait to read what was on her turquoise grocery bag. I reached for it and read out loud, "You know it's going to be a bad day when you get out of bed and miss the floor." I laughed, and hugged Mom and Liv and handed them each a glass of wine.

By the time Lucia arrived, I'd had a second glass of wine and was dancing to "Build me up Buttercup" in the kitchen. Lucia looked a little ragged. She was still wearing a pacifier on a rope around her neck, and I figured she had gotten the kids fed and to bed before leaving them to Mark. She joined the dancing in the kitchen, and I snatched the paci off over her head.

"You won't be needing this tonight." She'd have stayed and participated with us no matter what just to get a night away from the twins. She reached inside her shirt and pulled out two more pacifiers.

"Or these," she said matter-of-factly.

She always did that; reach into her bra and pull stuff out; pacis, her phone, lipstick. I wondered where she had room for all that stuff. In fact, I had the ridiculous urge to pull on her shirt and look down to see what else was there. I restrained myself.

Seishin arrived last. She is even more of an introvert than me and when she got there, we were all giggling like schoolgirls and singing to Billy Joel's, "Only the Good Die Young."

Even Mom was into it. Seishin looked a little dismayed, and for a moment, I feared she might turn and run, but she joined us in a drink if not a song.

I made a dish I found in an Italian cookbook that Lucia gave me, and everyone loved it. I sautéed shrimp in white wine, bacon, garlic, and red onions and put it over a bed of pasta and spinach leaves. It smelled divine. A little parmesan shaved on top and it was a great success.

Then we cleared the table and set up a cutting station on one end of the dining room table and the sewing machine on the other end. They cut the pieces of fabric, and I sewed them in an assembly line fashion. We turned on the Lifetime channel and half watched some sappy chick flick while we worked. I was able to sew seven bags in the time it took me to sew one all by myself. And they cut enough fabric pieces for me to have plenty to sew after work and on the weekends. I never did put the sewing machine away. I left the dining room as a sewing room and ate in the kitchen after that. Every month the girls came back and we set up TV trays and ate in front of another Lifetime movie that we hardy watched.

Chapter 15

Driving home from work on Wednesday, I listened to the 60s radio station because it puts me in a good mood. Not this day; I was in a dark mood. It was Kevin's and my wedding anniversary, and it would have been twenty-seven years had he not dumped me. In fact, just to fuck with me, the DJ played our song, Good Vibrations.

I've been prone to feeling sorry for myself a lot lately (*a fact that I'm not proud of*) but this day I was fueled by a rage that burned in my belly. If I'd have seen Kevin at that moment, I could have torn him limb from limb. I was near my neighborhood on Gael Drive, and I stopped to let a white Volvo out from a side street. A huge tricked out, red Ford pickup truck behind me laid on the horn.

Redneck I thought. *Probably from Alabama.*

That led to thoughts of Cathy and this time they weren't funny. All of this coupled with my already dark mood pissed me off so much I heard the keys jangle in reaction to my anger. I didn't care. I wanted to sit there all evening and make that bastard wait. If I couldn't get back at Kevin then this guy would serve as a great stand in.

Traffic was backed up from the light at the intersection anyway, so I just took my foot off the brake and coasted, inching my way forward, leaving a larger and larger space between me and the Volvo. I saw the guy in the truck in my rearview mirror flipping me the bird and yelling curses at me. That fueled the anger in my belly even more. I felt powerful that he couldn't do a thing except wait behind me.

I was mistaken, however, and I watched wide-eyed in my rearview mirror as he jerked his huge truck right up over the curb through someone's perfectly manicured front lawn. He gunned his engine and skidded through their yard leaving huge "S" shaped ruts in his wake. He careened back onto the street narrowly missing me and another car in the opposite lane. That car swerved away and jumped the other curb, nearly hitting a young woman pushing her child in a stroller. I heard her scream. As he accelerated with a squeal of his tires, he sprayed mud and grass all over my windshield. Then he repeated the same stunt to get around the Volvo I had let in front of me.

That son of a bitch. I was furious. His actions alone were enough to fuel the anger that flared in me, but my already sour mood fanned the fire. Traffic was congested so the whole dangerous stunt only got him two car lengths ahead. That pissed me off even more.

I tromped on the gas and accelerated behind the Volvo. My intention was to get the license plate of the truck, and I cursed myself for being nice to the woman in the Volvo.

No good deed ever goes unpunished.

All the frustration, shame, anger, fear, and anxiety I had felt after the divorce was now aimed at the bastard in the red truck. I saw a huge concrete drainage culvert off to my right and wished he'd end up with his big, red truck upside down in the bottom of it. That would show him. I craned my neck to see around the Volvo and get his license number while I reached in my console for a pen.

I noticed the interior of my car getting smaller. The circle of my vision decreased, and I felt the now familiar surge of anxiety and nausea well up in me. The keys jangled wildly in the ignition. No sooner did I comprehend what was happening, than to my shock and horror, his huge red pickup truck skidded sideways toward the culvert and then tipped and rolled side over side down into a twenty foot drainage ditch.

The keys stopped jangling, and I knew I was going to vomit. I had to get out the car as much to throw up as to check on him. Other people were already exiting their vehicles and going down to help. I saw smoke rising from the ditch and really panicked.

What if his truck exploded and killed him?

I flung open my door and ran to the side of the road afraid to look down and see what I'd caused. I forced myself to look down into the culvert and saw the truck on its roof and the driver crawling out from the smoke. I threw up right there on the side of the road. I heaved and heaved until I had nothing left inside me. I heard people screaming to call 911. I was aware of people running into the ditch. Someone was yelling "fire, fire." Another person screamed over the din that it was the tires smoking. Then I smelled the burning rubber. I dry heaved yet again. All the while I stood with my head hanging down over my vomited lunch feeling hatred for myself. I wished I were dead.

What he had done that infuriated me so much was nothing compared to what I had just done. I took one more look down in the ditch and saw that the driver was walking around. I eased back to my car and slipped away. No one noticed my leaving as all eyes were in the culvert. I didn't have a clue how the witnesses would describe what happened, but I knew I had caused it, and I had to get away.

I couldn't even call Gene. I wished I had a place like Julian's Church here in Atlanta. But instead, I drove home longing for the sanctuary of my back yard. I grabbed a glass of wine on my way out and sat in the grass with my back against the stone retaining wall and sobbed. I sobbed and prayed and cussed and stomped my feet.

After I had expended every ounce of energy to rail against Kevin and God and even the goddess Dealan, I just sat. The wine glass was empty, and I wanted more but I couldn't gather the energy to get it. I shoved the glass away and lay on my back in the cool grass. I felt as empty as the glass I had carelessly tossed away.

A still quiet came over me. I felt the setting sun on my face, saw the green of the leaves, felt the cool blades of grass on my neck. It was as if I could watch all the past months play out like a movie. And for the first time, I saw myself as the whining, angry victim I had become. I had depended far too much on Gene. I couldn't understand why he'd even want to be around me. I used to be the "fun aunt." Now what was I? I hardly talked with my daughters anymore. What must they think? I was disgusted with myself. And furthermore, my ass was as wide as the side of a barn.

I needed to get my life in order. I wanted the old Brava back. I knew at that moment I had a choice. I could continue wishing for my old life and blaming Kevin and God and anyone else I could think of. If I kept that up, I could see my future in front of me. I'd end up on a TV commercial for a weight loss reality show. Or selling "fat jeans" at the mall of North Georgia, eating lunch every day in the food court. I'd get so fat I'd explode. I could see the headlines now, "Fat Woman Explodes in Busy Food Court. Injures Six."

Or I could go forward toward a new life and shape my own destiny. In that instant, I chose the latter. I would work hard to be happy and healthy. Or at the very least stop whining and feeling sorry for myself and stuffing my face with sandwiches and chips.

I laid there as the sun set over the house and the grass cooled. I saw the first star appear and watched the crescent moon rise. I thought that a red-tailed hawk sat in the tree, but I think it was my imagination. I was cold and stiff by the time I dragged myself up off the ground and went inside. I called rather than texted Gene. It was late, and he was surprised to hear from me. I asked him if I could pick him up to spend the night. That was an unusual request on a school night so he knew something was up.

"Are you OK?" He asked me that a lot lately, and I told him so.

"I'm more than OK, and I'd like to share it with you. You've been party to my whining long enough. Can I come get you?"

"I'm waiting at the front door."

I met Gene with a smile that I realized had been absent for a long time. It even felt good on my own face. I caught him up on what happened with the red truck, and after that in the backyard. He was a little more freaked about the truck than I had expected. He grabbed his laptop and searched the local news channels for the story. He found none and we discussed it, playing out different scenarios. We eventually surmised that people "saw" what their brains could rationalize, rather than the impossible thing that really happened. Eventually, he relaxed about it.

We actually laughed and joked about my being a superhero. It felt like the old times, and I was thankful for the lightness. I had an idea I shared with Gene. I'd look this minute and find a superhero movie and watch it to learn. I was exhausted from the terrible evening and knew I should go to bed, but I simply had to start my new life at this very moment. I began with the action/ adventure category on Netflix and came up with Spiderman 2. I congratulated myself on such a good choice.

"By the second movie, I'm sure he's got this superhero gig down pat," I told Gene.

Gene had seen it before, but it had been years and besides, he said, "They all run together." He couldn't remember the plot of this one.

I was barely ten minutes into the movie when the day caught up with me. I could hardly hold my head up and was nodding off, but I was determined. I was about halfway into the movie when I realized my misjudgment. Peter Parker whined and pissed and moaned even worse than I had these last few months. I didn't need a lesson in feeling sorry for myself. I had been living that to the max. I turned it off, and Gene and I went to bed. I was still determined but frustrated. I'd choose another superhero movie and another until I found one I could emulate.

Chapter 16

The next day, work went slightly better than the previous weeks. I used my app a little less and felt more in control of everything. I still taped quite a few stones on my body just in case. Despite the hypoallergenic tape, the constant use of it irritated my skin. I had been forced to move the stones around to different places on my body as my ankles and wrists were suffering from the rash. I had linear patches of red in various shades of healing all over my torso and legs. When anyone noticed, I told them I had gotten poison ivy from working in the garden. I knew I simply had to find another solution. But what?

It was Saturday a few weeks later, and I was meeting Olivia for lunch. I wanted to look nice because I always felt frumpy next to Olivia. I chose some navy cotton capris with a red and white striped cotton top and white low-heeled sandals. It was a hot day, and I liked the nautical theme because it reminded me of the ocean. I looked at myself in the full-length mirror and aside from criticizing my hips, I thought I looked nice. I grabbed my large straw bag and left the house feeling good. It was my first foray into a restaurant with real silverware, and I was a little worried. My wrists and ankles were bare so the stones would show if I taped them there, but I had a few extra Julian stones taped and tucked in various locations.

I arrived before Liv at JJJ and B, nicknamed J3B, the newest and best restaurant in Atlanta, and ordered a glass of merlot. I hoped that the wine would help keep me calm so the silverware wouldn't get away from me. I could just picture my fork skittering along the floor while the haughty waiter chased it saying, "No worries Madam, that's perfectly natural; happens all the time."

The restaurant is owned by four chefs from Food Network TV. I don't remember their names, except for Julianna, my favorite, but they all begin with J and B. It's an interesting concept. Each chef has a different culinary style, and they post a schedule on their website if you want to see who's cooking. I think much of their success lies in the adventure of going and then finding out. That's what Liv and I were doing today. I was delighted to see that it was Julianna. I inhaled the aroma of garlic, oregano, basil and fennel. Mom and I are both good cooks, especially Italian food. Liv is only good at making reservations. Chef Julianna is a master, and I love to choose dishes that I don't know how to cook and then try to imitate them.

I perused the menu while I waited for Liv, and I knew the minute she arrived. There was a hush as she swept into the room. Olivia doesn't walk; she sweeps or sashays or floats into a room. Seeing her, I realized I had gone wrong with my outfit yet again. She was wearing a cream colored crepe de chine designer outfit. I knew it was designer because that's all Liv wears, and because it fit her body in that way only designer clothes fit. Her shoes were soft leather Italian wedge sandals with dainty seashells. Apparently, she also went with the nautical theme, just way more elegantly than me. She had accented it with gold jewelry and a gold clutch.

I felt like Raggedy Andy wearing a sailor suit and playing dress up at a fancy restaurant.

Watching Liv enter a room is like watching a movie. All the eyes of every man between the ages of puberty and death turned toward her. Time slowed. I swear I could hear the lilting music. Conversations stopped. And Olivia is utterly unaware of the effect she has.

She was clearly delighted to see me, and we hugged as she sat down. Olivia is the most charming person I have ever known. She's probably the most charming person that anyone has known. And her total unawareness is part of that charm.

The best thing about our relationship is that we always laugh when we're together. We can both tell stories better than most native southerners, and they have the patent on storytelling. But our family is fodder enough for a good laugh. We were remembering our recent trip to Italy taken to cheer me up post-divorce.

That was the time Mom told them Kevin was dead. We recalled Mom's near perfect Sicilian. We had never heard her fluency prior to that.

I said to Liv, "I think there's a gene that lives in our brain that gets triggered sometimes. It's like a genetic memory from our ancestors. It must have gotten triggered or something."

Liv responded with her theory, "Or she simply remembered Grandma and Grandpa talking Sicilian and recalled the words."

"I like the gene theory. Kevin always said I carried a Sicilian "grudge gene" in my head, because according to him if anyone ever crossed me or my family I carried a grudge forever. What's wrong with that?"

Liv laughed. "Maybe he was right because we all carry a grudge against him, hunh?"

At the table, I told Liv, "I can't believe I was upset that she said he was dead. It's almost like he is, and it would be so much more sympathetic to be a widow. You should see people's faces when I explain what really happened. I've considered keeping with Mom's story when I meet someone new; especially if I start dating, which I've considered."

"Seriously Brava? Why didn't you tell me? I can hook you up with Brian's friend, the neurologist. You've met him briefly, I think."

"Oh my God, Olivia, I never should have told you I was considering it. I've only gone so far as to fill out a profile on an internet dating site. I hover my mouse over divorced and widowed and then freak out and hit escape. Divorce just comes with so much baggage that I don't have. I guess I should be grateful to Kevin for that."

My sweet sister Olivia, who rarely has a bad word to say about anyone said sternly, "Do not use the words gratitude and Kevin in the same sentence ever again."

I was grateful when the waiter interrupted the dating conversation and took our orders. I ordered the red snapper with a white wine reduction sauce over spinach, and a green salad with the house dressing. Liv ordered the pasta Napoli, which is a saffron cream sauce over linguini and a Caesar salad.

The extra stones taped to my body, coupled with the wine, were helping me relax. The dating conversation was fraught with danger, and I was glad it was over. I was counting on the fact that I was with Liv, and it would be fun. I did far better when I was relaxed.

So far so good with the silverware.

The waiter brought bread to the table, and I dipped a small crust into some peppered olive oil and nibbled it as I sipped my wine and worried about my ass getting broader. Olivia eats like a lumberjack and never gains an ounce. She had four pieces of bread slathered in butter and dipped in oil before the meal came. She got a second glass of wine and asked for extra bread when the meal arrived. I took half my meal home for dinner. Liv wolfed every bite of hers. Sometimes I can't believe the size of her bites. It's as if she's afraid if she doesn't get it all in quick, someone's gonna take it away. It's so unfair she's a size four. I'd hate her if I didn't love her so much.

"Did Gene tell you about last Saturday night?" she asked.

"No. What happened?" I was curiously hurt because I thought Gene shared everything with me. Then I realized that was ridiculous. I didn't know the half of it.

"He got in really late, like two a.m., smelling of beer and cigarettes, and Brian was waiting up for him."

"No way! Gene was drinking and smoking?"

"Apparently. I thought Brian was gonna kill him. I awoke to the screaming and ran downstairs to hear Brian say he was going to lock Gene up in a cage in the basement until he was twenty-one."

"Brian? Said that? He's always so calm."

"I know. He lost his shit. I've never seen him so mad."

"What did you do?"

"I calmed them both down, sent Gene to bed, and talked some sense into Brian. As far as I'm concerned, it could be far worse."

I secretly thought Liv was relieved that Gene did something so normal, but didn't mention it to her.

"No wonder he didn't share it with me, huh?"

The waiter hovered until I stopped talking and looked at him. He asked if everything was delectable.

"Delectable? Who says that?" I wondered.

Liv and I were both laughing really hard at the re-telling so some leg crossing was in order. I excused myself and went to the bathroom as much to pee as to use my app so the lightning wouldn't show. I was sorry to see the lunch end. It was a wonderful reprieve.

Chapter 17

The caller ID on the phone at work showed that it was Dad calling from his mobile phone.

I answered with "Everything OK, Dad? You never call me at work."

"I'm concerned about your mom, Brava," he said, getting right to the point.

Anxiety welled up inside of me. I have a red alert button that gets pushed easily when it comes to my parents. Since the lightning, it gets pushed even more easily and with far worse consequences.

"What is it, Dad? What's wrong with Mom?" The scissors skittered across my desk, I grabbed them and took a few deep breaths.

"She's just off. It's really not reason for panic. Settle down. She's not eating much or sleeping well. It's only been going on for four or five days. I've asked her about it several times, but she does that thing waving her hands around like she's swatting flies and waves me off. She says she's fine so I sent her in to see Dr. Jack. You know she adores him, and maybe he can figure it out."

"OK Dad, he's with a patient now, but I'll get her in to see him in a little while."

"Love you Brava."

"Love you too, Dad."

Looking up a short while later, I saw Mom coming up the walk, and even from a distance I knew she was in trouble. We're not an emergency clinic, but I know one when I see one. I ran to the door to help her into the office.

She was extremely agitated and was breathing rapidly, but it seemed like her chest wasn't moving at all. She was staring but not really seeing me, and I could see the sheen of sweat on her brow, and her face was a ghostly white. She was shaking violently.

"Oh my God, Mom what happened?" I had a brief moment of fury at my dad for letting her drive in that condition, then realized he hadn't. He had no sound of alarm in his voice. This must have happened since she left home.

"I made a terrible, terrible mistake, Brava. My family should hate me. I wish I could die. Your father should leave me."

I felt an awful sinking feeling come over me. "My God, Mom what happened to you? Have you been in an accident?"

She was shutting down. On one level I knew she couldn't answer me in her present state, but my own fear got the best of me, and I peppered her with questions.

"Mom what happened? Talk to me, please." I got nothing in response.

I was half dragging, half carrying her toward a treatment room as she seemed too weak to walk. Passing the room Dr. Jack was in, I pounded on the door and screamed, "Dr. Jack help me."

I got her into room three and had barely got her up on the table when Dr. Jack came running. He was immediately in doctor mode.

"Get the table flat. Get a cuff on her. Get her heart rate."

I did as he instructed, dropping the exam table into position and wrapping the automatic blood pressure cuff around her arm.

"Pulse is 121. BP is 150/98," I reported.

He rummaged in the cupboards and came out with a pill that he stuck under her tongue and held her mouth closed. She was flailing and fighting, but he calmly held her mouth closed and her arms down at the same time.

I thought of screaming for Sheila when she came running. She ran to the head of the table and cupped my mom's head in her hands.

"Eugenia listen to me. Focus on my voice. Blow all your air out. Blow it out. Just blow it out. We've got you. You're going to be OK. Blow. There you go."

Mama exhaled with a loud hiss and gasped a breath in, and Sheila said again, "Blow it out again Mama Eugenia."

As all of this was happening, I realized that panic was setting in on me. I began to shake, and the instruments on the counter vibrated. My vision telescoped.

Dr. Jack saw it about the same time I realized I was in trouble. He'd seen me through many panic attacks in the months after Kevin left though he had no idea how different this one was.

"Get out," he roared. "I don't need two patients in here."

I ran to the bathroom and grabbed under the sink for the rubber gloves I kept stashed there. I just barely got them on and made it to the toilet before emptying my guts. I was crying and heaving and gasping for a breath. I reached for my phone and used the app to calm my breathing and energy.

It seemed like forever until I got a hold of myself. Sheila came in and found me. I had just enough time to rip off my gloves and check that nothing was vibrating. She helped me up off the floor and hugged me hard and long, steadying me. She asked no questions. She just stood with her hand on my back and waited while I washed my face with cold water, drying the mascara streaks with a paper towel. She walked with me back to Mom's treatment room.

Dr. Jack scrutinized me at the door before stepping aside to let me in.

"She'll be fine," he reassured me. "If she were younger, I wouldn't worry so much, but with her age I am worried. If I had any god-dammed confidence in the hospital, I'd send her there for observation. But they're so understaffed, she'll be forgotten. We'll keep her here for the remainder of the day. Talk to her for a minute and then cancel the rest of the afternoon. And figure out what caused this if you can, but don't upset her."

Dr. Jack was always so calm. I'd never heard him raise his voice or swear so I knew this had really shaken him up. That made two of us. I took in the room. The EKG machine had leads dangling and was askew beside the table. The graphs were strewn across the counter. The air smelled of alcohol and Mom's perfume, and I noticed the swabs thrown on the floor near to the medicine wrappers. Sheila walked in ahead of me and stood beside the table holding Mom's hand.

"Is she OK?" I asked.

"Yes, Brava. Your mom is a strong woman. She is OK now."

"Mom, what happened? Dad called and said you seemed agitated, but nothing prepared me for this."

"I made a terrible, terrible mistake, Brava. My family should hate me. I wish I could die. Your father doesn't deserve what I've done. He should leave me." She was getting worked up again, and her hands began to wave around.

I forgot Dr. Jack's warning as my own fear escalated.

"What on earth could you have ever done for your family to hate you? Don't be ridiculous. We'd never hate you."

"I can't talk about it. I made a terrible mistake. I can't eat or sleep. You'll find out soon enough. I made a terrible money mistake. I got scammed." Now she was getting really worked up. Sheila gave me a look, and I backed off as she calmed my mother again.

Horrible thoughts ran through my head. *Did she drain the savings? Were my parents now destitute? How much money, what scam? When?*

I couldn't let it go.

"Mama if it's money we don't care, just please tell me what happened. I am so scared to see you like this."

"Stop Brava, I can't talk about it. I wish I could die." Sheila was giving me the look again, but my anxiety was coming back with a vengeance, and we were all going to be in trouble if it did.

"Who scammed you? How much money Mama?"

"I can't say it. Don't make me say it." She was yanking her arms away from Sheila who was trying to calm Mom *and* shut me up and failing at both.

"Mama just answer this. Was it more than $10,000? $20,000?" I was shouting out numbers and looking for any response. But I got none.

I couldn't get any more out of Mom that day. Dr. Jackson and Sheila put a stop to my trying. Liv came to the office and drove Mom's car to their house, and I followed with Mom silent in the passenger seat. Dad looked stricken when we delivered her to him. We were all terrified and had endless dire possibilities in our minds. All we knew was that she had been scammed out of a lot of money.

I took Liv back to the office to pick up her car, and we worried all the way back. Would they have to live with one of us? It would most likely be me since I had the room. How in God's name would I ever hide what was going on with me if they were living in my home? A hundred unanswerable questions parried back and forth between us as we dreamed up more and more terrible possibilities.

We finally agreed that we'd just call it a day and go home. We'd wait and see if Dad got anything out of her tomorrow. I was sick and scared so the lightning reared up. I had a terrible time trying to get something to eat despite the fact that most of my utensils were now plastic. But I felt like throwing up anyway, so I went to bed hungry. It was a long, sleepless night. The hawk was outside my window again.

Was it a dream or real?

For the first time since the lightning I seriously pondered becoming a superhero. *What if I figured out who did this to Mom and got their money back?* Revenge would feel so sweet. I was reluctant to tell Gene I was contemplating it as he'd take the idea and run with it.

I did my daily routine the next day taping some extra stones to contain the lightning. It was always much worse when I was riled up. Keeping my mind on work was almost impossible and the docs felt for me so they gave me a lot of leeway.

Dad called near to noon and said Mom was still in bed; sleeping or pretending to sleep, no doubt to avoid discussion. He knew better than to push her. If you tried, she'd dig in her heels even harder. I would have been berating her to get the details, but he was right, it wouldn't work; never had. She'd talk when she was ready and he'd help her get there better than any of us. He said he'd let us know.

"Brava no matter what, we'll all get through this as a family. We always have."

Thank heavens Dr. Jackson gave me the following day off. It was almost worse than the day before. I was feeling more agitated, rather than less. I laid on the sofa and watched Home and Garden TV and the Food Network. I felt sorry for myself and indulged in a pity party. I drank too much coffee, and then had a toasted cheese sandwich and tomato soup for lunch. I changed to chocolate candy in the afternoon and by four o'clock it was wine. Everything I had counted on in my life looked different; Kevin, the lightning, now my parents' financial situation. I never thought I'd be this unsure and scared in my life. I had only thought the divorce was the worst of it.

That day and the next went by in agonizing slowness. I went to work the third day but felt miserable. Mom still wasn't talking. She had gotten out of bed and cried the second day, only to return again without Dad learning anything useful. He was going through online banking accounts and had come up with $50,000 missing. I threw up when he told me that. I don't know Mom and Dad's financial situation. They had a grocery store in Pennsylvania and sold out to a chain and retired here. They lived like they hadn't a nickel to spare, but I figured they were pretty well off.

Dad said Mom went out for a bit that third day and came home acting like her normal self. She said "Don't you worry, Alfred I'll take care of this. I caused it. I'll fix it."

When Dad told me that we both agreed that was scarier than her lying in bed and crying all day.

Dad told me, "Brava, I asked her to trust me and tell me what happened so I could run some numbers and see where we're at financially and plan our future. I reassured her that I was sorry it happened to her but didn't blame her. Far as I can tell it's $50,000. I don't think it's more."

"Oh God, Dad, what will you do? Does that completely wipe you out?"

"We have some money tied up in accounts, but I can't get to it without penalty for six months. I'll make this work Brava, and I don't want to burden you, but we may need to stay with you a while. It nearly wiped us out; at least for a while. We can't live off our Social Security without that extra money."

"Whatever I can do to help Dad. You know I'll do it."

I was wearing extra stones taped with non-allergenic tape everywhere. I kept my phone on the app and sucked and blew on that gold flag every second someone wasn't looking at me. The doctors probably thought I had a bladder infection because I spent half my day in the bathroom. They thought I was peeing, but I was breathing.

I got a text from Gene that day.

"U OK?"

"Not great. I probably weigh twenty pounds more with the stones I'm wearing. The lightning is hard to control."

"Do you know what happened yet?" Gene asked.

"She's not talking. I'm scared she is going to do something stupid. Or stupider on top of whatever happened in the first place."

"Yea. I'm worried too. Pick me up after school. Will ya?"

"I'll be there. Luv ya."

"Me too."

Sheila stopped by my desk between clients. She was wearing a full, denim skirt with a sea green and pink silk blouse and sheer jacket to match. She wore a stunning set of earrings and a necklace crafted from beach glass and seashells. Added to her ensemble were six silver bracelets; three on each arm. She jingled when she walked. The earrings had three tiers of small green glass beads and beach pebbles with tiny pink shells. On her fingers she wore several white and pink shell rings we had gotten on a beach trip to Gulf Shores, Alabama.

"Hanging in Brava?" she asked with concern on her face.

"By a thread."

"Do you know what happened, or is she still not talking?" Sheila asked.

"Still not talking, but she is acting back to normal and says she'll take care of it. That is NOT a good thing. We're afraid she's gonna go off like some vigilante. You know how she is. I wish she'd come talk to you, but she won't hear of it. Even before this she wouldn't. Sheila, I think she lost $50,000, and Dad says they might have to move in with me for about six months."

I teared up and continued. "I feel awful for Mom and Dad and awful for me, then I feel guilty for thinking of myself. This is dreadful." I was starting to blubber, so I got a tissue and wiped at my eyes and tried to recover my senses.

"Sorry," I said to Sheila. "You do enough therapy in your room without doing it at the front desk."

"Don't be ridiculous, Brava. I love you and I'm your friend, not your therapist. I asked how you were, and I don't want you faking it for my benefit. That would be an insult to our friendship."

Just then, we were interrupted by her next client. Following her client, she turned around and mouthed, "Later, OK?"

I smiled despite my despair, feeling lucky to have such a good friend. I wished I could tell Sheila about the lightning, but so far Gene was the only one I could bring myself to share that with. I was still hoping it would go away, and I wouldn't ever have to talk about it.

Chapter 18

I picked Gene up after school and we went to my house. I fixed spaghetti and meatballs, his favorite. The kitchen was filled with the aroma of garlic and onions and tomato sauce. I sipped a glass of wine, and Gene sat at the kitchen table so we could talk. I could manage the lightning in my kitchen with Gene and some wine. When I was relaxed, it was better.

Gene was tight-lipped regarding the subject of Mom, and I was suspicious that he knew more than he was telling, but it still felt good to talk of other subjects.

"How's your Kung Fu?" I asked.

"Pretty good," Gene answered. "But you know Sifu. He's not big on the compliments. It's hard to tell."

"Has he told you your Kung Fu was like watching a train wreck?" I asked.

Gene laughed. "Not exactly that, but it sounds as if you're speaking from experience."

"Yea, I am. One day I was doing my form and having a hard time concentrating. He told me he could read my mind by looking at my body and when I made a mistake it was like watching a train wreck in slow motion. When I came home

A K Robbins

and told your Uncle Kevin how upset I was, he laughed at me. I couldn't understand what was so funny and told him so.

He said, 'Brava I just never heard you care *that* much about what anyone thought of you before.'"

I remembered Kevin laughing as he went on to say, "I wish you cared that much about what I think."

At the time, I had punched him in the arm and he had kissed me. I didn't share that with Gene. The good memories were the most painful.

Gene laughed. "I know. Sometimes I hate Sifu, yet I want to please him too. What's up with that?"

"I don't know Gene, but he gets in your head and lives there."

Gene laughed, and we commiserated about what it was about Sifu to make you want to do good even if you rarely got a compliment out of it. We ate our pasta and talked some more about Sifu and his maddening ways and about the trials of Kung Fu. It felt good to forget about Mom for a while.

Dad called the next day and asked me to meet him for lunch. He didn't mention Mom   coming, so I knew something was up, and I readily agreed. We met at the Varsity, an Atlanta landmark that serves hot dogs, a favorite food for both of us. You have to learn a whole new language to order correctly at the varsity. When you walk in the door, all the counter people start yelling "What'll ya have, what'll ya have?" Tourists don't know the language. I got my dog "all the way," that is with onions. Dad got a naked dog with an

138

FO and a bag o' rags. That's a dog with nothing on it and a frosted orange and chips. I think Dad orders that because he likes to say it! I ordered onion rings and we shared. Despite the anxiety around Mom, I relished meeting Dad alone for lunch as it was a rarity. He explained what he had found out so far.

"Apparently your mom was shopping on Saturday over at the shopping center near your house; the one with the Dollar Tree and the Goodwill and the Peruvian, or Ecuadorian, or Colombian restaurant. Whichever. It has the Bank of Atlanta right there."

"Yea, I know it. It's the one we love because it has all the deal stores."

I had the random thought that that might be why I look so frumpy because I shop for deals, and Olivia always looks like a million bucks because that's about what she spends. Her favorite shopping center is Phipp's Plaza where they have stores like Saks Fifth avenue and Tiffany's.

He continued, "Some woman came up to her and showed her a bank bag stuffed with money and asked your mother if she'd dropped it. Well, your mom's nothing if not honest, so, of course, she said it wasn't hers. I'm not sure I've got the whole story from her, but the scam went something like this. She told your mom that she found this money and showed her the bank bag full. They could split it, but her boss, some unseen guy, was going to do something with the serial numbers so it couldn't be traced."

"How did it go from sharing a bank bag full of money to mom losing all your savings, Dad?"

"That's apparently the scam, Brava. This lady said your mom had to give her $5000 dollars for her boss to do that."

I interrupted. "Fifty thousand dollars or five thousand dollars?"

"Five thousand."

"Well how the hell did it turn into fifty thousand?" I had raised my voice, and I looked around because I didn't want people to hear me.

"Your mother went to the ATM and withdrew $5000. When the con lady met your mom, presumably to split the found money, your mom still had the ATM receipt in her hands. She grabbed it. The balance on the receipt was $45,000. I think that's how she knew exactly how much to ask for.

She told your mom that she knew everything about her family. She said that we lived in Lamplighter Village, a gated community in Canton. She knew we went to St. Francis Episcopal Church. She threatened your mom that if she didn't go back in the bank and get $45,000 she knew where her whole family was and she would kill all of us in our sleep."

"Oh, my God, Dad, how did she know all that?"

"Brava, I've really thought about it. I don't think she did. I think she simply looked at your mom's car. The plates are from Cherokee county and the dealership is in Canton. We have a property owners' tag on the windshield to get us through the gates. She didn't know it was a gated trailer park. And we have a Saint Francis decal on the back window."

"But Dad how did she know about the rest of us?"

"I don't think she did, Brava. She had just enough true information, your mom believed all of it. Just like you did."

"So Mom walked back in the bank and emptied the account? Why didn't she call the police from inside the bank?"

"You saw her, Brava, and that was what, five days later? Can you imagine what she was like when she thought the woman would kill her whole family? She was in shock and must have been terrified. And you know she'd do anything to protect her family."

"Oh my God, Dad, she just walked back in the bank, withdrew $45,000 and handed it over?"

"Yep Brava. I think the con artist manipulated her and scared her so much that your mom believed we were going to die. You know how dramatic she is. I think that woman played right into it, so she did what the woman said."

"Aren't you furious with her, Dad?"

"Brava, it would be easy to be furious with her, I'll admit. But I keep thinking what could have happened, and how frightened she must have been, and how we nearly lost her. When I think about the last few days, honestly I am so glad to have her. Nothing else matters, and I'll figure something out regarding the money."

"Have you gone to the police?"

"Yea, we called the police, and they said they'd send a detective out to take a report within seventy-two hours."

"Are you shitting me? In three days, they'd take a report?" I was incredulous.

"Yep, that's what they said. So we marched ourselves down to the Atlanta police station and insisted someone meet with us. That was yesterday. A detective reluctantly met with us. He looked about twelve years old and acted so disinterested that I fear they don't give a damn. He treated your mom like she was an idiot for what she did."

"Dad, what are the chances you'll get that money back? If the police don't care enough to "take a report," I marked the quotes with my fingers, "for three days, what do you think they'll do to find the scammers?"

"Brava, I'm certain they don't give a damn. I believe they think your mother is a doddering old fool and deserved what she got. At least that's my take on it. I don't think they'll do one thing further. I'm just figuring out ways to get by without the money."

"How bad is your financial situation, Dad?" Dad was pensive for a moment.

"Brava, we did all right when we sold the store. We'd have had plenty of money to live out very long lives and travel or spend freely. And we are frugal as you know."

I nodded. They were indeed frugal.

"We will be OK. But if I withdraw any money before six months, we'll take too big of a hit on top of what she lost. We can't make it on our Social Security alone, so I have to ask you something I never thought I'd do."

"Anything Dad. I'll do anything for you and Mom. You know that."

"If we sell our second car, drop that car insurance, utilities and food and a few other things, we can make it on Social Security. But we'd have to live in town and sometimes share a car with you as well as a lot of other sacrifices; yours as well as ours. I'm sorry Brava. After six months, I can withdraw some money and we can live OK; if a bit more frugally than before."

"Of course Dad. You and Mom come right away." I said that and meant it sincerely, but I cursed the lightning because I didn't know how I'd ever keep it hidden. I'd have to hold it together and keep the stones taped on me 24/7. My heart was so willing to help them, but I couldn't imagine them living with me even before the lightning, let alone now. I returned to work with a heavy heart and made it through the day, though I know not how.

I had imagined Mom and Dad arriving with a few suitcases, but on Saturday morning they pulled up towing a small U-Haul. Mom acted as if they were coming to take care of me, and at first it made me furious. Then I realized it was just a defense. I was initially so angry that the keys hanging by the door jangled like a wind chime. Mom looked at them horrified, and I brushed against them with my jacket to cover it. I went into the bathroom with my breathing app, and I called Lucia.

"It's not even been an hour, and I am a wreck. How can I last six months?"

"On my way."

When Lucia came to the door, Mom handed her a martini.

"We're celebrating!" Mom exclaimed.

Lucia looked at me wide-eyed and whispered, "It's only eleven a.m. and they moved here because your mom lost $50,000. What are we celebrating? I can't drink a martini this early."

"If you stay here for long you'll need it. If you don't, I will."

I saw Lucia casting surreptitious glances into the living room. Mom shopped at warehouses that sold in bulk, but my house is really small, and I don't have a lot of storage space. Piled like an end table beside the sofa were two cases of Straubs beer, a gallon of cheap screw top wine, and a garbage bag size of Cheetos. Straubs was a small local Pennsylvania brewery before local brews became vogue. In high school, we drank it because it was cheap. I didn't even know you could get it here.

Lucia said, "Well, it's good to know that if the end of the world comes tomorrow, you've got plenty of cheap liquor and junk food."

She had to scream to be heard over the TV. Dad had a baseball game on. Pittsburgh Pirates versus the Cincinnati Reds. It was so loud it probably hurt Maggie, my neighbor's Bassett hound's ears.

I wished I had trusted Lucia with my secret but now hardly seemed like an ideal time to spring it on her. We walked out back and sat on the porch swing drinking our martinis at eleven a.m.

"Actually, I prefer drinking in the morning," I told her with all seriousness.

She gave me a sidelong glance. "I know a place where a whole group of people who think just like you meet in a room for an hour every week."

I laughed, "Good point. But it reduces the morning hangover."

"And you know about that, how?"

"When Kevin and I used to go to the redneck Riviera every summer with his family, I had no rules against drinking in the morning. In fact, I needed it. This is a similar situation. I'm not sure I can make it without copious amounts of alcohol."

She didn't know the half of it either. If the lightning got away from me, I could become a weapon.

Lucia couldn't stay for long because the twins had therapy so she drank half her martini and handed me the glass. I gulped the rest as she pulled out of the driveway and actually considered running after her screaming, "Take me with you."

Chapter 19

By Monday, I was actually relieved to go to work. Both Mom and Dad needed a car so Dad dropped me off and was going to return at three to pick me up. I felt trapped without a car and rattled by the whole situation, so I asked Liv to pick me up and take me out to an early lunch. She readily agreed because she was desperate to find out more about Mom and Dad's situation. So far, Dad had only talked to me about it. Not necessarily to keep anything from Liv but because they were moving in with me. I had the room since my kids were gone. It made the most sense to everyone. But no one knew that lightning lived in me, and I was a tornado if I got upset.

I told Liv I only had a short lunch so we wouldn't end up at a restaurant with real silverware. I knew I'd feel upset telling her everything, and I feared flying forks! For safety, I picked a sandwich shop near the office that served lunch in plastic baskets.

I had a Reuben sandwich with onion rings, and I wolfed it greedily without really tasting it. I had eaten little on the weekend because I was so nervous, and the smells of Mom's constant cooking had left me nauseated. Today I was so stressed and overly hungry that I forgot to worry about my weight and pick at my food. Olivia had the deluxe cheeseburger and fries and ate every bite with her usual gusto.

I told her everything I knew. She said that she and Brian could help Mom and Dad financially, and she'd even offered it to Dad but he wouldn't hear of it. I selfishly wished he would have accepted and they wouldn't be living with me. Then I felt like a bitch.

I asked Liv, "How much does Gene know?"

"Probably more than we do, knowing Gene. You know how he is. I didn't tell Venice though."

Venice was studying in Italy, and Liv didn't want her to be worried while she was so far away. I hadn't told my girls much either. They just thought Mom and Dad were staying with me for a brief time because of a financial snafu.

Liv said, "Remember in Sicily when our guide said we would never be in danger of a violent crime?"

Our guide had explained that violence drew the "policia" and the mafia didn't want them so they threw the criminals in the sea. The people on the tour bus had tittered at that but by the look on his face it was apparent he was serious. The tittering had died away.

Liv continued, "Now I wish we had that here. At least the mafia do something. It sure would beat the hell of being a victim and then being victimized by the cops on top of it."

I wondered if we had the mafia in Atlanta. If so, I wanted to meet them. Maybe they could help. It appeared the cops wouldn't. I wondered if I could help, but at the moment, the mafia seemed preferable.

As always, no matter how bad things were, when Liv and I got together we were bound to laugh. And we did!

It was a Cathy story that got us laughing. I told her about the time one of the nephews went hunting wild boar and came home proudly sporting three of them and boasting that he was the king of the jungle.

"Kevin and I and the girls were there when the brat came home from hunting, but we left the next morning. Come to find out two days later that in addition to the fact that it was two boars over the legal limit, they happened to be domestic pigs from a nearby farm. The farmer demanded that Bubba pay him nearly $6000 that Bubba, of course, didn't have. The farmer threatened to call the Game Warden. Apparently they have more power in Alabama then the IRS. So guess who Cathy called?"

We were laughing so hard that it was Liv who had to run to the bathroom to pee. I used the moment to breathe with my app. I was doing OK, but no sense taking any chances.

After the foray to the restroom, Liv said, "How much money did Kevin give that damn sister and her redneck brood? Maybe you're better off divorced from him. The kids probably got worse the older they got and you might not have had anything left."

"Yea, I wonder who bails her out now."

It felt so good to be with Liv and to laugh that I hated for lunch to end. When I got back from work, I got a text from Gene. "Pick me up after school. I found out something. Need to talk."

I could do that after Dad picked me up. I texted back "OK. I'll be there." I wondered what he had found out. I was curious if it had to do with Mom, or with the lightning in me.

Dad came to get me after work, and I took him back to my house and then went to get Gene. We were used to hanging out at my house, but we went to the pavilion at Piedmont Park instead.

As we walked into the park, I recalled a time when the girls were little and we had spent sunny days playing there. I had met a young Muslim woman who brought her son to the same play area. Her husband accompanied her and hovered over the boy and mother. In a rare moment alone, she mentioned that she had recently been a university student wearing blue jeans and rebelling against her Southern Baptist upbringing.

"Yes, but that's a far cry from marrying a Muslim man, wearing a burka and raising a Muslim son." That's exactly what came out of my mouth. I remember it perfectly well even after all these years because at the time I wished I could have hit rewind.

I asked my new Muslim friend how she met her husband and how long they dated before marrying. She explained that dating was forbidden to Muslims. The women at the mosque had introduced her to several eligible men. She met with her husband a couple of times while in the company of other people from the mosque. They were married shortly after.

When I asked her how she could jump into a situation like that, especially having been raised so differently, she responded matter-of-factly, "Divorce is not forbidden in Islam."

Little did I know at the time that those words would come back to haunt me.

I wondered how much Gene knew about Mom's situation but realized it was a foolish thought. He knew everything and then some. Gene never missed a thing, even as a little boy.

"Brava, we've got to do something. Grammy isn't the only one this happened to. It's been happening for nearly a year in exactly the same way in several different parking lots."

I was right. He knew more than all of us. I asked him, "How do you even know what happened much less that it's a pattern?"

I got "that look."

"Dear God, Gene, tell me you did NOT hack into the Atlanta Police Department files?"

"I didn't." He readily protested, then hesitated and admitted, "But I could, and I have before."

"Oh, my God, you are going to end up in jail, and I'm not going to be able to get you out."

"Brava, seriously you've got to listen. Almost everything I found out is from public records."

"Almost everything?" I asked.

"Almost. But listen Brava, I've got to tell you what I found out."

I decided to let him tell me and deal with his hacking later; or not. I had plenty else to manage in the moment.

"Aunt Brava, these scams have been happening with almost certain regularity every couple weeks or so in three different parking lots around the city. But all three lots are in different police districts and a different cop has handled each one, so no one but me has seen the pattern. It's all right there, Brava. They just don't give a shit so no one bothered to follow up or investigate."

"Then we have to go to the police with this Gene. Maybe they'll listen and get Mom and Dad's money back. Then they won't have to live in my house."

"Brava, you are so naive it makes me wonder how you made it so far in life."

That really hurt my feelings, and I was so raw already. Lately, I felt like my skin had been flayed, and I was just nerves and bones.

"Thanks, Gene. I didn't know you thought so little of me."

"I'm sorry Aunt Brava, you know I love you and love that about you. But do you think if the cops don't care now, that when I go to them and tell them what I found out and make them look like a bunch of idiots, they'll care more? Plus, maybe it wasn't *all* in public records."

"I knew it." I sighed and rolled my eyes. "Go on tell me the rest. What are you thinking?" I was afraid to find out.

"Besides," he continued almost as if I hadn't spoken. "Even if the cops got these guys, do you really believe they'd recover the money Grammy lost and return it to her? We've got to figure a way to get it back, and Dealan will help. It's a huge injustice; just the kind of thing you were meant to right."

Deep down, I knew Gene would head in that direction. "I'm afraid to ask what exactly you have in mind. But I'm also desperate. I hate what they did to my mom. And it's aged my dad ten years. Have you seen him?"

Gene had, and agreed with me. But then he just used that as additional leverage to further his superhero campaign. He was relentless if he was anything. But for the first time since the lightning, I was in agreement. Well, actually the second time. Brad was the first, but that was a spur of the moment decision.

"What do you have in mind?" I wasn't entirely sure I wanted to know, but revenge is in my DNA so I couldn't help myself.

"I thought you'd never ask." Gene sneered and then grinned.

He continued, "Here's the deal. The scams have taken place in three parking lots and it's always a Saturday. I think the scammers have a day job with regular hours. They rotate the parking lots on a fairly consistent schedule. It's not entirely predictable, but they never hit the same place two Saturdays in a row. Also, it's not every single Saturday, but three out of four or five. We stake out one parking lot and watch for them. Even if we miss it one or two weekends, we're sure to hit it, right."

"First of all," I interjected, "how do we know it's them? And second of all, what do we do about it?"

"Aunt Brava, that's the thing that makes me so sick about the cops. The reports are surprisingly detailed and all similar. If even one cop made an effort or gave a damn, they'd have seen the pattern. So number one, don't worry, we'll know them. And number two, Aunt Brava, you must remember, we have Dealan and the lightning on our side."

"I still don't know how to control the lightning, let alone how to make it happen. I can see it now. It will be just like the cans in the back yard. I'll try to stop the bad guys, and they'll just feel a tickle while they whip out their guns and shoot us."

Gene was clearly frustrated with me. "Will you stop trying to get rid of the lightning, and stop trying to figure it out? I've told you a thousand times. Dealan put the lightning in you to mete out justice with her help. The two times you used it, there were injustices. Both Terry and Brad, especially Terry." He paused. "But Brad was funnier."

We both laughed, remembering. Gene began to act out Brad slapping his ass and balls and running to the lake. We were both laughing almost as hard as the day it happened.

When we got a hold of ourselves, Gene continued. "The victims in the police reports all say the scammer is a white woman in her late forties, early fifties with medium length graying hair. She's average height and slightly overweight so that's no big help but they all agree that she leaves in a white delivery type of van. The guy driving the van is described as a white male wearing a ball cap and sunglasses."

"Great Gene, we are looking for two people who look like everybody else and drive a white van."

"Do you want to help Grammy and Grandpa or not?"

"More than anything, but I don't want to get us, especially you, killed in the process."

"Look Brava, just shut up for a minute please and listen to me. I really do have a plan that I think will work. And whether you believe it or not, we have special forces on our side."

I took a deep breath and resigned myself to listen to what Gene had to say without arguing or interrupting. I had nothing to lose. And so far, I hadn't come up with a better plan or any plan for that matter. I was simply exhausted and frazzled and totally unable to think it through.

"OK Gene. I'm sorry I've been so disagreeable since the lightning. It rocked my world and this thing with Mom and Dad hasn't helped. I promise I will listen, but no promises that I'll agree to do it."

"Fair enough. Here's the plan. They hit the lots on Saturday between ten a.m. and two p.m. while they are at their busiest. We can better our odds if we pick one lot and go at ten and watch for the white van. I think we should go to the same one where it happened to Grammy, the Plaza on Buford Highway. My guess is that he drops off the con lady and then parks nearby so he can watch it go down. So we spot them, keep our eye on them and watch the scam the whole way through. I hate it for the vic, but we need to wait and follow the scammers to where they go afterward."

I found myself looking out over the green of Lake Clara Meer and absorbing every detail of Gene's plan. I noticed a great blue heron fishing in the shallows. I heard the sounds of the traffic in the distance. I felt the sun warming my bare arms, and for just a moment, I felt a wave of well-being wash over me. I so rarely had well-being of late that I wondered if Dealan was real and had reassured me. I realized that I had gone from fighting tooth and nail to becoming totally invested in Gene's plan in a few short moments.

Gene was so absorbed in relaying the details of his plan that he didn't notice the change in me until I asked if we were going to start this Saturday. He looked puzzled as if he didn't understand the question and then awareness dawned on his face that I was "in."

He grinned and said, "Finally. I knew Dealan would change your mind. We're going to do this Brava. We are going to get them, and get Grammy's money back."

For the first time since the lightning, I dared to believe.

Chapter 20

My house looked as if a cyclone had hit. Mom had had the audacity to re-arrange all my kitchen utensils in the drawers and then proudly show me around my kitchen like she was conducting a home tour. Dad's golf clubs were leaning against the bathroom door so I couldn't close it to use the toilet. In my living room, they had put up a huge clothes rack like you'd find in a department store.

Where had that come from?

They had pulled my sofa into the middle of the room and put the clothes rack with all their Bermuda shorts and Hawaiian shirts behind the sofa. Bras and stockings were hung over the shower curtain, and there were six bottles of shampoo and conditioner on the tiny bathroom shelf that once housed my single bottle of each; which to my horror, were missing!

Dad was ensconced in Kevin's recliner watching Jeopardy. Alex Trebek was screaming in the pompous tone like he knows all the answers; like he doesn't have a cheat sheet right in front of him. I hate game shows and Jeopardy is the worst because the jingle gets stuck in my head for days.

Mom had fish in the oven and collards on top of the stove so the whole house stunk. My sanctuary had turned into a nuthouse. I texted Gene. "If I wasn't fully invested in the plan before, I am now."

He sent back, "What happened? Grammy?"

"Homicide is a sin. It's even worse if you kill your parents. That breaks two commandments. Saturday can't come too soon."

I surreptitiously photographed the house to show Sheila. I'd need her to help me through this. And I didn't want her to think I was exaggerating when I told her I was losing my mind. I taped a few more Julian stones to my body and took my app to the bathroom where I moved the golf clubs so I could close the door. I texted Gene some of the photos too.

Gene texted back. "Come get me. Grammy needs help with her computer, and I can see the madness for myself."

I got Gene and brought him back to my house. His look was one of astonishment. "Aunt Brava this is almost as bad as after the lightning."

"I know. I'm losing it."

I was interrupted by Mom. "Gene, I'm so glad you're here. I didn't do anything wrong. I don't know what's the matter with that damn computer."

Gene put his arm around Mom and towered over her so it choked me up. He said, "Come on Grammy, we'll figure it out together."

They set her laptop on the dining room table that was now a sewing room, and I heard him saying, "Grammy, do you see all these tabs that are open? They're locking up your computer. There are forty-two tabs for Publisher's Clearing House. What's up with that?"

"I'm going to win the jackpot, and they send an email every day to remind me to sign up. Isn't that lovely of them? It increases my chances," Mom explained patiently to Gene.

"OK Grammy, I see. But opening all these tabs is causing the problem so I'm going to close them now." He continued, "Do you really think you're going to win? I think Publisher's Clearing House is bogus."

"I've seen the commercials so Publisher's Clearing House has to be unanimously true all over the world."

I mouthed the words "unanimously true all over the world," to Gene behind Mom's back.

I heard Gene attempting to explain to Mom that when she signs up for those giveaways it makes it easier for hackers to breach her security. He was doing that thing he does when he wants to make a point. He goes on and on with technical information far over anyone's head save for his. It works against him; at least with me. And with Mom.

I had to laugh when I heard Mom respond. "Besides, if you never enter, you'll never win."

I retreated to the bedroom.

Chapter 21

I was struggling with the tape allergy almost as much as the lightning. With Mom and Dad living there, I couldn't get a respite from the stones so I kept them on all day. I had to figure out another way to use more talismans and less tape, or I would end up in a rubber burka or a rubber room.

Sheila stopped by my desk the next morning to bring me coffee and chat as usual. I showed her the photos of my house, and she hugged, me but I could tell she was laughing behind my back.

"You're laughing at my misfortune. That's terrible of you", I said, but my tone belied the seriousness. Actually I had to laugh as well when I looked at the photos.

Sheila was squinting at my phone. "What is piled beside your sofa? It looks like a garbage sized bag of cheese curls."

"It is a garbage-sized bag of cheese curls," I said with a deadpan expression. I continued, "Sitting on a case of cheap beer."

She threw her head back and laughed loudly. "Your mom is a hoot." Then she turned serious and said, "Schedule yourself in my book today, and I'll do a relaxation treatment on you. You need it!"

Oh, how I needed it! It was one of the worst days since the lightning. All the small desk items acted as if they had a life of their own. Every time I reached for something it slithered or skittered a few inches.

The whole week was like that too. On Thursday, I skipped lunch intending to catch up on my work but found myself instead in a comfortable chair in the waiting room using my breathing app. Dr. Jackson and Sheila had both left the office over an hour ago, and weren't due back for at least another thirty minutes. I was absentmindedly scratching my wrists and ankles where the tape had caused a rash. I got the idea to look through Dr. Jackson's cabinets and see if I could find a better itch cream than the over-the-counter ones. I was rummaging through the cabinets when I heard a rustle behind me. Guiltily I turned my head slowly toward the door. What I saw was even more shocking than if Dr. Jackson had caught me. It was Mrs. Pierce, still dressed in her paper gown, clutching the top together with both hands as if she was clutching a life rope.

"Uh, hello Brava."

"Uh, hello Mrs. Pierce. Uh …" I was trying to find a polite way to ask, "What are you still doing here, and why are you still in that ridiculous paper gown?"

Thankfully she continued before I asked.

"I, uh, am in the room next door waiting for Dr. Jackson to see me, uh and I know he's really busy but I just wanted to check and see how long he'd be."

Had he not taken care of her before leaving? Is that what she just said? I was mentally going through the appointment book. *When was Mrs. Pierce scheduled; before or after Sheila's patient, Sue Ellen? Oh my God before. And before Mr. Jones, a patient of Dr. Jack's. That meant she'd been here for over two hours.*

She went on to say, "He surely must be here because these are his glasses."

Only then did I notice the brown spectacles clutched in one of the hands still holding the top of her gown.

"Of course, Mrs. Pierce." I had recovered my wits a bit at this point, and only wanted to get her back in the treatment room before she figured out that Dr. Jackson was having a nice lunch at his country club. I continued talking in a tone that could calm a suicide jumper off a ledge. "He had an emergency that he is tending to. I am so sorry I didn't let you know. In fact, I was just now rummaging through these cabinets to get something for his emergency patient."

I was rambling.

She nodded happily. "I knew he didn't forget about me."

"No never that, Mrs. Pierce. Now let me get you settled back in your treatment room, and I'll see about getting Dr. Jackson in to see you as soon as his emergency is stable."

Mrs. Pierce turned to go back in her treatment room, and I was gifted with the image of her bare ass hanging out the back of the open gown. I offered to help her get dressed and reschedule her if she couldn't wait on Dr. Jack today. I stammered apologies and offered her coffee.

She insisted that she would happily wait for Dr. Jackson today. "I am just so looking forward to talking with him about my new grandbaby and my visit to Arizona to be with my kids."

Great.

I settled Mrs. Pierce in her treatment room, got her a magazine and gave her a weak smile.

Where did Dr. Jack say he was going to lunch? Did he mention the country club or did I just think it?"

My thoughts were racing, wondering how soon he could get back to the office.

I raced to the desk and called him on his cell phone. *Pick up, pick up, pick up.*

I heard, "Hello this is Dr. Jackson, I'm unavailable …" I was frantic as to what I'd do now. *Would I cop to the truth to Mrs. Pierce?* Then I realized I had a call waiting.

"Doctor's office, Brava speaking."

"Brava, It's Dr. Jack. I couldn't get to my cellpho …"

"Get back here right now." I was doing that thing my mom does when she's upset; a half whisper, half scream.

"Excuse me?" I'd never spoken to Dr. Jackson like that. I was sure he was shocked.

"Mrs. Pierce is still in room two, naked under her paper gown and clutching your glasses, waiting for you to see her."

Dead silence. I could almost read his mind, doing exactly what I'd done moments before, calculating how long she'd been there.

"It's been nearly two hours. She was before Mr. Jones." Mr. Jones had been a quick med check prior to Dr. Jackson leaving for lunch.

Dr. Jackson had recovered somewhat and said, "Brava, can't you handle this? Just make some excuse and reschedule her. Give it to her complimentarily."

Figures he doesn't want to face her. Handle it Brava.

"I tried that already. You know I would have done that before I called you." My voice took on a false happy tone, dripping in sarcasm. "She's just so excited to see you that she will happily wait to tell you about bla, bla, bla. Just get back here."

"On my way."

"Where are you anyway? How long until you get here?"

"'At the country club. I'll just tell them to put it on my tab and walk out the door in five. I'm twenty minutes away."

"Speed."

Talk about things rattling around on my desk. And if I was itchy before, now I was hot and nervous and even itchier. I gave Mrs. Pierce a "report" on Dr. Jack's emergency patient and said he'd be a few more minutes. I got her a drink of water and a blanket.

Well, if I had to deal with this, I felt even more entitled to the prescription skin cream. I dug through his cabinets and found some with a high percentage of cortisone in it. When Dr. Jack returned he raced right into the room with

Mrs. Pierce, and I raced into the bathroom to smear cream on my body.

The next day, Mrs. Pierce brought chocolate oatmeal cookies to Dr. Jackson, "because he was so wonderful to me after that dreadful emergency, the poor dear man."

I ate five of those damn cookies before I gave any to Dr. Jack.

When I got home, Mom had fourteen quart jars of spaghetti sauce on the counter. Every pan in my kitchen was dirty. There were seven bras and four pairs of panty hose hanging from the shower curtain. She was on the phone with Mrs. Cohen. Mom screams into her cell phone for some reason I fail to understand. But she was screaming into her phone and Dad was watching an ancient rerun of Walker, Texas Ranger. Maybe Mom screams into her phone because Dad plays the TV so loud. The neighbors had to be able to hear it. I debated joining Dad on the sofa because I actually love Chuck Norris, but instead went to my room and screamed into a pillow.

Chapter 22

That Saturday morning I texted Sifu, "Family situation again. Gene and I will miss today."

"Good luck with that. See you Tuesday. Remember last Tuesday? That was just a taste. Sifu Evil."

I wanted to scream. I knew he would lie awake at night to determine our punishment. I worried that I'd get so frustrated the swords really would fly off the walls. Then I hoped that I'd get so frustrated the swords would fly off the walls. He deserved it.

Gene and I parked in the center of the lot of the plaza so we could see in all directions, facing toward the Bank of Atlanta. Gene had taken over the driving and I sat sipping my coffee in the passenger seat. I was so nervous that the keys kept jangling in the ignition. Finally, Gene pulled the keys from the console and stuck them in his pocket.

I saw a white van and screamed, "Gene, Gene look it's them. Oh, God, what are we gonna do? It's them. I know it."

From out of the van stepped a young Latino woman with her four stair step children following like little baby geese behind her.

"Relax Aunt Brava. I never knew there were so many white vans until this happened, and now I see them everywhere. I think we're going to have a lot of false alarms before we find the right one."

I drew a deep breath and attempted to calm my mind. I was reaching for my relaxing app when I spotted another white van.

"Oh, my God, Gene that's it. I know it. I feel it. Oh, my God, what are we going to do?"

Out of the second white van stepped four young men around fifteen or sixteen years old wearing tie-dyed T-shirts to match their tie-dyed hair, or maybe they matched their hair to their shirts.

"Brava, relax. Let's just watch and wait."

I grabbed my app. I was inhaling and exhaling with a sucking sound in an attempt to calm myself. At that moment, another white van cruised slowly through the lot. Gene and I cast a glance at each other and back toward the van. This one had tinted windows and was passing available parking slots, coasting toward a blue-haired woman in a blue flowered dress.

"That's the mark, Gene. They're going after that lady in the blue dress. What are we going to do? Oh God, this is crazy. It's them, and I don't know what to do."

At that precise moment, the van veered into a parking space and a man stepped out. He was only about five feet six inches tall but had to weigh three hundred pounds. His pants were hanging below his pendulous abdomen and a tool belt hung dangerously lower than his pants. He turned to walk toward the hardware store, and we got a great view of a five inch butt crack.

The direction the van faced as he parked allowed Gene to notice the logo on the side. He read it to me. "Got a Leak. I'll take a Peak."

"A real plumber's crack? This is my life. A farce. Rubber gloves and plumber's cracks."

The four hours continued like that. I was beyond exhaustion by two o'clock. And I think Gene was way past exhaustion from dealing with my hysterics. I dropped him off, went home and told my parents I needed a nap. They assumed it was because of Kung Fu, and I didn't correct their misconception. I slept fitfully for four hours and dreamed of crows and piles of money. I awoke feeling worse than I did before my nap.

I knew next Saturday was going to be a repeat of today, and perhaps several more Saturdays until we found the scammers. I worried that we wouldn't find them soon, then I worried that we would, and I worried that I would die from what Sifu had in mind for torture.

On Sunday, Gene and I deconstructed the day and formulated a plan for going forward.

"Brava, I've been thinking about when we find them. We'll follow them. I have a feeling they'll go home. I mean it's not like they're going to go to a bank and make a cash deposit of how ever many thousand dollars they just stole."

"Yea, I see your point. It makes sense they'd take the money home. What do we do when we confront them?"

"Dealan will take care of that, I feel sure." Gene was so confident.

Being a fifteen-year-old boy made him bulletproof. I had a running joke with Kevin about that. I always told him I wished I were a fifteen-year-old boy. He'd laugh and say, "I'm glad you're not." And pinch my ass.

"Gene, I need a plan. I can't hope that a Celtic goddess will show up." It occurred to me that if Dealan really did exist, maybe I could have that feeling of invincibility. But I just wasn't so sure.

"You better hope she shows up. Otherwise, we need a gun."

"Thanks, Gene. That relieved my anxiety," I said as sarcastically as I could. "I'm also worried about them going to the police about us."

"Seriously? What exactly do you think they'd say? 'We've been scamming money out of little old ladies for eleven months and then this red-headed, middle-aged bitch tortured us and took back the money?'"

"You have a point. But still, I feel like I need a disguise. I need to at least cover my red hair. It makes me so memorable. Most of the time I love that, but it worries me now."

"You could wear a burka." Gene laughed. "That would cover everything."

I was almost excited about the idea until I realized that some people thought all Muslims were terrorists so that might work against me. *And* the ridiculous irony that I would be wearing a burka after my husband left me to convert to Islam. I said as much to Gene.

His response tickled me. "Have you ever noticed that your life is more ironic than most people's? Or is it just me?"

We had a good laugh over it.

"I could simply tie a scarf over my hair and look like a cancer patient, but my ass is too fat for anyone to believe I'm getting chemo."

Gene said, "You could wear a veil and look like a nun. Far as I know no nuns have ever bombed a stadium or anything."

"Actually I like that. I can make that work. I'll make a veil and wear a navy blue skirt with a white blouse and sensible shoes. I'll hang a big cross around my neck and even drop a rosary from my belt. They'll be talismans, and I'll feel protected as well as disguised."

"Whatever works," Gene answered with a grin. And I could tell he was actually glad I was getting into it.

"I want you to be in disguise too, Gene. I don't want anyone to try to hurt you later."

Gene said, "I'll wear a baseball hat and aviator sunglasses, and a University of Georgia T-shirt. Like I'd ever go there!"

I laughed because UGA is a college that majors in football. "Perfect disguise. No one would ever believe you'd wear a Georgia shirt."

Chapter 23

On Tuesday evening, Sifu met us with a glare as Gene and I walked into Kung Fu. "Don't plan on going anywhere after class. You'll be here a while. And if you think last week was tough, think again."

I had an hour and a half to worry about what he had in store for us. I was glad I had taped more stones to my ankles and halfway up my calves or I feared the swords on the wall shelves would fly out and hurt someone.

Sifu made me hold horse stance with my sword held over my head for twenty minutes. And this time he sparred with Gene rather than having Gene just hit the heavy bag. I was shaking and sweating so I tried to ease up on my stance a little and drop my arms; just enough that Sifu wouldn't notice. I watched Sifu pummel Gene.

"Brava, don't even think about it. I see you."

I swear he could see us with his back turned, and I'd told him so before. "How can you do that? You're not even looking at me and you can tell what I did wrong. Do you feel a change in the air currents or what?"

Sifu commanded, "Get your guard up, Gene. I'm going easy on you now, but if you drop your guard like that again, I'm not gonna pull my next punch."

Gene was already soaked in sweat and exhausted after ninety minutes of a particularly grueling Kung Fu class. I don't think it was grueling by accident either. Sifu was fresh because he'd just been barking commands for ninety minutes. He even looked evil like his nickname.

I was furious with him for treating us this way, especially Gene. He didn't understand the situation. And I couldn't figure out a way to tell him. Sifu didn't have any family. At least any family he shared his life with. His mom had passed away young, and he didn't have any contact with his dad. So he had no patience with people who let family "get in the way of their training."

I began to feel nauseated, and the world started to close in until all I could see was the altar with the photos of our dead ancestors. The candle we lit prior to each class was winking and dancing. I couldn't hear Gene and Sifu sparring.

"Oh, my God," I panicked. *It's going to happen again. I'm going to cause an accident if I think mean things. Think about ice cream,* I commanded myself. *Think about happy things like vacations and the beach. That's it. Go to the beach.*

And what popped into my head? The time I nearly drowned. The vivid picture of me washed up on the sand like a beached whale. I felt the nausea and that weird anxious feeling rise up. If I didn't get a hold of this soon, we were all in trouble. I had to change my thoughts and fast! I called up images of happier times with Kevin and our family.

The relaxing sun and sand baking my bones. The kids making sand castles during the beach vacations with Liv and Brian and their kids. Breathe Brava, I told myself. Breathe. Picture the app. You don't need it. Just picture it. Focus on your breath.

I felt my breath deepen and the circle of my vision began to expand and gradually include the rest of the room. The nausea and anxiety in the pit of my solar plexus dissipated.

At the exact moment, I wondered how long I'd been "gone." Sifu yelled, "Brava. You can put your sword down." He was looking at me curiously.

"Are you OK?" he asked. "I called "stop" three times before you heard me."

"I was just doing what you expected. I was breathing and holding my sword." I looked him dead in the eye.

He continued to hold my stare for an eternity and then he looked away first.

"Score one for Brava," I thought. I was pissed and relieved at the same time. I had just averted a really bad incident. I was sure of that.

But what did I learn? I wondered. What caused them and what stopped them? It was the second time I felt I had control of the lightning. The first was with Brad when I used it and now when I'd stopped it. And why did it come up in the first place? I did feel as if Sifu were treating us unjustly. Maybe Gene had a point about the injustice thing. I'd have to talk with him after we got out of here.

I managed to sheath my sword and get my bag of gear and out the door without any further trouble. Gene followed close on my heels.

"Brava, what happened back there?"

"I started to lose it Gene, but I got it back. I focused on my breathing and ice cream and I pictured our family vacations when all you kids were young. It worked."

"Thank God," Gene said. "I thought that was what was happening, and I was so scared. I was half watching you, and I dropped my guard. Sifu nailed me right in the mouth. He pulled his punch a little so he didn't injure me, but he made sure I felt it."

"I wish he would cut us some slack over all this. I'm so angry at him; it's scary to even go to class."

Gene said, "You're scared to go to class? At least he doesn't fight you. Think what I feel?"

"I know what you feel, remember. I was getting my ass whipped by him when you were still a toddler."

I went home and had a drink and attempted an Epsom salt bath. It didn't go so well. I was worked up and sore, as well as itchy from the tape so I'd removed my stones. My vibrations made the water splash and slosh over the tub to soak the floor. I considered getting my rubber gloves. It was so bad that I'd need my rubber boots too, but that sort of defeated the purpose. So I had another drink. I knew I would be sore tomorrow and even more the next day. Nor was I any further ahead in figuring out the lightning.

Work was grueling, and I could hardly walk two days later. It was agony to bend over the file cabinet, and the small desk items jumped and jiggled more than usual. I made more trips to the bathroom and used my app repeatedly.

Sheila stopped by the desk and checked in as usual. I assured her that I was fine, but she could see through that. I hated keeping the truth from my dearest friend. I hoped that I would find a way to trust her about the lightning, when I came to grips with it myself. But for now I just couldn't, so I told her I'd slept poorly and was sore from a particularly grueling Kung Fu class. It was true enough.

I looked up to see Mr. Landon coming through the door. I forgot he had an appointment with Dr. Jackson today. He owed Dr. Jackson $800 for visits over the years that he refused to pay even though he drove a Jaguar and was dripping in dough. I tried to talk Dr. Jackson into dropping him as a patient because he took advantage of him, but Dr. Jack was too good-hearted to turn anyone away.

Several years ago, the doctors had hired a decorator to renovate the office. She suggested an open floor plan so it would have a homey atmosphere. It was meant to make the patients feel more relaxed while they waited. But in reality it just meant I was the patients' sounding board. I used to sit behind a glass window that I could close to get my work done. But now if patients were waiting, they downloaded to me. I hated the new environment, and I'd been hating it for nearly seven years.

Mr. Landon sailed in with expensive cologne wafting in his wake. He was dressed in white linen trousers and an untucked, pink, button-down dress shirt. He had on deck shoes and no socks. He looked like he'd just stepped off his yacht, and in fact he may have. He was wearing what looked like an eighteen karat gold anchor around his neck and a gold Rolex watch. I was so pissed off because he hadn't paid Dr. Jack for his wonderful care. If I'd have taken the call from him asking for an appointment, I wouldn't have booked him, but he had the audacity to call Dr. Jack's cell phone! I cut through the pleasantries and asked him the reason for his appointment. I was trying to be professional but was filled with resentment.

He began describing in great detail the boil on his anus. Resentment turned to revulsion. Many times since the office reno I had longed for the old glass wall, but I never wished for it more than now.

I tried several times to interrupt him to get him to take a seat but to no avail. He seemed to enjoy describing his anus problem. I was getting agitated and the familiar nausea welled up in me. I knew that this could be trouble, and I desperately searched for my phone. *Where was it?* I needed my breathing app or something bad was going to happen.

Mr. Landon could sense I wasn't listening to him, and so he leaned in closer. I was really fumbling for my phone now. I wished he'd have to stick his lips through the hole in the glass to tell me about his anus. Abruptly he stopped, and his head jerked back just as if he banged his head. I was puzzled, and he was even more puzzled so he tried again. *Dumb ass.* This time he banged his head even harder, and I giggled to myself because I knew what had happened.

Sometimes I even like having super powers. I had put up the old glass window that I longed for every time I had to hear about treasure boxes and anuses. Mr. Landon was finally dazed enough after banging into the "glass" several times that he went and sat in the waiting room with a stupefied look on his face. I went to the bathroom, more to giggle than to breathe into my app.

Chapter 24

The second Saturday that Gene and I were staking out the Plaza, I awoke as usual at seven and put on my Kung Fu uniform. I said goodbye to Mom and Dad and told them I'd be home around three or so. I had my nun costume stowed in the duffel bag with my martial arts gear.

Mom said, "I'm going to the garage sale at St. Wolfgang's with Mrs. Cohen. She's meeting me there."

Mom was wearing a long dress with giant, lime green sea turtles on a black background. She had a red scarf tied around her neck and brown flat sandals. With white socks.

St. Wolfgang's is the largest Catholic Church in Atlanta and located on Peachtree Road in an exclusive area of town. It is so well attended, the city actually closes the road for the sale. All the debutantes go and it's the event of the year. It's quite prestigious to say "I got this at the St. Wolf's yard sale." Mom had never missed it since she'd moved to Georgia and would come home with bags of "treasures" she didn't need.

I saw that she already had her bag packed and it was lying on the chair by the door. I checked it out hoping for a laugh on my way out. It was bright yellow with black letters that read, "I laughed so hard tears ran down my leg." It was the tag line for a big Urology Group in town. I knew that because they advertised on the radio all the time, and Dr. Jack referred his prostate patients to them for a router procedure so they could pee.

Where does she get these? I wondered and left the house laughing.

I picked Gene up and we went to Dunkin Donuts. I had a Bavarian crème filled donut with chocolate icing and Gene had two custard filled ones with powdered sugar on top. I laughed at him as he ate because he got the white sugar all over his beard stubble. He pointed out that I had some chocolate in the corner of my mouth.

The day was starting out with both of us in a good mood, and I hoped that was a favorable omen. Maybe today would be the day we'd catch the con artists and get Mom's money back and by tomorrow I'd have my sanctuary at home again.

One can always hope.

I didn't bother to text Sifu. I didn't want to hear what he'd answer back. I figured it would only spoil the mood. Gene and I made our familiar trek to the Plaza on Buford Highway. I yanked off my Kung Fu Uniform and slipped on the nun costume in the back seat while Gene drove. He left the house in jeans and the T-shirt so only had to don the sunglasses and baseball cap.

We took up our position in the corner of the parking lot with the best vantage point for the entire lot and most especially the bank. I hoped that this would be the day. I couldn't believe how many white vans there were. The first one that I was certain contained the con artists disgorged a pirate. Seriously. It was a guy in black capri slacks, black crocs, a red, striped T-shirt and a patch over his right eye. I didn't even know they made Capris for men. They shouldn't. But I guess they do.

The next white van that did not contain the con artists was a handicapped van. After the ramp came down, out came a guy in an electric wheelchair tricked out like Jeff Gordon's racing car. It was painted red and black with "Dupont" and the number "24" stenciled on the chair. He was wearing a Dupont ballcap, and he even had a checkered flag flying above. I'm not a Nascar fan, but even I had heard of Jeff Gordon. If you live in the south, you can't help it.

Gene was mocking each one of the "characters who were not our cons" as he called them.

He was talking like a pirate. "Arrrrrr, I'm a swashbucklin' scallywag o' th' sea, I am."

I was laughing so hard I was at risk of peeing my pants when I saw a car that looked just like Mom's. I knew she was at the garage sale, so I didn't pay it much attention at first.

"Gene stop, you'll make me pee my pants. I never knew this Plaza had so much entertainment. Even if we don't find the cons today, it might be worth missing Kung Fu for this."

"Never that," he said. "At this very minute, Sifu is cooking up some devious punishment for us."

"What more can he do to us?"

"Aunt Brava, take those words back this instant. Just uttering them out loud is asking for trouble."

The white PT Cruiser that looked like Mom's parked on the other side of the plaza near the pawn shop and had its rear end toward us when I noticed the bumper sticker.

"I get along with God just fine. It's his fan clubs that I can't stand." Mom gets on a tirade about religious fanatics, and Dad isn't much better. No doubt it's a sore subject for both of them due to their strict upbringing. Hence the bumper sticker.

"Gene, that's Grammy's car. Look over by the pawn shop."

"Brava, there are only about a million white PT Cruisers just like there are about a million white vans."

"I thought so too, but how many of them have the same bumper sticker as Mom?"

He jerked his head and looked again. "You're right."

Gene turned on the ignition and slammed the car into reverse so fast it nearly smacked me into the dashboard. He wheeled the car backward around the side of the building so just the nose was sticking out.

I looked at him stunned.

"That way we can see them, but they can't really see us."

Gene was always a quick thinker. It had amazed me even when he was little. I need time to process things.

He probably would have the perfect retort for Cow Patty, I reckoned.

Gene leaned closer to the windshield. "Look. Someone else is in the car with her."

"It must be Mrs. Cohen. They were meeting at the sale. It must not have been good this year." I squinted and said, "Wait, Gene, it looks like a man. Is it Grandpa?" I asked.

"It's too short to be a man. And Grandpa is tall. That's why he hates driving in the PT Cruiser. Among other more embarrassing reasons. I don't blame him. I hide my face when Grammy takes me places in it."

I laughed then grew serious. "She wouldn't have had time to even make the Wolfgang sale and get back here. And I can't believe she'd miss it for anything. She's been coming to it since she moved to Georgia. And if she didn't go there, she lied to Dad and me. I've never known my mom to lie."

As we watched them talking in the car, my mind raced. *Why would Mom lie to us?*

Was she having an affair?

I said as much to Gene, who answered, "That is a disturbing thought on so many levels."

I mused, "Why else would she lie to Dad and me?"

As we watched, a man got out of the car. Despite the heat, he was wearing a black suit with shiny, black leather shoes. He was short and had a huge, barrel-shaped upper body. I thought he looked kinda fat but guessed it was all muscle. I'd seen other men built like him; one of them was my Uncle Alberto. He had huge hands and feet out of proportion to the short stature. He worked in the stockyards in Pittsburgh. He'd been dead many years, and I remembered him fondly. He was "a man's man" who drank and cursed and probably did all kinds of other "manly" things, but he loved all of us nieces and nephews. He growled and chased us and swung us into the air with much laughter.

This guy got out of the car carrying a large silver-colored metal briefcase. It looked like the kind movie gangsters use to carry money or weapons.

"He's headed toward the pawn shop Gene."

"That case looks like it's got drugs or weapons in it. What's he doing?" Gene asked.

I hadn't thought of drugs. I said "he might be buying a gun." Gene reminded me that there's a waiting period for guns.

"Well, he could be picking it up today," I said.

There was something kinda familiar about him, but I assumed it was simply that he looked like my Uncle Alberto. He disappeared into the pawn shop and Mom stayed in the car.

"If you were going to have an affair, would you go to the pawn shop on Buford Highway?" Gene asked.

"You have a point. You keep watching for the white van, Gene. I'll keep my eyes on Mom's car."

About ten minutes passed in agonizing slowness before the guy walked out of the pawn shop still carrying the briefcase

"Does it look heavier?" I asked Gene. "I can't tell."

Gene couldn't either. When I saw him from the front, he looked even more familiar. He had a rugged face and his thick salt and pepper hair was swept straight back from his forehead.

"Gene, I recognize him, but I can't think from where."

"It'll come to you. Quit trying to remember."

"We watched as he got back in mom's car. They sat there in the parking lot, as did we. It was driving me crazy wondering what was going on with them. We watched a few more white vans that were hopefuls but not the cons.

It was nearing two o'clock, and we were debating about whether to leave when Mom got out of her car and went into Goodwill. I was still hung up on the fact that Mom had lied to Dad and me, so I assumed it had to be an affair, but Gene was right. Why have an affair and sit in the parking lot of a shopping center and shop separately in the pawn shop and Goodwill? *What were they up to?*

A few minutes later she came out and they left. We followed shortly after as it was now past two o'clock. Gene made a quick stop in the electronics store and then we went to my house. I changed back into my Kung Fu uniform in the back seat and stowed the nun costume in my martial arts bag. When we got to home, the PT Cruiser was there.

"Brava, don't say anything about seeing Grandma. I want to hear what she says about it."

"I want to confront her right now Gene, but you're right. She'll clam up, and we'll never figure it out. Plus, I don't want Dad to know if it is an affair."

Gene was impatient. "Get over the affair notion please Brava. It puts images in my head that are too painful to bear. But realistically it just doesn't make sense. It's much more likely that Grammy is out for vengeance herself and has got some yo-yo to go along with it. She could really be in danger."

I hadn't thought of that, and I felt stupid; a feeling I frequently felt with Gene even though he never contributed to my feeling that way. As I walked past her car, I saw the empty Goodwill bag lying on the floor of the back seat. We got in the house, and I saw Mom and Dad talking in the dining room.

Mom had laid out on the dining room table a Jesus statue, two elephant bookends, and a huge, fake yellow sunflower in a red pot. "Look at the treasures I got from St. Wolfgang's. It was one of the biggest sales ever."

Gene and I cast a glance at each other.

"Really Mom? Did they close the road?"

"Yes, of course, Dear. They always do."

I asked more questions, trying further to trip her up. "How is Mrs. Cohen?"

"Fine Brava. She is furious with her stepchildren but what's new with that? The oldest daughter broke into their trailer and stole her diamond ring from Edgar. That bitch only got a fake diamond from Home Shopping Network. Serves her right. Mrs. Cohen keeps her real one in the safe deposit box."

Chapter 25

I dreaded going to Kung Fu all day Tuesday and worried that Sifu would make the punishment so harsh I wouldn't be able to control the lightning. I went to class early and asked Sifu if I could talk with him. I tried explaining that we had a difficult family situation that I couldn't talk about and that Gene and I may miss some additional Saturdays.

"Miss all you want, but plan on spending time after class to take your punishment," he answered.

"Sifu please cut us some slack. I'm afraid if this continues, someone is going to get hurt."

"Brava you know I have control and I'd never hurt Gene." He misunderstood what I meant. But how could I explain that I was the threat? In his mind, that was laughable.

I changed tactics. "Sifu, you are asking us to choose between Kung Fu and family. In our world, family is always first. You're just making it harder to come here at all. If this keeps up, I fear we'll just quit until after we've resolved the family situation. Is that what you want?"

It was really hard for me to even think that, let alone say it to him. I loved going to Kung Fu with Gene and Sifu. I respected Sifu so much and appreciated him and maybe even loved him. Furthermore, I needed Kung Fu now more than ever.

Sifu stared at me a long time before answering. "The practice of Kung Fu needs to be in your life the most during the tough times, Brava. It's what teaches you to get through those times. It's what quiets your mind so you can figure out the solutions. That's why I'm so hard on people for missing class. It's not really that I like being Sifu Evil."

I raised one eyebrow and cocked my head at him.

"Well, I do sort of like it, but seriously I meant what I said about the tough times. You *need* to be here and so does Gene. I can see something is wrong. It's on both of your faces."

Tears welled up in my eyes and threatened to leak out. I really did appreciate him. I just forgot that perhaps he had my interest at heart. I hung my head and asked, "It's going to be a few more Saturdays, Sifu. I can't change that. Is there any way we can work this out without feeling like we're being punished with the family situation and again with you?"

"Sure, Brava. All you had to do is ask. I come here every Sunday anyway to train. You and Gene can come then."

It was that easy? All I had to do was ask?

"Brava, I know you think I'm mean, and it puzzles me that you've studied under me for so many years and yet you still don't know that I have your best interests at heart. Always. What's it going to take for you to trust me?"

I was so grateful. I felt awful for being so angry with him

and not trusting him to help us. All I could see was the punishment. I felt like a naughty child.

Training on Sunday solved two problems. It would get us out of the doghouse with Sifu AND got me out of my house with my parents. As I contemplated all of this, the tears began to fall. Sifu is uncomfortable with emotional displays so he pretended not to notice, and said harshly, "Now get your sword. I want to go over your next move before class."

Gene had gotten a friend to drop him off and walked in at that moment. He looked at me curiously, and I mouthed, "It's OK."

Our latest punishment had consisted of practicing "falls" on the mats one hundred times. I was already sore, and my back and stomach ached. In two days, I'd probably be puking.

We sat in the car and talked in the parking lot as Gene told me of his most recent caper.

"I know what's up with Grammy." I turned in my seat and looked at Gene.

"What? How do you know? Tell me it's not an affair."

"Just stop talking and I'll tell ya." Gene grinned.

"How did you find out? What have you done?" I continued peppering him with questions.

He stopped and looked at me and waited with a grin on his face. "Promise you won't tell Mom?"

"Oh God, it involves hacking," I said.

"No. Skipping school," Gene admitted.

"Well," I said my voice dripping with sarcasm, "that's so much better than hacking."

"It sort of included hacking too. I had to change the attendance records in the school's program."

That shut me up. I waited for the story that would come out in Gene's good time.

"Well, I got a text that Grammy was on the move."

"What do you mean you got a text that she was on the move? A text from who?"

"Oh yea ... about that." Gene continued. "Do you remember when I ran into the electronics store last Saturday?"

"Yea. I do now. But at the time I didn't take much notice."

"Well, I got a tracker for Grammy's car so I could monitor her movements and see what she's up to. I was worried she might be in danger."

"This kid amazes me," I thought. My heart swelled at the thought of him watching over his Grammy to keep her safe. Then I became intrigued with this tracker thing and forgot my pride in Gene for a moment.

"What tracker thing and who texts you? And when did you put it on her car?"

"Patience, Aunt Brava. Shut up for one moment."

"OK. OK." I "zipped" my lips with my finger.

"Well, I got the tracker from Joe at the electronics store. I put it on Grammy's car that day while you and she were making dinner. It monitors her car's movements by way of a GPS and texts me her location in real time."

I feared a lengthy explanation of electronics and I was impatient again. Also, I couldn't imagine something like that except in spy novels and wondered how much it cost. I interrupted Gene yet again.

"How do you even know that technology exists, and how ever much did it cost?"

"If it's technology, I know it exists. And as for the cost, it's expensive but Joe owes me so he gave it to me free to use for a while."

"Dare I ask what you did for Joe?"

"No, it involves hacking."

"OK, go on. You're off the hook this time cuz I'm dying to know what's up with Mom."

"Well, I got a text in history class that she was on the move like I said. But I figured it was probably just to the grocery store or something. I've been watching her since Saturday."

I was confused. "Is it a camera or what?"

"No, look here." Gene whipped out his phone. "I get a text that says she's on the move, and I log into a website that follows her by GPS on a map. Here's the map of where she went this morning."

I looked over his shoulder at his phone.

He continued. "Before today, she'd only gone to Publix, and the thrift store and a few other local stores. But this morning, I saw her going down Ponce toward the Old 4th Ward."

He pointed to his map. "I knew that wasn't in her usual stomping ground, and it's not the best part of town."

"Yea, it's transitional," I said thinking of the area.

"So, I got Jordan to take me to follow her."

"Who's Jordan?" I asked. I didn't remember Gene talking about a kid named Jordan and I knew most of his friends.

"He's a senior."

"How do you know him well enough to get him to skip school and take you on a spy mission?"

"I told him the president of the United States was going to be at the Martin Luther King Center, and we wouldn't want to miss such an important historical event."

"Is the president in town?" I asked.

Gene rolled his eyes. "No, Aunt Brava. Really, do you think it's hard to get someone to skip school? And besides, he owed me one."

"Everyone owes you. What did you do for Jordan?"

"I helped him with a math problem."

"You tutored him?" I felt proud of Gene.

"Not exactly. Do you want to know where Grammy went or not?"

"I do. I do." I forgot all about Jordan.

"Well, we followed her using the GPS down to the 4ᵗʰ ward and onto Boulevard. You know where those shipping docks are down near the Greyhound Bus Station?"

"I don't think I do."

"Anyway, when we were still on Boulevard we saw that she had stopped, so we caught up to her. She was at that Sporelli Italian Import Store."

Realization dawned. "I do know the area. We went there once when Mom first moved here. She wanted some special kind of olive oil and they order it for her. Now I know who that guy was; Mr. Sporelli." I exclaimed. "She knew the Sporellis in Pennsylvania."

I continued on, "His son played soccer with Louma when they were really little. I haven't seen them in years. His son was peculiar."

Gene interrupted. "Gaetano Sporelli is rumored to be the mafia don in Atlanta and has ties to the New York mob. They're really strong in Pittsburgh too. I've done a little homework this afternoon. Do you know what his son does now?"

"No. I'd totally forgotten about them over the years."

"His son is Antonio Sporelli, the psychic medium who runs the Decatur Ghost Tour. I bet that goes over really well with his dad."

"No way," I exclaimed. "I took that tour with Lucia a few years ago. I had no recollection of him being that Louma's friend."

I recalled the tour. We walked all around Decatur stopping at different private homes and restaurants, and learned all about the ghosts who "appeared" regularly at those locations. We'd taken photos and even had "orbs" show up on our photos. It was a fun diversion, but I wasn't sure the orbs were anything other than dust on the camera lens.

I thought some more about it. "Wait," I told Gene. "The tour guide's name was Boo, not Antonio."

Gene replied, "I guess the Decatur Ghost tour led by Antonio Sporelli doesn't exactly have the same ring to it as the Decatur Ghost tour led by Boo Sporelli."

"You've got a point."

I still found it odd that I hadn't made the connection. Antonio had even come to our house to play with Louma. In my mind, I recalled him as an adult and then I could see the resemblance. He had the Sporelli hairline and even wore his hair combed back off his forehead like his dad. As a kid, he had lighter hair but it had darkened over the years. It was just so out of context that I hadn't seen it.

"So what was Mom doing at Sporelli's anyway?" I asked. "He ships her olive oil to the house."

"Think Brava. He's the mafia don. Where else would my Italian Grammy go if she were seeking revenge?"

"You think so, Gene?" I stopped and thought about it. "It would explain them being at the scene of the crime, wouldn't it?"

"Jordan and I waited outside the store for about forty-five minutes and then Grammy came out. I ducked down in his car so she wouldn't see me. Then I watched on the GPS, and she went home, so I went back to school."

"What do you think they're up to?" I asked.

"I'm not positive, but I have a pretty good idea that it's revenge. It worries me. Grammy may be in debt to the mob after this. She was so afraid of that bitch hurting her family that she handed over $50,000. That mafia guy ain't doing this for free for the love of Grammy."

"What are we going to do Gene? My mother is going to be the death of me ... if I don't kill her first."

"Aunt Brava, we are going to do exactly what we've been doing, and we are going to get those scammers before the mafia has a chance to. Then Grammy won't be so much in their debt. I'm still worried though."

Me too. Also, I lacked Gene's faith in our getting the scammers first.

Chapter 26

It happened the third Saturday. I, in my nun habit and Gene as a UGA fan, were sitting in the same parking lot watching white vans that were not the cons come and go. We didn't see Mom's PT Cruiser so we assumed the mafia wasn't involved; at least not this week at this parking lot.

It was nearing two o'clock, and I feared that we'd missed them yet again. We were debating whether to go home or wait a little longer. It was Gene who wanted to wait, so I reluctantly agreed. Then we saw it: a white van circling the parking lot and going up and down the aisles of parking lanes. It stopped near the hardware store. An elderly woman with blue hair, wearing a green, polyester slack suit exited from a newer model Cadillac Sedan. Even from some distance away, she reeked of money. Her wrists were dripping in gold, and diamonds flashed on her fingers. She began to walk toward the fabric store.

Out of the van came a middle-aged woman wearing blue jeans and a sweatshirt. She had grey hair and glasses just like the description in the police reports. She was average height and a little frumpy. She walked up to the blue haired lady and a conversation ensued. We couldn't hear but could guess how it went.

We watched as the con lady held out a paper bag and opened it conspiratorially so the other woman could peek inside. More conversation and lots of nodding and pointing toward the bank. The con woman put a hand on the blue haired lady's elbow and smiled and nudged her toward the ATM. The blue haired lady followed meekly. We watched her withdraw some money and hand it over to the con lady who surreptitiously looked at the old lady's bank receipt. There must not have been much money in the account. She handed over the bank bag that we knew was filled with plain paper and took off toward the van.

I felt so sorry for the blue haired lady because I knew she'd lost some money, but we couldn't help her in the moment. I hoped we could get some of it back to her. I got the Cadillac's license plate and wrote it down on a Post-it note I kept in the console. I guessed that Gene could get the address from the license plate. I didn't want to know how though.

Gene looked at me and said, "Why didn't you just take a picture with your cell phone? Paper and pens are antiquated."

The van exited the parking lot with us following close behind. We followed it north on Buford Highway where we passed a lot of apartment complexes, fast food restaurants and strip clubs. I was looking in the side view mirror when I noticed a black Cadillac sedan following us closely.

"Change lanes Gene." I hoped that the Cadillac wouldn't follow us.

"I see it Brava, and it's definitely following us. I didn't see it at the Plaza, but it followed us out. It looks like a mafia car, and we have to lose it."

"What's if it's the cops?" I asked.

"They don't drive Caddies."

Gene was driving faster now to keep up with the white van that was flying north on Buford Highway. As we approached Clairmont Road, the light turned yellow and the van flew across the intersection.

"Run it Gene. We can't lose them."

"I'm on it, Brava."

I was turned backwards in my seat watching the black Cadillac. They also ran the red light and then I was sure they were following us. I heard the sirens before I saw them. A cop car pulled out of the food mart and chased the Cadillac.

"Thank God, Gene. We don't have to worry about them anymore." I craned my neck forward to see if we were still on the tail of the white van.

"Brava, they may not stop for the cops. Throw down some tacks in front of their tires."

We were quickly getting out of sight of the Cadillac. I was confused. "Gene, I don't have any tacks."

"Use Dealan, Brava. Think!"

I called upon Dealan and pictured the tacks in front of the tires, but I wasn't sure it worked. I didn't feel the nausea and anxiety.

"I don't think it will work. I don't think Dealan is here."

"Call on her, Brava. We need her."

I looked in the side mirror and then turned around in my seat but didn't see the Cadillac. "I think we got away Gene." I turned back to look out of the windshield and saw that we were still some distance behind, but within sight of the white van.

Gene followed the van as they took a right on Dering Circle. It was a post-World War II neighborhood that had become Latino. Kevin and I used to drive around here at Christmas and hold a contest for the tackiest Christmas light display. The houses were originally two bedroom, two bath brick homes that had been added onto. The additions were painted in hues of lime green, royal blue, and bright yellow. Old car tires had become planters in many front yards, and there were more than a few Mary statues sporting plastic flowers.

I was aware that Gene was staying a good distance behind the van, and for a moment I feared we'd lose them, but suddenly it was as if there was another part of me that was calm and quiet, and watching from a distance. I trusted the driving to Gene and implored Dealan, "Please show up. Please be real."

The van turned into a brick house with a parking pad out front. The carport had been enclosed with odd scraps of wood and was painted bright yellow. No other cars were in the driveway. Gene drove past that house and backed into an empty driveway four houses down. We could see the van, but it was obvious the cons hadn't noticed us.

The woman exited the van first, and I almost didn't recognize her. The frumpiness was gone. The sway of her hips reminded me of the gangs of teenage Latino girls outside the movie theater. I wondered if perhaps she wasn't Caucasian at all, or as old as her description. The man exited next. It was the first time I'd seen him. He was dark skinned and looked over six feet tall and had at least 240 or 250 pounds on him. He looked more African American than Latino. She walked directly up to him swiveled her hips suggestively. He did a groin pump and they high-fived and headed toward the house.

I was furious at their celebration of others' misfortune; especially my parents. As I watched, I felt the familiar anxiety rise up in the pit of my stomach. I knew in that instant Dealan was here. I looked at Gene. "I've got this."

I jumped out of the van wearing my nun outfit and took a posture much like the con lady had taken in the parking lot. I was sure I looked as unimposing as she had only moments before.

"Well, two can play at that game," I thought. I approached them in the driveway and said in a whiny voice, "Excuse me, but did you drop this?"

I had grabbed an old fast food bag from my back seat before I left the car. I was aware of Gene behind me. His vigilance was almost palpable. The woman answered over her shoulder with a toss of her hair "We don't want any." She turned back toward the man and rubbed her hands on his crotch right in front of me; a nun, no less. She had no respect. She obviously hadn't heard what I said.

I said it again. "Did you lose this?"

Awareness dawned first on her and then on him. I could actually see it when she realized what I'd said. They both turned around warily. But their shoulders visibly relaxed when they saw a "nun."

She said, "Sister, can I help you?"

A third time, I asked, "Did you drop this?" I held out the bag with one hand and fingered the rosaries at my belt with the other.

I saw wariness come into both their eyes. I watched as his posture became defensive. My awareness only included the three of us as the world closed in. I wasn't even aware of Gene anymore.

I knew I had to immobilize the man first. I remembered Mr. Landon with his anus boil and decided in an instant that the glass wall worked exceptionally well. Before I could even think further, a vision of a huge Lucite box came into my mind, and I dropped it right over his head. It enclosed him on all sides and the top, but no one could see it. I recalled Mr. Landon banging his head at the office and hoped this would work.

Then I nicely asked the con lady if we could exchange bags. I reached out my hand with the empty fast food bag. She said, "You stupid bitch," and I heard the Hispanic accent. I was right about the Latin blood in her.

She looked at him and said, "Charlie, handle her," with a jerk of her head.

Gene stepped forward, and I thrust my arm out to the side like a seatbelt. "I'm OK. Dealan is here."

Charlie lunged forward and banged into the nothing that was really a lucite cage. It would have been a great comedy skit under different circumstances. He hit so hard that his nose and entire face squashed in, and he rocked back about three feet. He was so stunned, I guess it made him stupid so he tried again.

First old man Landon and now this guy.

This time his face was tilted up slightly, and he hit his chin first, jamming his jaw and knocking himself out cold. He fell back like a redwood tree, going down hard.

The harder they fall.

It was as if I were outside myself and watching someone else. It felt surreal.

I turned back to the woman and said in my sweetest voice. "How about we step inside with my partner here and talk about this?" I had to be careful not to say "my nephew" as I didn't want to give anything away.

She was standing there with her mouth agape. All the cockiness of a few short minutes ago was gone, and she looked far more like the non-threatening woman from the parking lot. She looked to Charlie and to Gene and back to me. Then she headed toward the door, and Gene and I followed her inside. I mouthed to Gene, "A glass cage," and pointed toward Charlie. He nodded understanding.

The house smelled of spicy food and cooking grease but was furnished quite expensively. There was a leather sofa, a couple of matching leather recliners and a 56" flat screen TV. A sound system surrounding the TV looked like some space age communication station.

I said to Gene, "I don't know where they work during the week, but it looks as if they've spent at least some of that money on furnishings." There was a huge painting of Our Lady of Guadalupe above the fireplace.

"How did she reconcile that with her crimes?" I wondered.

Gene explained to her all that we knew about the scams. He told her which weekends she'd been at which parking lot. He described in great detail what we had just witnessed in the Plaza. It was evident we knew plenty, but she wasn't ready to back down yet.

She tried to bargain and offer us half her stash. I wasn't sure just how long Dealan would keep my powers up. As far as I knew, it was a one shot deal and I had just used it. But I wanted to play along to get the money. I kept up the pretense of being a nun and asked her to repent and give us the money.

She cussed me like a sailor.

So much for that.

I just had to trust that Dealan would help me. I figured the fire ants worked on Brad, so I might as well start with that. I turned my attention to her feet and legs and pictured angry fire ants biting her feet and ankles. I noticed her begin to wiggle and move her feet around just like Brad did. I upped the energy and moved it higher to her calves and knees. With Brad, I was just pissed, but I wanted justice for this bitch. I pictured thousands of ants swarming her crotch. She began screaming and yelled at me first in English and then in Spanish. I pictured some red and orange flames of real fire along with the ants. She deserved far worse than Brad.

"You bitch. You ain't no nun. What the hell?" Then "Te voy a matar, estúpida puta."

I didn't understand Spanish, but I knew "puta" wasn't nice. I kept it up. She, like Brad, was slapping her ass and pulling at her clothes. I had no remorse. In fact, I was feeling good. She'd injured so many people and their families. I pictured the scene with Mom at the office. I pictured Dr. Jack and Sheila and how worried they were. I knew that it could have nearly caused Mom to have a heart attack. I pictured my dad and how much this had aged him. I thought of the families I didn't even know and the pain and shame they had felt. I wondered if it had killed any of them. I thought of the fragile little blue haired lady we had just seen. I even thought about the rack of Bermuda shorts and Hawaiian shirts in my living room. Her words became incomprehensible screams after that.

I pulled back a little and took a deep breath. "Get us the money you've stolen, and I'll make it stop. Get us every penny, bitch."

I backed off a little more but never let the ants completely leave my mind.

"Don't try anything funny. This is just a taste of what I will do to you." I wasn't as sure of myself as I sounded. Maybe my whole bag of tricks was just spent, but I wasn't gonna let her know that.

"Put your hands behind your back," I commanded. She complied, and I pictured handcuffs on her wrists, and I saw her pull and tug at the invisible restraints so I knew they were secure. I kicked the coffee table out of the way and pointed to the middle of the room a distance away from any furniture.

"OK, you're going to sit down right there on the floor and tell us where the rest of the money is."

She kept looking toward the front door, no doubt hoping for Charlie to show up. I was worried too.

"Did this stuff work long distance?" I wondered to myself.

I nodded toward the door and said to Gene, "Check on Charlie."

He walked backwards to the open front door still keeping his eyes on the woman on the floor. I saw him out of the corner of my eye as he looked toward the driveway.

And then he laughed and slapped his thigh. "We're good."

I wondered what was so funny, but I was starting to worry that I couldn't hold this much longer. I wanted the money, and I wanted out of there. One more burst of fire at her crotch put some more fear in her.

"Tell us where you hid the money. My partner is going to get it while I stay with you. If it isn't there, I will burn you up like the witch you are. Start talking right now."

I gave her yet another quick burst of fire, and I pulled back. She jumped and screamed, but the fire stopped abruptly and so did her screams.

She took one last look at the door, and Gene said, "He ain't coming."

Then she pointed with her head to a credenza between the well-appointed living and dining room. Gene walked over to it and slid open the doors on the front. He reached inside, and I was torn between watching him and keeping my eye on her. I kept my eye on her. She was whimpering and squirming and rubbing her butt on the rug like a dog with worms.

I could hear Gene rummaging through the cabinet. He came within my line of sight and showed me an armful of individual paper bags stuffed with money.

He said, "There are seven of them. They've done twelve scams including today."

"Where's the rest?" I didn't know if there was "the rest" but I wasn't about to let her know that, and I wanted every penny.

I gave her another burst of pure flames up her crotch and included her torso this time. She screamed and peed her pants. I was beginning to feel uncomfortable and a little sorry about what I was doing, so I again pictured in vivid detail the image of my mom lying on Dr. Jack's table with EKG graphs strewn on the counter and the medicine wrappers littering the floor. That worked. I gave her another burst of fire and felt good about it this time.

"In the pink room," she gestured with her head toward a hallway off the living room, "between the mattresses."

I said without looking at Gene, "I've got this. Check on Charlie and go look. Also look around for any weapons."

He took another look out to the driveway and reassured me that we were fine before sprinting down the hallway.

I could hear him rummaging around, and it seemed to go on forever. I was getting worried, but then he came back holding several more bags.

"We'll never know for sure if this is all of it, but it's a lot. I think there are several hundred thousand dollars here."

I said, "Get her purse. It's on the chair by the door. Empty it on the coffee table."

He did, and I said "Any weapons?"

Gene shook his head. "They don't need them, the way they do it."

I asked, "What's in her wallet?"

He narrated the items. "Money, credit cards, a driver's license and insurance card. We'll take those. She's Rosita Lorenzo. And here's a work ID badge for "Speedy Recovery Company." It has an address on the back in case it's lost. It's on Buford Highway. We'll take that too."

"Leave her insurance card, she may need that."

I took one last look at the whimpering, urine soaked and burned woman who had harmed so many people. She didn't look much like the sweet middle-aged con woman and even less like the cocky hip-swiveling Latino the driveway.

I leaned down lower to the floor so I was sure she could hear me. I said, "If I could carry it, I'd take your damn fifty-six inch television too. But I know who you are, and where you live and work. I will watch you. If you ever try to come after us or do anything like this con again, I will burn your body inch by inch until you are nothing but charcoal. Do you understand me?"

She nodded her head but didn't look up. I gave her one more, hard burst of real fire and pictured it licking over her nipples.

"Take that you puta." I spit the words.

We turned and walked out of the house leaving her with her wrists bound behind her back, her head hanging down on her chest, and sitting in her own urine.

When we saw Charlie, Gene just had to laugh despite the circumstances. Charlie looked like a mime walking around inside the box and placing his hands on the invisible walls and ceiling. By his expression, I could tell he was saying things we didn't want to hear.

Then Gene slapped his thigh and said, "Look over there. It's big pile of shit. Charlie didn't shit his pants. He pulled them down and took a shit. If anyone were driving by they wouldn't know he was in a glass cage, they'd just think he was taking a shit in the driveway."

I glared at Gene. "I don't quite see the humor in it. How long do you think this will last?"

"No idea, but I suggest we leave him like that and get out of here. We can decide what to do later."

As we walked toward the car, I felt faint from exhaustion, relief, and perhaps a few other emotions I couldn't name. I nearly swooned and leaned in hard on Gene's arm.

At that precise moment, we heard the roar of an engine. Both Gene and I whirled our heads around just in time to see the Cadillac barreling down Dering Street. Gene grabbed me and dragged me behind a parked car, pushing my head under his arm. The jerking movement made me feel like I'd throw up but I stayed put.

Gene narrated. "It's them. Stay down. The driver is getting out. Sporelli's in the back."

Gene continued, "He's walking up the driveway, Brava. A few more feet and he's gonna figure out that Charlie's in the glass. Can you make it go away?"

I felt too weak to do anything. I couldn't even begin to try, but I implored Dealan to do it. I didn't even dare to look up.

Gene continued narrating. "I think you did it Brava. Charlie just fell over on the driveway. Sporelli's getting out of the car. We need to get out of here before they spot us."

Gene continued to watch what was going on in the driveway while I just hung my head. He said, "They're talking to Charlie, and they're all going inside. When I say 'go' we'll run to the car."

We ran, with Gene supporting me, to the car and got in without further incident. Gene gunned it out of the driveway and went the back way out of the neighborhood.

He looked at me and said, "So they don't see our license plate." I was glad he'd thought of that.

I began to recover a bit as we drove. I yanked off my veil and tousled my hair. "I don't know how they wear those damn things on their head. I have a terrible headache."

"You think it's the veil that's giving you a headache?" Gene cast me a sidelong glance. "That was pretty intense. By the way, well done Aunt Brava, I'm impressed. I've never seen you like that."

"I guess I never needed to be like that before. But I watch a lot of movies." I laughed. "Seriously. I believe in Dealan now. Holy shit, huh? I don't know where I came up with some of that shit. It had to be her."

When we got to Buford Highway, I said, "Go easy here. There are a lot of cops on this road."

"Yea, thank God they got Sporelli's goon for running the red light. But where were they when the scams went down?"

I smirked, "Yea, right?"

I was worried about what the scammers were telling the mafia. When had the word "scammers" and "mafia" come into my vocabulary? I'd lived fifty-something years without those words in my life.

Chapter 27

Mom and Dad had gone to check on things at their trailer, so as we neared the house I said to Gene, "Go slow and make sure their car isn't in the driveway. If it is, keep going and we'll make a new plan."

The coast was clear, so we gathered up the bags of money and took them into the house. I made sure to lock the front door behind us and followed Gene into the dining room to find him dumping the money out on the dining room table. It was piled high with mostly twenty dollar bills.

I said to Gene, "You start counting, and I'll call Mom and Dad and get a feel for how long we have."

Mom and Dad were visiting with the Cohens and not planning to return until after dinner. Thankfully Mom was distracted by the Cohens so it was a short call.

When I returned to Gene, he had stacks of twenties and was pointing at each, "$140,000, $160,000 and still counting."

I stayed silent and let him finish.

He whistled. "Two hundred and eighty thousand dollars."

We were both stunned into silence. After a long moment, I asked him if he could figure out who they scammed and how much they took.

"I already know everything. It's in the police reports. There were eleven scams before today."

"How much is that per scam? You do the math," I said

"Well, it averages about $23,000 per scam but she got $50,000 from Grammy. And she only got $8000 today. But it's all in the police reports."

"Well, all I care about at the moment is giving Mom and Dad back their $50,000. I want their worried looks to go away. And also, I confess I want them to move back home."

"Aunt Brava, I think it would be more fair if we figure out how much they got from everybody and then give each victim an equal percentage back."

I was speechless. My heart welled up with pride in my nephew. He was wiser and more generous than me. I was ashamed of my selfishness.

"Gene, you amaze me. I can't believe what a wonderful man you are growing up to be. I am so proud of you. And more than a little ashamed of me. Of course, you thought of that. Speaking of that, how are we going to get the money back to everyone? Do you have a way to find out who the victims are and where they live?"

He gave me that look he gave me when I asked a stupid question.

"How did you know we'd even recover any of the money?" I queried.

"Faith. Ever heard of it?"

"OK, show me up yet again. If you've got it all figured out, just tell me how much money we can give back to Mom and Dad. And since I'm being so shallow at the moment, I'd like to know when they can go home."

"How long do we have before Grammy and Grandpa get here?" Gene asked.

"They're staying for dinner with the Cohens, so we're OK for several hours. Why?"

"I'm hungry. And you probably need to eat too, so let me get on the computer. I'll figure out all the details while you cook."

Gene continued, "But I'm more worried about Sporelli. And I'm worried about what the scammers told him and his goon."

"Do you think Sporelli's guys could figure out who we are?"

"They had plenty of time to get our license number. And if I can get an address from that, so can they. One good thing is that the scammers didn't get anything on us. I'm confident of that. It's the mafia I'm more worried about."

"Will Mom still be in their debt if they didn't get the money back?"

"I think the fact that they tried to get it back puts her in their debt, but I don't know anything about the mafia. But you know Grammy, she can charm anyone. Let's just hope that includes the mafia don, Mr. Sporelli."

Gene set about figuring the amounts we could give back to each victim and where they lived. I grilled some poblano peppers from the garden and wrapped two Vidalia onions in aluminum foil with salt, pepper and olive oil and tossed them on the grill too. I made hamburger patties into which I stuffed the peppers, goat cheese, garlic and thyme and added them to the grill with the onions. Then I tossed a salad with blood oranges, cranberries and goat cheese with a raspberry vinaigrette. Sipping a glass of Italian red wine, I inhaled the fragrance of the food and realized how hungry I was. I was also relieved that this saga was nearing its end. Maybe I could go back to my old life.

Well my old life after lightning but before my parents moved in.

Gene walked into the kitchen just as I was dishing up our plates. He told me that each victim could get back 83% of what was taken.

"How much is that for Mom and Dad?"

"$41,500," Gene answered.

Initially, I felt relieved, then that Sicilian grudge gene reared its ugly head. "But that means that bitch got $8500 from my mom, Gene. I want to go back and hurt her some more."

"How did I know you'd say that?" He grinned and rolled his eyes.

"How much did they get total from all the victims?"

"You mean the amount we didn't recover, right?" He was stalling.

I glared.

"Fifty something thousand as far as I can tell."

"You can tell, and you know to the penny. Tell me."

$56,800."

"I'm gonna go back and kill them."

Gene sniffed the air. "I'm gonna eat this meal and let you calm down. You know you're not going to murder anyone, and so do I. Be glad Dealan helped us get this much back. It changes Grammy and Grandpa's future, and yours. Now eat while I tell you of my plan to return the money."

"I hadn't gotten that far. Somehow I just pictured us walking up to them and handing them a bag of money."

"Yea Brava, that wouldn't raise any suspicions."

"You're always one step ahead of me."

"That's why you need me, Aunt Brava. And I didn't tell you enough earlier. You were amazing. That was the best thing I've ever seen in real life OR a movie."

"It was something, Gene, but it wasn't me. I guess I have to believe in Dealan now. I couldn't have done that alone."

I saw Gene's smile though he tried to hide it.

I said, "I know what you're thinking."

"What?" he asked with feigned innocence.

"'I told you so!' Right?"

Gene just grinned.

When he explained his plan to get the money back to all eleven people, minus Mom and Dad, I was amused.

"But Gene this could take weeks doing it your way."

"Yea, but think of the fun we'll have."

He continued, "Well there's Mrs. Elbright. She's a teacher at the Alston Academy. A society is giving her an award for being such an influential teacher."

"What society?"

"Brava, our society that we make up."

"Oh. I get it."

I got into the game. "I can wear my nun costume again and drop the money at the school for them to give to her. What shall we name our society?"

"How about the Society for Heroic and Influential Teachers?"

"That's great, Gene. Did you just make that up off the top of your head, or have you been thinking about it?"

"That's how I amuse myself thinking up ways to mess with people. Think about the name again and consider the acronym."

"Society, Heroic, Influential, Tea ... Oh my gosh, it's shit! Gene I'm not calling it that."

"Brava, have some fun with it. Besides you've got time to decide. Tonight we give Grammy and Grandpa the good news and get their money back to them. They'll probably move out tomorrow."

"Hallelujah is all I can say. What are we going to tell them? I suppose you've already got that figured out too."

"You know how Grammy signs up for Publisher's Clearing House every single day?"

"Yes, I delete those damn emails every time she has me check her computer for something."

"Me too," Gene said and continued, "Well, Grammy just won $41,500 from Publisher's Clearing House."

"Seriously?" I was laughing as I said it.

"Yep, and they came by the house today to give it to her, but she wasn't here, so they told us."

'But she doesn't live here."

"Already figured that out. They went to the trailer park yesterday and someone gave them this address. They failed to get that kind person's name. Imagine how frustrated they were that they went to their house yesterday and here today and missed her both times!" Gene's voice was rising and falling with fake enthusiasm.

"Well, you do have it all figured out, don't ya?"

"Yep, we're gonna go right now to Office Depot and print a huge check that PCH left with us this afternoon. We'll pick up some balloons too."

"I'll drop you at Office Depot, and I'll go get the balloons and come back for you. What time is it?"

Gene said, "It's only 4:30 so we've got several hours to get it ready and get our stories straight. It's not Grammy that I worry about figuring out the details, it's your dad."

"Yea. I know what you mean. Mom lives on emotions and she'll be so excited she won't think beyond that. Dad will be more analytical. He'll ask a lot of questions."

Gene said that he had two senior guys who owed him a favor. I didn't even ask what he'd done for them. He'd already called the boys so we could get photos of them holding the check.

"I told them to wear something nerdy and traditional. They'll be here by six so let's go."

Gene's friends were great! They showed up driving a 1957 turquoise blue Chevy Coup restored to all its glory. Three of them piled out. They had enlisted the help of a third boy to "film" the event. The two in suits looked about twelve years old. The other one was in jeans holding a video camera and huge microphone. It was perfect except for their obvious youthfulness, but I didn't think either Mom or Dad would notice. Probably everyone under fifty looks twelve to them.

We had a grand time playing it up. The boys thought it was just a prank we were playing. Only Gene and I knew the truth. When Mom and Dad got home, around eight, Gene met them at the car while I waited on the steps with the huge check. Dad looked bewildered when we told them that Mom had finally won the jackpot from Publisher's Clearing House. He kept trying to catch my eye, which I avoided, but Mom was all excited about it.

Then things took an unexpected turn. Mom turned self-righteous. "I've told you all these years that someone had to win. And every one of you in this room," she pointed to each one of us, "told me I'd never win. And I never lost hope, no I didn't, and now look."

She kept on and on. I almost regretted this plan that seemed so perfect. We were going to hear about this forever. But then I remembered that it meant getting my home back, and I decided I could live with the self-righteousness.

I think Dad was suspicious, but I was surprised how fast he came to the conclusion that he could move back to the trailer. He began making plans to move tomorrow and asked Gene if he could help. It almost hurt my feelings for a second until I looked at the Bermuda clothes rack jammed in my living room.

I figured we'd have martinis and celebrate, but Mom took another detour.

"God provided this money for me, and it is a miracle."

She dropped to her knees and began to pray the rosary and made us join in. She took the lead with the "Hail Mary full of grace" part and Gene, Dad and I answered with the second half beginning "Holy Mary Mother of God." It took an hour. After we were done, she lit candles all over the house "in celebration of our miracle."

I longed for a martini. This day had exhausted me with its range of emotions. I was weak in the knees as I contemplated it and it felt like days had passed since finding the scammers. I finally interrupted Mom from her candle lighting and handed her and my dad both a martini. I even offered one to Gene. I figured he deserved it, and I didn't care if I was corrupting a minor. He refused one of his own but had some of mine. I had two. Gene slept over, and we all went to bed a little tipsy and a lot relieved.

Chapter 28

We feasted on blueberry, cottage cheese crepes with real whipped cream for breakfast while Gene and Dad planned the move. Mom was on the phone with all her neighbors at the trailer park telling them of the "miracle." She hadn't told them the whole story of the scam because she was so ashamed, but they knew she had been robbed and that they had to move in with me for a while.

After we got them settled back in Canton, Gene and I went back to my house to plan the return of the rest of the money. The house looked like a cyclone had come through, but nearly all of Mom and Dad's stuff was gone. It smelled of my mom's fragrance, and I felt a moment's sadness that I hadn't enjoyed them more, but then I remembered the mess. It looked more like my sanctuary than it had only hours before so I was happy. I'd take a few more loads of little things back to Mom and Dad over the next week.

"Tomorrow night we are going to the Colonnade for dinner."

I pictured the restaurant, an Atlanta landmark for meat and threes. Its nickname is Gays and Grays because that's who eats there. It's on Cheshire Bridge Road, a street that's only about a mile in length and has several of the best and oldest restaurants in the city, along with strip clubs, gay leather bars, package stores, ethnic groceries, antique stores and tattoo parlors. Mom and I once did a progressive dinner down Cheshire Bridge Road, stopping at several different ethnic restaurants to share an appetizer and drink and ending with dessert at the Greek restaurant near the Mexican Grocery.

"Are you hungry for a meat and three with the old folks who eat there, or is this part of our caper to return money?"

"One of the guys who got scammed is a waiter who's been at the Colonnade for nearly forty years. They did a piece on him in the newspaper that I found doing my research; that's how I know. Anyway, those scumbags got $40,000 from him. I imagine it was nearly all he had."

"Oh my God, that poor man. He was probably devastated. And now he believes he'll have to face working at the Colonnade for another forty years before he can retire. He'll be as old as Methusela."

"Who? Oh, never mind," Gene continued. "That's why I want to get the money back to him as soon as we can. I figure we can just eat there and leave $33,200 as a tip. Maybe we can even hide so we can see his face."

I was delighted. "Who else can we give the money to this week?" I laughed and Gene did too because he was happy I was into the spirit of it.

And so it went with Gene delighting me with his schemes. It was fun just talking about it. I couldn't wait 'til we did them.

We counted out the $33,200 dollars for the waiter. It was a huge pile of money, and we worried how we'd get it to him on the table. We put it in a plastic baggie and squeezed the air out. It brought the huge stack down to two more manageable stacks just a few inches thick.

Gene created an official sounding letter on letterhead from a fictitious law firm complete with a logo and partners. The letter stated that an anonymous patron left John Gaylord $33,200 in his will for serving him many delightful meals during his life. It was very realistic. But if John Gaylord pursued it, he'd find no law firm with that name, and of course, a law firm would have sent a check. I was curious if he'd try, or just accept the cash without question. We'd never know.

All day Monday, I couldn't wait to get out of work so we could eat at the Colonnade. I was excited about getting the money back to that poor waiter and also my mouth was watering for good Southern food. We got there around 6:30 and there was a wait. In addition, we asked for John Gaylord to serve us, so it was an hour and a half before we got seated. I was starved and getting cranky even though I was excited about our mission.

I ordered chicken fried steak with a wedge of iceberg lettuce with blue cheese dressing, and macaroni and cheese. Gene got the fried chicken with macaroni and cheese and creamed corn. They brought cornbread and rolls to the table. I wolfed three rolls in quick succession before I slowed down. I didn't want to ruin the meal. We planned where we would hide so we could watch John when he got his "tip."

After I ate most of my meal and Gene ate all of his and finished mine (I was counting on a doggy bag but didn't complain), we got our check. I paid with cash and put that and the letter and baggie of money in the little black case on the center of the table. It was bulging and popped open, but it would have to do. We stepped away and hid in the hallway that led to the bathrooms. I had a heart lurching moment when the busboy came by first and cleared the table, but he never touched the money.

John grabbed for the black case and stuffed it in his apron, then he slowly withdrew it and read the letter right there at the table. I saw tears well up in his eyes. He scanned the restaurant, but we went out through the bar before he spotted us.

Gene high-fived me in the car, and I teared up. This was so much fun. I was grateful that Dealan had given me the chance to right a terrible injustice that was done to so many innocent people in our city, including my mom. Maybe I really could be a good superhero worthy of Dealan's powers. I shared my thoughts with Gene, who laughed and punched me in the arm.

Chapter 29

Mentally planning my outfit for the day and running late as usual, I dove in the shower only to feel an icy trickle come out of the shower head. I jumped from the shower, naked and damp, grabbing a towel to wrap carelessly around me, and went to the basement to figure out the problem. The cellar was flooded with about an inch of water and as I stepped into it, water splashed out behind me like a wake from a jet ski. I jumped backward to the steps.

Oh yea, lightning and water don't mix. I recalled the Epsom salt bath.

I could take a shower without incident if I wore my stones around my neck, but hadn't managed a bath since the lightning. Perhaps because most times I'm upset and taking it in an attempt to relax. Still naked and wrapped in a towel, I grabbed my rubber rain boots and gloves and went back down, stopping on the bottom step just above the water.

It was quickly evident that the water was coming from my hot water heater. I needed to turn off the water to the house but didn't know where it was. Kevin always handled these types of things. I missed that so much.

I asked myself, "Did I appreciate him enough when he was here?"

I felt guilty for a minute then I remembered the way he dumped me and felt rage. In that moment, I was so angry at Kevin for leaving that I wondered if the lightning would work long distance. I pictured squeezing Kevin's head like a pimple and watching his brains shoot out the top of his head like pus.

Oh God, what if it did work long distance. I might have just killed him, and I'd never even know. I paused for a moment thinking of that possibility.

Well, it would be worse if I knew.

I managed to turn off the water to the house and did it wearing nothing but my rubber boots, gloves and a towel. I needed a plumber and worried that it would be expensive, and they might take advantage of me. Mom knew all kinds of shade tree mechanics, handy men and back door plumbers. I gave her a call at the same time I was pulling at my curls and tapping baby powder under my arms in lieu of a shower. I was going to be late as it was, and I was rattled. I would need a few extra stones taped here and there.

Mom answered, "Hello Brava, I was just washing the car since I got all that bird poop on it when your dad and I drove to Stone Mountain yesterday ..."

She always did that. It's as if she's just waiting for the phone to ring to tell someone what she's doing. She'll go from story to story for twenty minutes before I get to the reason I called, or worse, I get off the phone and have forgotten the reason I called.

"Mom," I interrupted. "I need your help with something."

"Are you OK?" she asked.

"Yes I ju–"

"Is Riley OK?"

"Yes Mom. I jus–"

"Is Louma OK?"

"Mom," I yelled. "We are all OK. Stop your litany. When are you going to realize that we are all almost always OK?"

"Well, I just worry you know. What's the matter?"

"I need a plumber. Don't you have a guy?"

"Yes, it's Bobby Joe down the street, the fourth trailer down from Mrs. Cohen. He's a wonderful, wonderful plumber. He saved Leeanne thousands of dollars when her septic tank backed up last Christmas and she had 25 people coming for dinner. He didn't even charge her extra for the holiday visit and brought his wet vac and cleaned up the shit water."

"How nice. How can anyone get 25 people in a trailer anyway? Don't answer that question. Do you think he can come and look at my hot water heater? It's leaking into my basement."

"Brava, I wish you'd give up that big house. There's a trailer right here for sale. You could live near your dad and me."

I thought, but didn't say *Yea, just what I need; redneck Peyton Place and a long commute to boot.*

She continued, "Bobby Joe works a day shift at the brewery, so he probably can't come until after four today, but I'll call him and call you back."

I reminded her I worked until seven and asked her to arrange that.

About twenty minutes later, she called back on my cell phone to tell me he'd be at my house by seven.

"You've met him, you know," she said.

I was pulling my shirt over my head and had her on speaker phone. "I don't think so Mom."

"Yes you did. About a month ago when you were here, he came to the door to talk to your dad about something. We were in the kitchen making spaghetti sauce. Remember?"

"Oh him." I moaned.

My dad never has a bad word to say to or about anybody. He lifts everyone else's spirits and sometimes people take advantage of that. This guy came to the door to talk to my dad and stayed forty minutes. I couldn't hear the conversation, but I got the tone; Bobby Joe all pissing and moaning, and my dad just saying good things to cheer him up.

Mom said, "Yes, I feel so sorry for him. His wife just up and left him after twenty years. He told me the whole sordid story. She called him a sad sack and said she'd jump off a tall building if she had to see his hound dog face for one more day. Can you believe it? She ran off with the country singer who plays at the Spuds and Spurs on Saturday night. Your dad and I see her there line dancing and hooting and drinking."

I yanked on navy blue slacks and slipped my bare feet into brown loafers. I snatched my toothbrush from its holder and squirted toothpaste while Mom babbled her sympathy for Sad Sack.

"Ew, ew, ew." I'd brushed my teeth with hair gel and had no water to rinse.

Mom feels sorry for everyone. I lack that kind of sympathy for others since Kevin left me. I save it for me.

She continued, "You know, Brava, I'd hate to die thinking you're all alone in the world. Maybe you could have him stay for dinner."

I'd considered some online dating sites recently though I hadn't shared that with mom. But I sure as hell wasn't gonna start dating sad sack.

"Mom, his wife left him by his own admission because he's a sad sack. Would you rather I have that or be alone? Don't give him any ideas about dinner. He's coming here to fix my hot water heater, nothing more."

I got off the phone and berated myself for not just looking online and finding a plumber. I worried about money so much that in order to get a deal, I got myself in these messes with Mom.

I went to work and was only a few minutes late. I felt disgusting having not taken a shower, so I'd sprayed some extra perfume on. I went to the bathroom at work and brushed my teeth. That felt a little better. So I washed my face and hands and up my arms. I had a wet paper towel and was washing my pits and it felt so good, I considered taking off my clothes and climbing into the sink, when Sheila walked in.

Does she have radar?

It wasn't the first time she found me in a compromising position in the bathroom. At least this time it was only because I had no hot water, not because I was having trouble with the lightning. We chatted for a few minutes.

She was wearing a lime green dress that hung in an angled hem down past her knees and billowed when she walked. She accessorized with a turquoise stone the size of a small hanging planet around her neck from a silver ribbon. Dangling from her ears were silver bells that tinkled when she moved, and matched a wrist and an ankle bracelet that also tinkled. She looked stunning and sounded like Christmas. On nearly all her fingers were multiple, tiny bands of silver and turquoise rings.

She is so pretty and fashionable. I felt even more disgusting after seeing her. *Oh well, maybe it will be a short day.*

After work, I met Sad Sack at the house. It took him about twenty minutes to fix the hot water heater, and he talked to me for forty more. I was tired, and stinky, both from BO and extra deodorant, and I was getting rattled. He kept droning on and I was so desperate to get him out of the house that I decided to use my powers. I looked out the window and saw his truck parked in my driveway. I sent a big wind to shake it and set off his car alarm.

He jumped and looked over his shoulder out the window toward his vehicle.

"I think I saw someone running away from your truck. He went that way." I pointed and Sad Sack took off running.

After I was sure he'd gone, I headed straight for the shower. It felt amazing, and I was afraid I'd stay in there forever, and never eat and then die all wet and naked and my neighbor's Bassett Hound would smell my dead, decomposed body. My mind can be a dangerous neighborhood. I dragged myself out of the shower and into the bed. I fell asleep planning mean retorts to Cow Patty.

Chapter 30

Friday began with Cow Patty and her usual meanness. Today she'd said, "I'm just gonna tell you, Brava, that hair is a color God never gave anybody."

I stammered, "It *is* the color God gave me."

Why do I defend myself to that bitch?

I do cover the gray, I admit. But the red is the color God gave me. In my opinion, God made a stupid mistake to make our hair turn gray when we still feel young. I mean to talk with him about that when I get to Heaven. That and a few other things like having periods every month.

Sheila was on the phone, and Dr. Jack was with a patient. Another patient was in the waiting room when a man in a three-piece suit and shiny shoes walked in. He had a red tie and a matching pocket handkerchief. I had him pegged as a salesman even before he got to the door.

When I first started working with the docs, I believed every lie that every salesman spun. "I went to school with Milton," or "I met Dr. Barry at a seminar and she asked me to come by," or "your doctors will be the only ones in the state to have this equipment. People will come from miles around to see them." I'd let them all back to take the doctor's time, and I got in so much trouble that I am a bulldog at the desk now.

If the president of the United States or Jesus in his white robes came to the door, I'd say, "The doctor is with patients. If you leave me some information, I will call you to arrange an appointment at a later date. It's policy."

This guy asked for Dr. Sheila Barry. I gave him the spiel to which he replied, "I think she will make an exception."

I was ready to launch into version two of the spiel which goes like this, "Listen sir, I'm going to save us both some time. You're not getting back there unless it's through me so your time would be better spent giving me the information, or sucking up to me with flowers or jewelry. Which would you prefer?"

He reached into his jacket and pulled out a badge which he discreetly flashed at me, hiding it from the patient in the waiting room. He then handed me a business card that said, "Federal Bureau of Investigation, John Grady, Special Agent, Fraud Division."

He allowed me a moment to study it and again, he said, "Perhaps Dr. Barry will make an exception to the policy. I am going to go outside and have a cigarette under that tree." He gestured toward the parking lot. "You show Dr. Barry my card."

I raced to her office waving my arms at her to get off the phone. She looked wide-eyed at me but stammered an excuse and hung up. "Sheila, do you see that guy under the tree out there?" I pointed out the window next to her desk.

Studying him for a moment she said, "He looks like a cop."

"He's FBI and he's here to see you. Sheila, what's this about?"

I saw the puzzled look on her face.

"He wants to see you right now. What should I do?"

"Do I need a lawyer?" she asked. I was shocked that she'd even considered that.

"Maybe you should just see what it's about, and then decide. I'll tell him I want to be in the room with you if you'd like a second pair of ears." I was being sincere in my offer to support my friend, but I confess I was nosy as hell, and it was a way to get the scoop.

Only after I said that did I think about the lightning getting away from me. There was grave danger lurking in this situation. But I couldn't figure a way out of it after I'd offered. heila said that she'd be fine for a brief interview with him. She seemed in control of herself, but I could hear from her voice that she was shaky.

I stepped outside and motioned FBI guy over. I said that Dr. Barry would make an exception to our office policy and meet with him immediately, but she only had twenty minutes before her next patient.

After he went in the room with her, I went to the restroom and used Gene's app. I calmed my breathing and grabbed my talismans tightly. When I felt calm enough, I went to the back hallway and tried to listen at Sheila's door. But she had the white noise machine spewing out ocean waves so I couldn't hear a thing. I slinked back to the front desk and wondered what he was investigating about my ex-nun best friend. I was indignant that she might have something in her past that she hadn't shared me. Then I remembered the lightning and realized I might not be the only one carrying around a secret.

I considered that he might be investigating one of Sheila's patients who had murdered their spouse or something. I tried to figure out who it might have been, and even went so far as to go online to the local news stations to see if a grisly murder had been reported. Only after my imagination had run totally away with me did I remember his card had said "fraud division."

After about thirty minutes (Sheila didn't really have a patient in twenty), FBI guy walked past my desk without a word. The nerve.

I yelled after him, "Smoking is bad for your health. You should quit."

I raced back to Sheila's office, certain that she'd be dying to tell me what had just gone on. I was shocked and oddly hurt when I found her door closed and the noise maker still running.

I went back to my desk and got caught up on some filing while my mind ran away with itself. Sheila's next patient was due in about twenty additional minutes. I prayed that she would come talk with me before Mr. Liles walked in, but she never came out at all. When her patient came in I called her on the intercom and told her, he was waiting.

She asked me to bring him back to her office. She never did that! She always came up to get them herself. She said I had enough to do without being an "escort" service too. We had laughed at her inadvertent choice of words when she said it. Then it became part of our lexicon. It was yet another of our running jokes.

Curiouser and curiouser. Secrets indeed.

Chapter 31

Relieved to be home for the weekend, I was kicking off my pants and washing the make-up off my face at the same time when the doorbell rang. I was down to bra and panties and had streaks of mascara running down my face, so I threw on some sweat pants and a T-shirt, dried my face and headed to the door. I peeked out of the spy hole and saw Sporelli's driver standing on my porch. I panicked. I ducked down and crab walked into the dining room where I could look out onto the street. There I saw the limo. No doubt Mr. Sporelli was in the back. No way was I answering that door. I laid down on the floor to wait until they went away.

The doorbell rang again. I laid still and prayed that he'd go away. It rang again and again in quick succession. I stayed perfectly still. Then I heard him walking around on the porch banging on the windows. He was right outside the window I was lying beneath. I was even holding my breath so he wouldn't know I was there.

"I know you're in there lady. We saw you come home."

Shit. Had they followed me, or staked out my house?

I still refused to answer. I wondered if I should call 911. But I wasn't sure I wanted the police involved any more than I wanted the mafia.

When had I begun to fear the mafia and the police?

Still I laid there, shaking but quiet. I wondered if he'd break in. I heard him leave the porch and hoped he'd gone but feared he'd simply gone out back. I quickly had my answer. I heard him banging on the rear windows and threatening to break in.

"Open the door Mrs. Falcone. Mr. Sporelli just wants to talk to you. I know you're in there."

Then I heard my cell phone ringing in my purse that I had flung on the dining table when I came home. "*Thank God,*" I thought. I scooted on my back and reached up over the edge of the table and pulled it off. Rummaging through my handbag, I found my phone that had stopped ringing by this time. I looked at the missed call and saw that it came from a private caller.

Sporelli, no doubt.

Gene had feared that the mafia would come after us for payment, but I hadn't listened. I was too caught up, initially in getting Mom's money back, and then in returning it to the victims.

Now what was I going to do? I sure as hell wasn't going to call Gene. I didn't want him in any danger. I'd rather they just hurt me.

I heard Sporelli's goon scratching at the lock at the back door, and I doubted it would be his first break in. A plan came to me. I would go out and meet them on the street. No way was I going to be alone with them in my house where they could torture me.

I didn't even think about it. I jumped up and ran to the front door and out on the porch. I yelled, "Hello, hello, who's there?"

Sporeli's guy came around the side of the house, and as he approached the front yard, I realized he'd have me pinned on my porch. I jumped down all five steps before he got there. It jarred my hip bones into their sockets and rattled my teeth.

"How long since I jumped?" I mused. You don't make a decision to stop jumping. It just simply happens. I remembered jumping as a kid, and it didn't jar my body that way. I felt old.

As he approached me, I felt afraid even though we were in plain sight. His bulging biceps so strained the sleeves of his suit jacket that I feared they might rip. He had a pockmarked face and one eye that went cockeyed. I couldn't tell if he was looking at me or Sporelli. Then I considered that he might have the ability to look at us both. Maybe having a cockeye was perfect for his job description.

"I was just washing my face and changing my clothes after work so I'm sorry I couldn't get to the door right away. You know how it is on Friday. You wanna wash that work right out of your hair." I was singing the words like the song, "I'm gonna wash that man right out of my hair."

I'm singing to mafia guy in my front yard. *I must be hysterical.*

He paused and looked at me quizzically. I wondered if it was to my advantage that he wasn't used to dealing with hysterical, middle-aged women.

He must have come to his senses. "Mr. Sporelli, my boss, wants to have a chat with you in the back of his limo. Right this way, Mrs. Falcone." He stepped toward me and reached out a hand toward my back to usher me toward the limo.

That kick-started me out of my hysteria and flattened my back tight against the porch railing. I considered acting all tough and indignant but intuitively knew that was the wrong approach.

I put on my sweetest, most charming Southern voice. "I didn't get your name sir, though I see you know mine."

He just said again, "Mr. Sporelli, my boss, wants to chat with you in his limo right there." He gestured toward the car.

"Why, my dear sir, you must know that a woman can't be too careful about her reputation even in these days of immorality. I simply couldn't get into that car alone with him. What would my neighbors think? I'd love for Mr. Sporelli to come up here in my front yard and have a chat with me. He's been so good to my ...

Mafia goon interrupted me. "Lady, cut the crap. And drop the southern accent. I know you're from Pennsylvania. You're no more a southern belle than I am."

Well, I was more a southern belle than he was. But I got the point.

Until that instant, I had forgotten that I have Dealan so I silently called for her now. Just to be sure she was here I pictured a few fire ants biting mafia goon's ankles. I watched for a reaction.

He kind of jumped and wiggled and looked down at the ground by his feet. He stepped away a few feet and inspected the ground again. I was beginning to feel grateful for fire ants.

I dropped the accent and the sugary sound to my voice. "What's the matter with your feet, 'Mr. Sporelli's employee with no name'?"

I knew Dealan was here so I felt more confident. "You can just ask Mr. Sporelli to come right here in my yard to chat with me. I'm not climbing in the back of that limo, now or ever."

The goon looked down again at his feet, stomped them and headed for the car. He leaned in the back seat and had a lengthy conversation. Just when I began to doubt that Sporelli would get out, he did. He came up the sidewalk toward the house. I was reminded of his unusual body type; short with a barrel chest and huge hands and feet. For a brief moment, I thought of my Uncle Alberto but jerked myself back to the present.

Sporelli wore a grey tailored suit that was almost silver in the sunlight, a starched white shirt and a purple silk tie. His diamond tie stud winked in the sunlight. It had to be three karats. His obviously expensive, Italian, brown leather Oxfords looked as soft as caramel. I wouldn't have thought to wear brown shoes with the grey suit but it looked great together.

I made a mental note to wear brown heels with my silvery grey dress. I was acutely aware that I was wearing sweat pants and a T-shirt and likely had mascara streaks running down my cheeks. I felt at a disadvantage.

What am I doing taking fashion notes when I'm facing the mafia don who's come to extort money from me?

I smiled and greeted him. "Mr. Sporelli, so nice to see you again. I've met you with my mom, Eugenia Falcone. I don't know if you remember."

"Of course I do, Brava. May I call you Brava?"

"Certainly, Mr. Sporelli."

I noticed that he didn't ask me to call him Gaetano.

He continued, "Eugenia is a delight. We go way back, you know? We knew each other in Pennsylvania."

"I did know that, Mr. Sporelli. And you and I have something else in common. Do you remember my daughter, Louma? Your son, Antonio, used to play soccer with her. In fact he's been at this very house many times; though it's been a few years! Your wife, Concetta brought him. How is she? I fear we've lost touch since our children grew up."

I was deliberately trying to make a personal connection. Maybe he'd be less likely to demand that we pay him some outrageous sum for helping mom.

"Concetta is well, thank you for asking. She's in Sicily now visiting family."

I waited. I felt nervous with the small talk and wanted to get to the point of this visit.

Thankfully, he obliged me. "Brava" he continued after a long moment, "I know about the scammer who got $50,000 from your mother."

I nodded but remained silent.

"In fact she came to me for help; to catch them and get her money back. I have some business connections that could enable me to assist her."

Business connections? I still remained silent.

"I took this matter into my own hands," he gestured with massive outstretched hands "rather than delegating it to my men because I respect your mother so very much. Our families are from the same region in the eastern part of Sicily."

"Yes Mr. Sporelli, I do recall that."

"What those people did to her is horrible and the cops were as bad as the scammers. The cops in this city aren't worth a damn."

One could assume the mafia and the cops aren't the best of buddies, but I agreed with him on this point. I nodded yet again. I was doing a lot of nodding. The anticipation was killing me. I just wanted him to get to the point. I nearly shouted out, "How much do we owe you?" Instead, I bit my tongue and waited.

"Week after week we staked out the parking lot where it happened."

I thought. "Week after week? It was two weeks."

He was really building up to a big payoff. I was worried. My relief at having Dealan was waning. What was I going to do, kill them both so I didn't leave any witnesses? Or hurt them like I did the woman? Actually, I considered putting

Mr. Sporelli and his goon in a lucite box, but they were at my house. I'd have to let them out sometime. No matter what I did to them, I'd have the rest of the mafia goons come after me.

I'd had enough of this small talk and the lead up was getting me anxious. I feared that something bad could happen if I got too nervous. I had to get Sporelli to cut to the chase.

"Mr. Sporelli, I don't know if you're aware of a recent event that has changed my mother's outlook. She recently won almost $42,000 from Publisher's Clearing House. Mom feels that it is God's way of returning the money to her, and she is no longer interested in revenge. She believes that punishment is best left in God's hands."

I continued before he could say anything, "We certainly appreciate your looking out for Mom. She is so lucky to know you. Do we owe you for the time you spent helping her?"

"Brava, you insult me. I looked after Eugenia in respect for our friendship and kinship as fellow Sicilians. I expect no payment for that."

The relief I felt nearly weakened my knees. No payment.

"I never meant to insult you Mr. Sporelli. I just wanted you to know how much we appreciated your efforts on Mom's behalf. I sincerely thank you for coming here to tell me personally that we don't owe you any money."

"Brava, money is not the reason I came here. Not to get it or forgive it."

My stomach did a flip flop. *If that wasn't the reason, what was?*

"Oh?" I waited.

Sporelli continued. "As I mentioned, we had been staking out the parking lot and we saw the scammers make the mark on the old woman. But when we went after them, someone ahead of us was chasing them. We got the license plate and only later learned that it was you. Then as bad luck would have it, the cops got us for running a red light. They did nothing all those weeks when the scammers worked, but they got us for a red light. Useless bastards."

He paused. "But you know this don't you?"

I just waited.

He continued. "By the time we searched the area and found their van and house, someone had gotten to them first. The lady was sitting in a puddle of piss. Looked like she had gotten beaten up pretty bad. The guy was in shock. Couldn't even finish a coherent sentence. He was standing over her and just kept repeating the words 'a sister, a sister.' We couldn't figure out what that meant."

I still stayed silent.

"We know you were there. You were following them. And you had someone else driving. We know who that was too."

Did they really know it was Gene or was this a bluff? I had to keep my mouth shut.

"Did you ask the scammers what happened, Mr. Sporelli?" I was desperate to figure out what he knew, and if he really knew it was Gene who was there. Also, I was buying time.

Sporelli answered. "They weren't talking. The guy couldn't put more than two words together, and the woman wouldn't. And we can be very persuasive."

He did a head nod and stretched out his massive hands to make his point. He continued "We searched the house and didn't find any of the money either. Now I wonder where that might have gone."

He stopped talking and pierced me with his eyes. I felt skewered.

"We were trying to do exactly what you were doing Mr. Sporelli. We wanted to get mom's money back. We did see them and followed them as you saw, but we lost them. I don't know what could have happened to them before you got there," I lied.

Mr. Sporelli studied me for a long time. I called on Dealan to keep me from showing my fear. I knew she was here because I felt a wave of well-being rush over me. I stood stock still, and I believed I looked calm on the outside.

"Brava, we are family. Nothing is more important to Sicilians than family. Tell me what happened. We must work together to right this injustice and take care of our famiglia."

"Mr. Sporelli, it looks like justice was done to the scammers, and Mom got her money back from Publisher's Clearing House so it all worked out in the end, right?"

I continued rambling. "I don't know what I, a receptionist in a doctor's office could ever do to help you, but I'm here if you ever need help; like in the office, or answering phones, or sewing. I have a little sewing busine–"

"Brava," he interrupted, "I don't need a receptionist or seamstress. I need someone who can do what you did to those scammers. I need an Enforcer. Think about it. I'd hate to think you'd let me down. It could be bad for you." He paused and finished with, "Or Gene."

Oh God, he really did know about Gene.

As I felt a rise of panic over the implications, he turned on his heel and was gone. It happened so fast I just found myself standing alone in my yard. The entire situation was so surreal that for an instant I even questioned if it had really happened. But his very expensive cologne lingered. Then I remembered the threat. *How had he worded it?* "It could be bad for you." And he knew about Gene. That scared me the most.

I went back inside and slammed and locked the door behind me. I leaned against it and tried to get my wits about me. I wanted a drink to calm my nerves, but thought I needed a clear head. Then I thought "fuck it" and got a shot of brandy and downed it in one gulp. As it burned in my belly, I felt calmer.

I asked Dealan for strength. I wondered if she were here to help *me*, or only when I needed to get justice for someone else. I wished I had paid more attention when Gene told me about the legend, but at the time I didn't believe it.

It was Friday night and Gene was going for pizza and a movie with some of his friends, so I didn't want to call him. Tomorrow, after Kung Fu, I would tell him what happened. Then I hoped we'd come up with a plan.

Even though I was home where I usually could keep my stones to a minimum, I was rattled so things wiggled and jiggled as I attempted to prepare something to eat. I gave up and called for pizza delivery and taped on more stones. I got a large pepperoni, ham and pineapple pizza and ate half of it. I saved the rest for breakfast. My ass was wide enough that I should have had a small salad instead, but I needed comfort.

I wondered if Dealan could make my ass smaller. Then I wondered what good it was to have superpowers when you had a fat ass and the mafia was stalking you. There was just so much to learn.

That gave me an idea that would fill the time until bedtime. I watched Wonder Woman, sure that it would help me learn to be a better superhero. By the end of the movie, I was more depressed than ever. Wonder Woman was descended from an immortal group of Amazonian women. Besides being immortal, she had big boobs and an impossibly tiny waist. And as if that wasn't enough she was bestowed with a golden truth lasso, bulletproof bracelets and an invisible plane.

An invisible plane? Seriously?

All I had were some stones from a creek in Pennsylvania that I affixed to my skin with tape. I was a poor superhero indeed. I guess it could be worse. I could look like the Incredible Hulk.

Chapter 32

I picked Gene up as usual for our Kung Fu class. I hadn't slept well the night before. I was rattled and had too much pizza and three shots of brandy before the night was over. I had bad dreams and woke up with a mild hangover. I sure as hell couldn't eat the pizza I'd saved for breakfast. So I just had a couple cups of coffee and headed to Gene's.

He didn't look quite awake this morning, either. I desperately wanted to wait until after Kung Fu to tell Gene about the mafia, but in my fragile state, I blurted it out the minute he got in my car

"Sporelli made a visit to my house last night, and he wants me to be his enforcer. And he knows about you too."

"Did you just say what I think you said?"

"Yep."

"Maybe you should tell me the whole story. I was worried about the mafia, and I was afraid they'd want something for helping Grammy. They don't do anything because of the love in their heart."

"Oh, you're wrong about that," I said with sarcasm. "He loves my mom. We're family and we stick together. He was insulted that I thought he'd want paid for helping famiglia."

I paused here for effect. "And if I don't become his Enforcer, and I quote here, 'it could go very bad for you, Brava. Or Gene.'"

"Does he know about your powers?"

"He knows something, but I don't think about the powers exactly." I told him that they tried to get information from the scammers but they wouldn't or couldn't talk.

I continued. "He said 'and we can be very persuasive.' Gene, I think they tortured those people. Not that they didn't deserve it, and not that I hadn't also. But ... well, I don't know. It just seems worse what they did."

"We can't go to Kung Fu today. I need to think this through, Brava. Turn around and let's go to Dunkin Donuts."

"I feel like I need Kung Fu today. And I don't need Dunkin Donuts, or for that matter, I don't need what Sifu will dish out if we skip. Let's just go and forget about this for ninety minutes and maybe something will come to us."

"More likely I'll still be thinking about it and get my ass whooped. But if you insist."

Class was particularly difficult that day. I often wonder who calls ahead to tell Sifu I'm having a bad day so he can make class even harder to torture me. But since no one knew about this, I guess he just picked it up out of the airwaves.

We did about a thousand kicking and punching drills until I was certain I'd throw up if we did one more. Thankfully we didn't. But then we broke up into groups. Gene's group was fighting, and I worried about his concentration; or lack of it.

My group was doing wrist locks and escapes. I hated these because I always got taken down and felt like I had whiplash when class was over. I was regretting my decision to come today. I went to the bathroom and lingered there, hoping for class to be over soon. I hoped Sifu hadn't noticed. *Yea, right.*

When I got back to class, he didn't say anything, he just used me to demonstrate five wristlocks with takedowns. I got whipped forward and backward and sideways and landed on my ass every time; except for the time I nearly landed on my face and Sifu snatched me up just in time.

Sometimes I wonder why I put up with this shit.

After an eternity, the ninety minutes was over. We usually hung around after class and had a cup of green tea with Sifu while we extinguished the candles on our ancestor's altar and cleared up the fruit offerings that were a week old. Today I told Sifu I had to be somewhere and left without the ritual I usually loved. I did have to be somewhere; Dunkin Donuts where a Bavarian crème donut with chocolate icing and a large coffee with cream awaited me. I grabbed the old fruit offering and chucked it in a dumpster on my way to the car.

Gene asked, "Regretting the decision to come to class?"

"With my whole heart and soul. Though not as much as I will tomorrow. Dunkin Donuts. You drive." I handed him my keys.

We drove there in silence. I'm sure we were considering the gravity of having the mafia know about my powers. Technically, they didn't know what I had (neither did I), but they knew something. And they were the worst people to know.

As we settled into our booth with our donuts and coffee, Gene said "Brava, this is bad. It's worse than I could have imagined. I can't believe the mafia wants to use you."

"But they don't really know anything."

"Tell me exactly what they said and what you said. How much do they know?"

"It seems they drove around looking for the scammers' place after the cops let them go. They found it. But we knew that. They went in and tried to get them to talk. They searched the house because he said they didn't find any money. Oh, and I almost forgot, the guy kept repeating "a sister, a sister," but Sporelli didn't know what that meant. He said she *wouldn't* talk and he *couldn't put more than two words together.* That's when he said the part about them being very persuasive."

"What did you say?" Gene queried.

"I didn't tell him anything. I was biting the inside of my mouth so I wouldn't. How are we going to get me out of this, Gene? I can't stand that they know about you. I'd die if anything ever happened to you."

"I feel the same way about you, Aunt Brava. I can take care of myself."

"Gene, I know you do Kung Fu and you are invincible, but I'm the one with powers. As much as I don't want them to know, I could use them. What can you do against the mafia? They have semi-automatic weapons."

"How do you know? Did they have one yesterday?" Gene sounded panicky.

"No," I reassured him. "I'm going by the movies."

Gene just shook his head.

"So do you have any ideas? I think we should do nothing and see if it just goes away. Maybe they'll forget all about it."

Gene rolled his eyes. "Yea, that's likely. They think they have a secret weapon in you, and they can use me to get to you. They'll probably forget all about it."

"You have a point."

Gene had already eaten three glazed donuts and slurped most of his coffee and was moving on to his Bavarian crème with confection sugar on top. I had nibbled some of my custard filled one and was licking the chocolate off the outside. I was feeling wired from the coffee and had sucked it down while it was still hot and burned the inside of my mouth.

Gene was thinking so I just waited quietly.

"I think we should set up a meeting with Mr. Sporelli at the store. That way we're more likely to be safe. Then we can get more information about what they think they know or what they want you to do. We play dumb and get as much information as we can. Let's pretend that you're really interested."

"I don't want you involved, Gene. I say I set up the meeting alone."

"Not a chance, Brava. I already am involved. Like it or not. And no one, you or me, is going anywhere near them alone. I'd already considered going without you. And as much as I'd still like to, it's too dangerous. Promise me and I'll promise you."

"OK, I promise. Now you."

"I promise."

Gene held up his hand and said "pinky swear?" I laughed.

"So we set up the meeting and find out what they want from me and go from there."

"How did you leave it with Sporelli?"

"I didn't. He just left."

Gene said, "We can call the store."

"Wait. I think I have his mobile number. I had a call come in during the time I was laying under the window in the dining room." I started scrolling through my phone. "Oh, no never mind. I think Sporelli did call me, but it was a private number. We'll just call the store."

"The sooner, the better. Do it now."

Chapter 33

Two hours later, Gene and I were sitting in the plush office at the back of Sporelli's import warehouse. A lovely young woman named Thomasina served us white wine from a chilled crystal decanter and set out a tray with Italian imported specialties; olives, prosciutto, buffalo mozzarella, tomatoes, rosemary bread, salami. It was set out on the typical southern Italian pottery hand-painted blue and yellow with lemons and olives.

I remarked on the dishes.

Sporelli explained, "They are from Caltagirone, in our beloved Sicily. Still crafted the same way as has been done for generations."

I had a wall hanging of a sun that I had purchased there but couldn't have ever afforded a whole set of dishes.

Mr. Sporelli acted just as polite as he did at my house. That in addition to the familiar comfort food and lovely dishes made it feel even more malevolent to me. He focused his attention toward Gene and repeated all that same stuff he told me about famiglia. I was even more anxious than I had been at my house and wanted him to get to the point of this visit, but I waited him out.

Finally, Sporelli turned his attention to me. "Now, Brava, I must tell you a story that will help you understand why I ask for your assistance."

I simply nodded and waited.

"You may have heard rumors that I am affiliated with the mafia up north."

I kept silent.

"Brava and Gene." He looked to each of us and paused. "In the movies, they portray the mafia as bad men, but in Sicilia (he pronounced it See Chee lee a) the mafia are protectors of the people. I act as a godfather would to his godchild. And in that role, I may need to help my godchild get on the right path. Occasionally the methods may seem harsh."

He continued as Gene and I remained silent.

"My father and his father before him have been godfathers in America. We are descended from many generations of godfathers in our native Sicily."

He gestured with his huge hands toward both Gene and me.

"Your ancestors and mine go back many generations on the island of Sicilia. That is the reason I am so close to Eugenia. My family came through Ellis Island as did yours and settled in Western Pennsylvania. There we stayed for three generations. But our children were leaving with our grandchildren to settle in the southern states. My father chose me to move to the south to be a protector of our children. He could no longer watch over the family from such a distance."

He went on "My job includes importing special products and delicacies from our native country to keep our culture alive. It is a calling that I am proud to answer. It is more than a job to me. And yes, it provides my family with a good life.

I nodded. Now it was my turn to make a family connection. "Mr. Sporelli, I have been pleased all these years to know Concetta and Antonio. We've lost touch a bit since our kids are grown, but we still consider each other friends."

Sporelli stood and walked around his office steepling his hands and appearing deep in thought. I sipped some wine and ate another cracker with prosciutto. Why not enjoy the feast? There was no point being anxious *and* hungry.

"Now, I want to tell you a story, Brava and Gene. There was a sixteen-year-old girl who ran away from her family and all the neighborhood came out to search for her. No one could understand why she ran away."

"I found her on a street corner selling her body. My assistant pretended to want her services and then grabbed her and dragged her into my limousine. She fought him and then me, even when she realized who I was. I calmed her and told her that I wanted to help her. I told her that everyone was so worried. And I asked her how she could sell her body in that way."

What she answered was chilling. She spat the answer, "Why not get paid for what my Papa gets for free?"

I gasped. Gene screwed up his face.

Sporelli continued. "She is my niece, the daughter of my brother, Salvatore. She told me how it had begun and that it had been going on for three years. I believed her. She was afraid that her father would start on her younger sisters. One was nearing thirteen. I promised to help her and assured her that I would make certain that her father never did that to any of my younger nieces."

He went on, "My brother, Salvatore has much ambition, but no brains and less of a heart. He wants to be the godfather of the south. He is not like me. I am good to my people; he is evil. My brother is evil.

I have spoken with my great uncle who resides in Palermo, Sicily. He is the greatest mafia don in history and is much loved by his people. He is willing to take Salvatore under his wing and assist him to channel his needs in a more positive direction. My fervent hope is that Salvatore can be molded. However, if he cannot, Vincente has ways of dealing with Salvatore that, shall I say, we do not have here in America."

Sporelli stopped talking. I waited. Gene waited.

After what seemed like an eternity but was probably only a few moments, Sporelli continued.

"Brava, I know you did something to those scammers. I can't imagine what you did or how you did it, but I need Salvatore to go to Italy, and it can't come back to me. He must never know that I took measures against him."

I still felt nervous, but relieved. Gene cast a sidelong glance at me, and I answered it with a glance of my own.

"So you just want me to persuade him to move back to Italy?"

"That is all Brava. Think what it will mean to the daughters who will be spared Salvatore's evil."

Gene reached into his pocket and pulled his phone out. "Aunt Brava, this is Grammy. Mr. Sporelli, we've got to take this. We'll step out."

"Please take it here. I need to check on some business matters. Make yourself at home and give Eugenia my best."

I tried to grab Gene's phone to talk with Mom, but he held it away from me. When Sporelli was out of the office, Gene said, "Cup your hands around your mouth when you talk to me." Gene demonstrated, and I almost giggled. He looked like a yodeler from the Swiss Alps.

"We're under surveillance here so be quiet. Grammy's not on the phone, Brava." He continued, "We need to talk so I bought us some time. Don't agree to anything Sporelli wants today. We need to get out of here and think things through."

"Gene, if I–"

Gene interrupted. "Cup your hands. I mean it. There are cameras in here. And whisper."

"How do you know there are cameras in here?"

"I have an app."

Of course.

"What's the big deal if I simply persuade a bad guy to get out of town, and Sporeli is happy? He'll leave us alone after that."

"Don't be so sure, Brava. It won't end there. It will just tie you in with the mob and get some even worse people after you. Please, Aunt Brava, let's get out of here. We can talk after we leave. I'm going to tell Sporelli that Grammy needs us because her pilot light went out. Go along with me."

Gene "answered" the phone again and told Mom we were on our way.

Sporelli returned almost immediately giving credence to Gene's supposition that we were being watched. We made our excuses and told Sporelli we'd get back to him just as soon as we could.

For a minute, I feared that he would tie us up and use some of those methods of persuasion on us, but he was gracious about our leaving. He walked us out to our car and held the passenger door for me.

Gene was already behind the wheel as Sporelli pinched my arm hard and said, "I look forward to hearing from you, dear."

"Ow, ow, ow," I exclaimed and rubbed my arm.

"What's the matter?" Gene asked and glanced out of the side of his eye before turning back to the road.

"Sporelli just squeezed the shit out of my arm as he said he looked forward to hearing from me and called me dear."

"You can't trust him, Brava. Regardless of what he says, he's mafia, and he is not our friend."

"But if I do this for him, he'll be in our debt and leave us alone. And we'll be doing a good thing."

"I'm not so sure, Aunt Brava. I fear that he has an ulterior motive. I'm just not sure what it is. But we need to buy some time. Maybe Grammy can help us with that."

"How?"

"Sporelli seems to genuinely like her. Maybe she can create a diversion."

"What are we going to do right now?" I asked

"I'm going home to do some research. You can do whatever you want. I'll let you know when I've found something."

"What are you going to do Gene? I don't want you getting into trouble or danger. We may be in over our heads. Remember our promise. It goes both ways."

"I don't have it all figured out yet, but when I do, I promise I'll let you know. I'll call ya later today either way."

Gene called me as promised, but had no information for me that day or for the next few days. I went to work as usual, and we went to Kung Fu on Tuesday. I was frantic that Sporelli was going to do something to me, or even worse to Gene.

Gene hatched a plan with Mom to call Sporelli and distract him from us. Mom was involved with the St. Peregrine's Cancer Foundation. They held craft shows and cook-offs to raise money for people needing help during cancer treatment of a family member.

She set up a meeting with Sporelli on Tuesday to ask for a donation. Then she cancelled at the last minute pleading mercy because she had broken a crown and had an emergency appointment at the dentist. Not exactly original, but it worked. Gene could get Mom to do anything, so she agreed and played her part like a charm. She rescheduled their appointment on Thursday and this time she made it.

She showed up at my door after her meeting. She was wearing a purple pantsuit and green sneakers. Her bag was yellow with fuscia writing that said, "If you're not supposed to eat at night, why is there a light bulb in the refrigerator?"

She launched right in with, "I ended up with a donation of an entire set of those dishes to be auctioned off for the foundation."

"I want those damn dishes. Can I buy them for $100 and give the money to the foundation?"

She laughed at me. "I'll get ten times that at auction."

"But they're only worth about $400. I just can't afford that."

"I know, but I can get those doctor's wives outbidding each other. Those old biddies are like a pack of dogs. If one wants it, they can't stand to let her get it. They pay way more than something's worth just to keep someone else from getting it. I'll get at least $1000 for those dishes." She looked smug.

Chapter 34

"Hello," I answered the phone at about 8:30 on Wednesday evening.

"Brava, what are you doing right now?" It was Sheila.

"Nothing big. What's up?"

"Can you come over? I really need to talk to you."

"I'm on my way. You OK?" I was already grabbing my purse and car keys.

"I'm fine. There is something I need to tell you. It can't wait any longer. It's been way too long as it is."

I knew she could hear the car door dinging, so I just said. "Be there in a minute." And hung up. Sheila lives only a few miles from me in a house almost exactly like mine. Both neighborhoods were built in the 1950s and the homes are one story brick ranches. The only difference is that her sunroom is on the back and mine is on the front. That and the color of our bathroom tiles. Mine are turquoise. I changed out my turquoise toilet when I moved in because I couldn't go in a toilet that made my pee look green.

She didn't sound hysterical or sick so I wasn't frantic. More curious than anything. I figured it had something to do with the FBI guy and I was dying to get the scoop. I arrived about ten minutes later and saw Sheila waiting at her door. She was still wearing the clothes she'd worn to work, and I wondered if she'd just gotten home.

As I climbed the steps, she handed me a piece of paper. It looked like an official document, and I stopped halfway up to read it. It was a warrant to search the premises. Stapled to it was the business card of John Grady, FBI guy.

"I found this on my counter when I came home."

"Inside your house? Did you just get home, Sheila?"

"No, I've been here for a couple hours, but when I found it I called my lawyer right away. I've been on the phone with him all this time."

"*Your* lawyer? What do you have a lawyer for?"

"He's my divorce lawyer."

I was stunned. Sheila is my best friend and I've known her for over ten years. I never even knew she had been married, let alone divorced. Had she been a nun before or after that? I was confused and hurt that she had kept it from me.

But then again, I have superpowers, and I hadn't told her. Somehow this seemed totally different.

Sheila continued. "Maybe we should go in and have a glass of wine, and I'll tell you the whole story."

"Maybe we should. And I need that glass of wine."

"You have no idea," Sheila said over her shoulder as she headed to the kitchen.

As Sheila poured our wine, I settled onto the sofa in front of the fireplace that was lit with a low fire. I tried to fit the timeline together. She had been a nun somewhere on the west coast, I knew that. But how long after leaving the convent had she come to Atlanta? I didn't really think I knew. And what had happened during that time?

Sheila handed me a glass, sat down on the opposite end of her sofa and looked at me. Her German shepherd, Thor, sat between us with his butt on the sofa and his front feet on the floor. I found it hilarious the way he sat almost like a person.

"I am sorry that I never shared this story with you, Brava. You're my best friend, and I should have, but it was something I wanted to forget. And I never thought it would come up."

"Never mind that, now, Sheila. Just tell me, however much you want. I guess we all have secrets."

I hoped she would have as much compassion for mine if she ever found out.

"I'd just left the convent a few months before when I met Sean. I was working at a Catholic Hospital in Laguna Beach and lived In San Juan Capistrano, just a few miles down the highway. I loved going to Mass at the mission. It's a tiny chapel with a small local congregation, so we all knew each other. One Sunday I searched the pew for a songbook and one came from behind me already opened to the correct hymn. I looked back to thank the person, and looked into the bluest eyes I'd ever seen."

She continued as I sipped my wine.

"He smiled and I turned back around, but my face was flaming. All through Mass I felt like his eyes were burning a hole through the back of my head. I wanted to turn around so badly I couldn't stand it. I didn't hear a word of the sermon. When we walked up to communion, he was so close behind me I imagined I could feel his breath on my neck. I got my host and turned around blushing to my hairline. I wouldn't dare look at him as he walked back down the aisle. I knelt and bowed my head, but I prayed 'don't let me look, don't let me look.'"

I laughed to ease the tension a bit. "Not exactly an approved post-communion prayer."

She smiled.

"But rather than going back to his pew, he stepped in beside me. I kept my head down and pretended to pray. At the final song, he opened up one hymnal and held it between us, and I just pretended to sing. After Mass, he asked me to go for a cup of coffee with him. There's a Starbuck's catty-corner from the mission."

"That was the beginning of a romantic, whirlwind courtship. He was an Irish Catholic lawyer who specialized in private adoptions to Catholic families; mostly from unwed Catholic mothers who chose adoption. We went to Mass on Wednesdays and Sundays. We went to the movies and dinner on Fridays. Saturdays we spent at Dana Point. We watched blue whales off the coast. We held hands as we walked among the yachts and watched the surfers. We ate outside at the cafes on the marina."

"It sounds incredibly romantic." I was a little impatient and wished she'd connect the dots that ended with Grady raiding her house.

"Only six weeks after we met we got married at the Serra Chapel at the Mission. I thought that the way we met was a sign from God that we were meant to be together."

I said, "It sounds perfect to me too."

"It was. The honeymoon was magical. He brought me roses and jewelry and breakfast in bed. We had a wonderful time exploring the beaches of southern California and had picnics of fruit and cheese and wine."

After the honeymoon, I moved into his apartment near the mission. I didn't have much in the way of material things anyway so it made sense. But I kinda felt like an interloper in his domain."

She continued. It seemed she had kept the story pent up for so long there was no stopping her.

"And he did things to make me feel that way. He'd move my purse or keys, and when I asked if he'd seen them, he'd tell me the wrong location. I'd run around looking for them and be late to work. Then he'd shame me for being forgetful. I began memorizing where I put things because I thought I was going crazy and I'd find them other places.

"He undermined everything I did or said by simply asking a question like 'are you sure?' or say 'really, is that right?' and I began to doubt myself."

I sipped some wine and she continued.

"He 'helped me,'" she put her fingers in quotation signs "with things I was quite capable of doing myself. He 'took me' places I could quite get to alone so I wouldn't get lost. It was a subtle, brilliant, decisive plan to undermine my confidence of which I had little anyway. It seemed sweet and helpful at first, but after a short while I felt sick all the time. He never let me be away from him except when I was at work.

"In the convent, I wasn't exactly alone, there were other nuns around, but I was alone with my thoughts. I could take a walk or sit outside or go to the chapel or cook without help or chatter or interference.

"With him I felt smothered. Then I felt guilty. He bought me gorgeous, expensive jewelry and told me how much he loved me. My co-workers and friends told me how lucky I was. They could never get their husbands to help them or go places with them and Sean did everything with me.

"I thought I was going crazy and seriously considered returning to the convent. I couldn't eat or sleep and lost a great deal of weight. In fact, I was hospitalized at one point and that's when my priest figured out something was dreadfully wrong. He visited me in the hospital and gently and patiently got me to talk. Here I was the psychologist, and he recognized the emotional abuse. I just couldn't see it.

"He helped me get out. I packed up my few belongings and left Sean while he was at work one day. I nearly left the jewelry, but at the last minute I thought 'I earned every last bauble.' I knew I'd never wear any but thought I might sell it and get a few dollars. I stayed in a shelter for a few days and then rented a room in a complex close to work.

"Father Casteel, my priest at the hospital, helped me begin the annulment process and find a divorce attorney. I had gone from being a nun, to getting a dispensation of my vows, to getting married, to filing for a divorce and an annulment in twenty some months.

"Sean showed up at my work. He called me constantly and left begging messages. He sent me flowers. He bought me more jewelry. He fought the divorce. He fought the annulment. He stalked me. He befriended my friends and turned them against me. And on and on. It was a relentless campaign to get me back. I tried to get a restraining order, but the judge said he wasn't threatening. He just sent flowers and jewelry.

"The divorce took twice as long as the marriage. Sean fought the annulment all the way to Rome. It took five years to get it. We were married nine months, and the annulment took five years.

My lawyer felt so sorry for me that he waived most of my bills, and we actually became friends and still stay in touch. Since he's in California, I caught him at the office when I came home to this."

She pointed at the search warrant.

"After all that was finally over, I moved here and have tried to forget about it. That is until John Grady showed up at the office. They're investigating Sean for money laundering. Seems he isn't a family law specialist; he's a corporate lawyer who buys businesses at a fraction of their worth and re-sells them to turn a huge profit. Apparently, he then hides large amounts of money in places like Switzerland and the Cayman Islands.

"I should have figured it out when I sold a couple of pieces of jewelry and got $13,000. A family lawyer doesn't make that kinda money. But I knew less than nothing about the world. I'd been locked up in a convent for fifteen years. Over the years, I've sold all the jewelry he gave me, and I've gotten somewhere in the neighborhood of $65,000."

I gasped at that.

"The FBI has been suspicious of Sean for years, and they want information from me. When I told Grady I didn't know anything about Sean's business and I thought he was a family lawyer, he so much as called me an idiot. I don't know how, but he knew how much money I got for the jewelry. He threatened to charge me as an accessory to money laundering and tax evasion because I profited from Sean's illegal dealings."

Sheila stopped and took a gulp of her wine. I did the same, and we both noticed that our glasses were empty.

I said, "I think we need another glass."

"I agree." Sheila went to the kitchen to fill our glasses. I felt angry for a moment and resentful, but I remembered my secret and let it go. Sort of. Not really. My situation was different.

When she returned, I asked. "How did the FBI get in? And how could they without you being here?"

"My sliding glass door is jimmied a little, and it's really hard to lock. I never worried about it because of Thor, but Grady braved this ferocious beast and walked right in. It's not breaking and entering if the door is unlocked. When I got home, I saw this on my counter and two seconds later Jack came banging on my door. She gestured with her head toward her neighbor's house. He said there were two FBI agents here; a man and a woman. They questioned him about my ex-husband and you can imagine his surprise. He didn't know I was married before either. No one did."

Sheila burst into tears at this point. "I am so ashamed that I didn't tell you or Jack. You've been the best friend I've ever had, and he's been a good friend to me too. How can either of you trust me? I feel sick to my stomach."

I had an intense urge to divulge my secrets; superpowers and mafia problems so she wouldn't feel so guilty. But I honestly couldn't think how I would begin.

Don't feel bad about that. Wait 'til you hear the secret I've been keeping from you.

Or *that's nothing. I am a superhero with powers from a Celtic goddess and the mafia wants to use me as an Enforcer.*

Or *watch this.* As conflicted as my emotions were, I was pretty sure I could scoot a little something across the coffee table.

But instead I said, "Sheila, I can only speak for myself, but I feel certain Jack feels the same. I love you. I understand why you wanted to forget that time in your life. I'm certain you don't know all about Jack's gay lovers. Or mine." I added that last part with a flip of my hair.

I asked, "What did your lawyer say?"

"He's looking into some things and will call me back; probably not until tomorrow. But there's more about Grady."

I felt sick. "What?"

"One weekend when Sean and I were married, we flew to the Cayman Islands with two of his clients. He told me they were a wealthy Catholic couple who couldn't conceive and had adopted two babies with Sean's help. They wanted to take us to the Caymans to thank him. I believed him. It was a remarkable weekend. They were lovely people. We sailed and snorkeled, and they dove with the Stingrays. I snorkeled above them. The rays felt like velvet.

"I'd never even been anywhere outside of Oregon and southern California, so it was a whole new world for me. He bought me more stunning jewelry there too. Grady says that was a trip to hide money. That's how he can get me for money laundering. The couple wasn't even married. And they didn't have kids; adopted or otherwise. They were business partners and they were hiding money in the Cayman's with Sean's help. Grady claims that I knew about it and was in on it. He can't believe anyone could be so stupid that they didn't know. His words 'so stupid.'"

"Did you tell him about you being a nun before that? That you were naïve, not stupid."

"Brava, I sang like a canary. I met him after work that day he came to the office. I told him everything. I threw myself on his mercy. But I guess he still didn't believe me, so he came here and searched."

"What was he looking for? Do you know? Or do you have anything?"

"I don't have anything from my time with Sean, except for the divorce and annulment papers. They're in my file cabinet." She pointed to the guest bedroom where I knew she had her desk and a filing cabinet beneath it.

"My lawyer says Grady probably doesn't want to charge me. He just wants Sean and is trying to get information, and when Grady finds out I don't have any, he'll leave me alone. But I'm not as confident as Scott. To me, Grady feels like a dog with a bone. He's been trying to get Sean for years and can't, and he's frustrated. I'm afraid he'll take out his frustrations on me precisely because I have nothing to give him."

Our conversation seemed to simply run out of gas. There was nothing we could do until Scott got back to Sheila tomorrow. There was little we could say. We just sat in silence and sipped the last of our wine.

Finally Sheila broke the silence. "Have you eaten dinner?"

It was nearly ten o'clock by now. "Yea, I ate after work. How about you?"

"No, but I couldn't possibly eat anything."

"Let me make you a piece of toast and some tea with honey. Go get ready for bed, then let me out. It may be a long night, but then again you may sleep from sheer exhaustion."

Sheila looked like she wanted to protest, then simply nodded and walked toward her bedroom. I made the tea and toast. She came out of the bedroom in a royal blue silk kimono with matching silk slippers.

I laid the cup and plate on her counter and gave her a huge hug. As I walked to the car, I wondered how an ex-nun had developed such a sense of style that even her pajamas were beautiful. I went home and got in my jammies; a pair of sweat pants and an old flannel shirt of Kevin's.

I doubted if I could sleep, but the two glasses of wine coupled with the emotional nature of the evening, did me in. I was asleep the instant my head hit the pillow.

It was a zoo at work the next day, and I never had an opportunity to talk with Sheila.

I grabbed her in the hall between patients. "Have you heard from Scott?"

She nodded, yes.

I said, "Come by my house after work."

"It has to be my house today." *Odd, we always alternated houses.*

It seemed like days later when we were finally sitting on her sofa having a cup of tea with a spinach and artichoke dip and bagel chips. She'd sliced up some apples and cheddar cheese too. We ate on TV trays, with the TV on but muted.

Sheila felt a little relieved after talking with Scott. He said that he still didn't think Grady was going to bring charges against her. She seemed less confident than Scott but was willing to trust his opinion.

It was a huge relief to me also. I didn't want Sheila to suffer any more than she already had. Despite feeling somewhat resentful, I understood her desire to leave her past in the past. But it appeared I was wrong about her neighbor, Jack, who wasn't speaking to her.

Sheila said, "That's why we had to come to my house. He

wouldn't let Thor out. Jack showed up after you left the other night and threw my key at me and demanded his key back. He was indignant that I should have trusted him. He waved his arms around like they were windmills."

"Gay men can be so dramatic. Women could learn from them!"

I hoped Jack would come around out of compassion, or when he needed her to take care of his dog.

We made it an early evening because Fridays started early and were busy, if not necessarily long. I listened to the comedy channel on my way home hoping I'd hear some insult that I could fling at Cow Patty tomorrow.

Chapter 35

Friday after work, I heard a knock at my door and freaked; certain that Sporelli was back to hurt me. Then the door opened, and Gene yelled "It's me." He has a key to my house, but we're usually together so he rarely uses it.

I looked out of the front door and saw Gene's friends from the Publisher's Clearing House event. They saw me and waved as they pulled out with the big Chevy engine roaring.

"Gene, I'm delighted. To what do I owe the pleasure of your company on a Friday evening?"

"It's business rather than pleasure, Brava. Mafia business."

I'd tried to put it out of my mind, and it wasn't too terribly difficult what with all that was going on with Sheila. But deep down, I knew it wasn't going away.

"OK Gene. Before we get to business, have you eaten?"

"No. I'm starving too."

"You're always starving. Let's go in the kitchen, and I'll rustle something up."

I popped open the cork on a bottle of wine and poured a glass while I made toasted cheese sandwiches and an iceberg lettuce salad with balsamic vinaigrette dressing. I sautéed some artichoke hearts and sprinkled lemon and parmesan cheese over them. I made two sandwiches for Gene.

After we ate at the kitchen table, we headed to the living room. There was a chill in the air, so I lit the gas logs and snuggled up with my fleece blanket around my knees and the second glass of wine in my hand.

"Dare I ask about Sporelli? I really don't want to know, do I?"

"Brava, I did a lot of research on the Sporelli family. They're in deep with mafia business, but it isn't all nice taking care of the family like Sporelli said. They've been investigated for money laundering, gambling, prostitution, murder, illeg–"

"Murder?" If they've committed murder, why aren't they in jail?"

"Nothing's been proven, Brava. They're slippery and have great lawyers. But where there is smoke, there's fire. And there's been a LOT of smoke."

Gene continued. "And there's more."

I rolled my eyes. "Great. More than murder."

Gene continued. "That whole story with his brother. I don't think any of it is true. I think Sporelli made it up to get your sympathy."

"How would you know if it's true or not?"

"I wouldn't for certain, but there are no rumors of it. That's not proof it didn't happen, but there *is* a lot of information that Salvatore is making a play to become the mafia don of the South. He has boatloads of money and no job. There's talk in the Italian community that Gaetano should step down. He's not ambitious enough. And Sal has a lot of people backing him. I think Gaetano is dangerous, and Sal may be even more so. I don't know exactly how to get you out of this, but we need to. I know that for sure."

"Great, now I'm in the middle of a mafia war. What good is Dealan if she can't help me?"

"Who says she can't help you? She will; I'm sure of that. It's only a matter of keeping the powers a secret from anyone in the mafia. So far, Sporelli doesn't know anything and you've not admitted anything. We're good for a minute."

"But if I just give in, and I do this one thing for Sporelli, surely he'll leave me alone."

"You're right smack dab in the middle of a mafia war. You just need to keep your head down until I figure something out."

"Gene how did you find out about Salvatore's money and business dealings?"

He gave me the look he always gave me when he'd hacked.

"Great. So I'm in the middle of a mafia war and you hacked into their financial records."

He smirked. "The difference is they don't know about my hacking."

I kept my head down as Gene suggested, going only to work and Kung Fu and home. I screened my calls and watched to be sure no one followed me.

Friday morning, Cow Patty showed up as usual. She wafted in on her perfume wearing a red plaid skirt that went down to the ground. I couldn't even guess what decade that came from. She had a lime green cardigan over a yellow shirt. The cardigan was held together with safety pins.

"Good morning Brava. I'm here to see Dr. Sheila."

No shit. Just like every Friday for the past ten years. I never would have guessed.

"Of course, Mrs. Patty. I'll call her for you."

"You look lovely today, Brava."

Did I just hear that? Therapy may be working after all.

"Well, thank you so much, Mrs. Patty." I smiled.

"That color of blue really downplays the ruddiness of your skin and one would hardly notice the concealer under your eyes. Did you sleep poorly, dear?"

Just at that moment, Sheila appeared. I couldn't come back with a mean retort if I had one. I bet Cow Patty was watching and timed it that way.

I was still fuming over that bitch when I looked up to see John Grady coming toward the door. This was turning into a nightmare of a day and it wasn't quite eleven a.m.

Grady walked in and looked around the waiting room. Dr. Jackson had two patients waiting, and Sheila's next patient was already there.

He asked me when Dr. Barry would be free.

"May I ask what this is about?"

"No, you may not."

"She's with someone now and has another patient waiting for eleven. We take lunch at twelve."

"I'll be back at twelve. It would not be in her best interest to leave before seeing me. Tell her that."

That felt ominous. I tried to convince myself that he just wanted to ask more questions. That's what her attorney thought. But then again, he was a divorce attorney.

The phone rang. "Doctor's office. Brava speaking."

"Is Dr. Barry available?" *Everyone's looking for her.*

"She's with a patient. May I take a message?"

"This is Scott Barrett. I'm calling from California, and I need to speak to her as soon as possible. When will she be available?"

I turned my back to the waiting room and walked into the hallway to get out of earshot. "Mr. Barrett, I am Sheila's friend as well as her secretary. I don't know what you are able to divulge, but I think you are her attorney. So I'm going to tell you something, and then I hope you will tell me what to do for her."

Mr. Barrett gave a non-committal, "OK."

I continued, "John Grady from the FBI was just here and said he's coming back at twelve and said she had better be here. I think he may charge her. She is with a patient now and will be coming out at 10:50. She has someone waiting, but I can cancel him. I think perhaps I should, then she should talk with you. Does that seem like a good idea, Mr. Barrett?"

"Yes I think that's a good idea."

I made apologies to Mr. Elliott, Sheila's eleven o'clock, begging a family emergency, and counted the minutes until 10:50 when the bitch left. I had a hard time managing the energy and used my app in the bathroom.

As soon as Cow Patty got out the door I grabbed Sheila's arm and dragged her to the bathroom. I gave her the note to call her attorney, told her I rescheduled Mr. Elliott and told her about Grady coming back at twelve.

I saw fear in her face, and I hated it for my wonderful friend.

Sheila called me back to her office at 11:45.

"I've just spent the last hour consulting with a criminal defense attorney. Now there are three words that I never thought I'd have in my life."

"I know, right?" I thought back to the last few weeks. *When had I begun to have the words "police" and "mafia" in my life.*

I continued. "Life comes at us fast."

"Scott was on the call too. They don't think he'll able to get me on accessory to money laundering. But Grady does have enough to charge me for tax evasion on the sale of the jewelry. It's a criminal offense. They still think Grady is just using me to give up information on Sean, but I have a bad feeling about him. Truth be told, I'd love for them to get Sean on something for what he put me through."

Sheila continued. "Scott and Parker – that's the criminal guy – got their research department to do a search on me to see if they could find anything to implicate me. They've been working on it for a while."

"What did they find?" I asked.

"They found the money from the jewelry sales and the trip to the Caymans just like Grady did but nothing else; because there is nothing else. That cost me $1500 that I'll never see again."

"Next time, let me know and Gene could do it for ya for free."

"Brava, they had a whole research team on this. What could a fifteen-year-old boy do?"

Plenty. I thought but let it drop. Gene didn't need to get found out.

"What did they think Grady is likely to do when he comes back?"

"They have information that he is coming here to charge me. They–"

I interrupted. "What do you mean? I thought you said they didn't find anything? Oh my God, Sheila, could you go to jail over this?"

I was babbling and I instantly regretted my outburst. "I'm so sorry. You don't need me getting all hysterical and jumping to conclusions. What can I do for you?"

"Look Brava, they can charge me with just about anything. They have enough to get that far, but the likelihood of me going to jail is low. The likelihood of them turning my life upside down and turning me over to the IRS is good. It's possible that they could get the tax evasion to stick."

I remarked, "You seem pretty calm."

"I'm not. My insides are running like a motor. I'm terrified. But I'm holding it together until I know exactly what I'm dealing with."

Grady arrived promptly at twelve, and I escorted him back to Sheila's office. She looked stricken. I'd never seen her face like that. As Grady walked in, I mouthed the words, "I'll be there," and pointed to the break room.

He didn't even give her the courtesy of closing the door. He said, "Sheila Barry, I am arresting you for the crimes of tax evasion and accessory to money laundering. You have the right to remain silent. You have the –" and he continued Mirandizing her while I stood there with my mouth agape.

Thank God, he didn't handcuff her and haul her away. He gave her a sheet of paper with the time and place for the arraignment. Then he turned on his heel and walked out of the office.

We were so stunned, we both stood still for what seemed like hours, but was only moments. Then I said, "Call the attorneys back. Right now."

While Sheila discussed her future with the attorneys, I ordered pizza to be delivered. I wondered if she could eat, but I was starving. I wolfed three pieces waiting for her to get off the phone and fill me in, but by the time she was done, the waiting room was filling up with patients. We made it through the rest of the day, and I needed ten glasses of wine to take the edge off. I didn't have nearly enough stones taped to me.

Mrs. Johnson dropped off a urine sample in a brown paper bag for us to test for a bladder infection. I carried it back to the lab to get away from the waiting room. *Might as well test it. Everyone's busy and it's Friday.* Then I could get Dr. Jackson to call in a script if she needed it.

When I opened the bag, I found five bananas. Five bananas. *The mafia is after me to become an enforcer because I have superpowers. Sheila just got arrested. I'm looking for urine and I found bananas.* And all I could picture was the person looking for the bananas and finding the urine. As Gene suggested, "Is your life more ironic than most people's?"

Apparently.

I laughed so hard, I started snorting and squeezing my legs together. When the tears start, so does the pee. I was becoming hysterical. Sheila found me there laughing with my head in my hands. I kept pointing and repeating, "Bananas. Bananas."

"Are you OK?" Sheila asked with a look of concern on her face.

"Bananas."

"Seriously Brava, are you OK or should I call Dr. Jackson?"

"I'm bananas. That's what. I'm bananas. God give me the weekend."

Chapter 36

I was home drinking wine when Gene walked in with three of his friends.

"I'm delighted, but don't you boys have someone better to hang with on a Friday night?"

"Aunt Brava, I've been worried about you. I've called your cell phone a half a dozen times since school got out."

I was puzzled because I hadn't heard it ring, so I went looking for my purse. I usually throw it on the dining room table but it wasn't there. Gene called my number, and we all searched. We followed the sound to the bathroom and found my purse with the ringing phone in the dirty clothes hamper. All four boys looked at me with questions on their faces.

"It was a really bad day. I looked for urine and found bananas, Sheila got arrested by the FBI, and ..."

Gene interrupted, "What? Ex-nun, perfect Sheila got what?"

"She got arrested for money laundering and tax evasion, but the money laundering probably won't stick."

Gene held up his hands palms out, in a "stop" gesture and looked at me out of the corner of his eye, "Brava, have you been drinking?"

I nodded. "Uh hunh. But not nearly enough."

I guess the boys thought I might be better entertainment than whatever they had planned, so they hung out with me for the evening. We ordered pizza, and I didn't even care that I'd had pizza for lunch and my ass was as wide as the side of a barn. But I only had one piece because that left more room for wine.

I was on my third glass when I got to the part of the day with the urine and bananas. All the boys were doubled over laughing. That started a pee joke fest.

Jared told the first joke. "A lifeguard blew his whistle at a boy in a public pool.

"Hey! Don't pee in the pool!' The boy yelled back, 'But everybody does!'

'Not from the diving board!"

Gene and the boys were laughing, and I think I laughed harder than all of them.

Kurt joined in "I can top that."

"Two drunk women stopped in a cemetery to take a pee. The first one had nothing to wipe with so she used her panties. Her friend squatted next to a grave with a wreath so she used the ribbon to wipe.

The next morning the first husband called the other. 'My wife came home with no panties!' 'That›s nothing' said the other, 'Mine came back with a ribbon stuck to her ass that said 'From all of us at the Fire Station. We›ll never forget you.'"

The last one was the best. "I got no superpowers. All I can do is turn water into pee."

Well that did it. The day, the wine, and the pee jokes sent me running to the bathroom squeezing my legs together. I almost made it.

Chapter 37

I t was Thanksgiving, my first without Kevin, and we all went to Mom and Dad's. My heart was heavy, but the food was to die for. Mom had outdone herself. She'd cooked a twenty-three pound turkey and we had sixteen sides and three kinds of pie. It was during the after-dinner hangover when everyone began clamoring for a Cathy story. Those stories had become the highlight of the Falcone family dinners since the divorce. I had a Thanksgiving one all prepared. I began weaving the story.

"One year Kevin and I and the girls got our asses up at five a.m. to go to Alabama to Cathy and Bubba's for Thanksgiving."

I continued, "On the way there, I asked Kevin what we were having. I was wondering if it was turkey or ham or both."

Kevin answered. "Turducken." Like I would know what that was.

Gene said, "I know what it is. I saw it on Duck Dynasty. It's a chicken stuffed inside a duck stuffed inside a turkey."

Everyone looked at Gene as if he were crazy. I giggled at the looks on their faces and continued with my story. "So Kevin answered me matter-of-factly just like Gene did. 'It's a chicken stuffed inside a duck, stuffed inside a turkey. But at the time I thought he was joking so I started to laugh. Then I realized he wasn't laughing."

I asked him again, "What is it?" At the time I was incredulous.

Gene was laughing harder at this point in my story.

"Kevin repeated himself in that maddening way he had as if by saying the same thing over and over I'd get it. 'A turducken.'"

"Is that a real thing? I can't even believe you can do that. Stuff one in the other that way. And I'm most sure it is disrespectful. Kinda like the Jews don't mix meat and dairy. If you're serious and it's a real thing, I'm not having any."

Dad said, "I've eaten it once with the guys I play cards with. It's actually pretty good."

"Well, I never got to try it. If I ever would have.

"So Bubba called us all outside to witness the moment that thing went into the fryer. Seems they debone those animal carcasses and jam them one inside the other and then deep fry it. Everyone was gathered around except the girls and me. So Bubba holds this thing up over his head like it's a holy offering and drops it in the hot grease."

I paused for effect.

"And the whole damn thing exploded!" Everyone broke up laughing.

"Figures." Olivia said, "How could you keep those stories to yourself all these years?"

"I was trying to be a good wife. And look what that got me?"

"Widowed?" laughed Olivia.

Everyone looked puzzled. We replayed our private joke for the rest of the family. They still looked puzzled.

"Guess you had to be there."

I brought them back to the Thanksgiving debacle.

"The thing was still partially frozen so it caused an explosion. Grease went flying and the "terfurk," or whatever it's called flew up in the air and landed on the ground in a pansy patch. Missy started screaming and everyone hovered around her as she'd gotten the worst of it. The grease had spattered her face and hair. She kept screaming so badly, I feared she was seriously injured even though I couldn't see anything, so I snatched her up and took her to the emergency room. They put a little ice on her face and said she'd be fine. Well then she was caterwauling about her hair. She'd just had it done the day before.

"Cathy and I tried to wash Missy's hair in the kitchen sink but the grease foiled all of our attempts. Then she was greasy *and* wet.

"Well, LuLuanne was Missy's hairdresser of thirty years. And God bless her, she went in on Thanksgiving. Missy was upside down in that sink for three hours while LuLu used Dawn dishwashing liquid like rescuers use on those poor sea birds after an oil spill.

"When we got her out of the sink she had a crick in her neck and couldn't turn her head. She wanted us to call her Chiropractor. At that point, I'd had enough. My family hadn't eaten since five a.m. and Kevin was just sitting on the sofa watching football with Bubba. There was no turkey, ham or other damn stuffed animal carcass. No food at all.

"I found a phone book and ordered Chinese food from the only restaurant in town that was opened. That's a cliché, huh?" They all laughed.

"I should have run screaming from the restaurant when I saw a sombrero hanging over a kimono. Can you imagine Mexicans cooking Chinese food? Why didn't they just have a Mexican restaurant?

"In the end, Kevin drove through a fast food place and we all ate hamburgers in the car. The kids slept the whole way home and then he carried them to bed. We were so exhausted we all slept with our clothes on. It was the worst Thanksgiving I've ever had."

Everyone was laughing really hard at this point.

In an instant, I went from laughing along with everyone to a terrible feeling of sadness. I missed Kevin. I wanted him with me this Thanksgiving. I wanted him with me every Thanksgiving for the rest of our lives.

I burst into tears and blurted out, "And he left me! I put up with all that shit from his family, and he left me!! That bastard." I stood there sobbing.

Everyone got really quiet. I heard Gene say "Awkward." I felt bad that I had ruined the moment.

Liv rescued the moment by saying "Maybe that's why he went to Turkey and became a Muslim; to get away from his family rather than to get away from you."

Even I had to laugh at that.

Chapter 38

A first Friday sewing circle was fast approaching, and I wondered how I would handle it. I hadn't touched the sewing machine since the lightning, in part because I was afraid I'd hurt myself and partly because every spare minute was taken up trying to manage it. I'd already cancelled several orders and was falling behind in the rest. I'd grown accustomed to the money from the purses, but I also had a good client base, and I didn't want to let them down.

I had figured out that wine helped me relax even better than the breathing app, so I decided to just start early and keep drinking and we'd all be OK. I longed for the simple, familiar things in my life, and I really looked forward to the food, the music and the friends. If I kept them plied with wine, maybe they wouldn't notice if scissors or pins wiggled or jiggled.

As Friday neared, I planned my menu; baked chicken breasts marinated in balsamic vinegar and rosemary with a sprinkle of lemon zest and parmesan cheese. I'd serve it on a bed of brown rice with steamed spinach. A nice white Riesling for everyone because it went better with the chicken, but I preferred red for myself.

It was necessary for me to sew prior to Friday just to be sure I didn't turn the sewing machine into a lethal weapon. So, on Wednesday evening, I went home from work and taped a few extra stones to the back of my hands and had a glass of wine. I found that I could handle it quite well. Then I realized the girls might notice that I had stones taped to the back of my hands, so I removed them. So far so good.

As I sewed I thought about the times my powers manifested and when they didn't. If I was ever going to be a superhero, I had to figure this out. I found it curious that I had begun to think of myself that way lately. I sipped my wine, and my thoughts wandered. I recalled the time Terry smashed into the fountain, when Brad had fire ants bite his balls, the red truck careening down the culvert, the male scammer in his lucite box, the woman being bitten much like Terry. I thought about the time in the backyard with Gene when I couldn't get the cans to move, the times at work when things wiggled and jiggled.

Before I knew it, I had finished one entire purse and had gotten an insight. Gene was right about there being injustices, but there was more. It was my emotional state, not my thoughts. That's why it seemed to so random. And that's why it didn't work when I "thought" about the cans. Each time I used my powers, I was frustrated or worried or angry. And each time the powers had a mind of their own, I was also emotional. I knew now why sometimes items didn't respond; because I was relaxed and happy; like with Lucia and Sheila. And when I had wine!

I couldn't wait to tell Gene, so I called him right away. He came over to spend the night, and I told him of my epiphany.

He was enthusiastic. "Of course, Brava! I should have figured it out sooner. Emotions have vibrations that can be measured with specialized equipment. If the vibrations are in harmony, it's called coherence and is related to the parasympathetic nervous sys–"

I interrupted. "You're doing that thing you do when you're enthusiastic. Talk in English to this mere mortal." I slowed my speech down and continued, "And talk slowly."

Gene could hardly contain himself but managed to slow down to breakneck speed rather than the speed of light.

"Remember when you first got the powers and we talked about hertz, and rate of vibration, and how your vibrations were raised by the lightning?"

I nodded. I find it best to keep words to a minimum when he's on a roll.

"Oh my gosh Brava, this makes so much sense. I can't believe I didn't get it until now."

"I believe I'm the one who 'got it' Gene. A little credit?"

"Sure, sure." But he continued on a mile a minute. "You change your vibrations with your emotions, raising them and lowering them so you can make objects move. But it's even more than that. It's fucking awesome. You can even create with your energy. The lucite cage for example."

"I can create? That's weird and scary." *Only God can create.*

He stopped and rolled his eyes upward like he could look inside his own brain and get the answer.

"Maybe you change their brain with your vibrations? Maybe the cage isn't there at all. They just think it is. The fire ants too. Brava we need to do some experiments."

"Gene, I'm exhausted. I was relieved that I understood the lightning better, but now I'm overwhelmed. I'm constantly trying to control these powers and you're constantly trying to get me to use them. I need to go to bed."

I left Gene pounding away on his laptop; no doubt researching vibrations, and I fell into a restless slumber. In my dreams, the hawk sat watchful on my windowsill.

I had work and Gene had school the next day, but it didn't stop him from following me around as I got ready. I felt lucky that he actually waited until I got out of the shower and got some clothes on. I was sucking down my coffee and leaning in toward the mirror, putting on my eyeliner while Gene babbled.

"Brava, it's so exciting. This opens so many new possibilities with your powers."

"Great. Just what I wanted." Sarcasm dripped off my words.

"No really Brava. Dealan has helped right injustices over thousands of years by raising vibrations, but never have we had such specialized instruments to measure them. We can hook you up to a machine and measure the rate of vibration as you feel each different emotion and then you can ..."

I pictured one of the old black and white spy films where they had the hero hooked up to a machine with aluminum foil electrodes taped to his head. It hadn't gone well for him. Gene prattled on with great enthusiasm all the while I put on my face and got breakfast and drove him to school. I added a few extra Julian stones since the knowledge rattled me more than calmed me.

Chapter 39

The radio was playing Elvis Presley's Suspicious Minds, and I was singing along as I drove.

"We're caught in a trap
I can't walk out
Because I love you too much baby."

Too bad Kevin didn't feel like that.

I needed some Sifu time but wondered if I was intruding on his Sunday workout. He seemed happy to see me. I could tell by his eye squint if not his snide comment.

"Brava, did you show up looking for some punishment?"

"No, Sifu. I just needed to soak up some good chi energy. I don't want to disturb your workout. Please pretend I'm not even here."

"No, I've been thinking about working with you on controlling your chi. This is a perfect opportunity. I can't do it when other students are in class."

"OK. I'm game for that."

In my mind, I envisioned holding poses for what seemed like hours while I "became" some random emotion.

"It's been a long time since we fought, Brava. I don't want you to lose the movements in your body. No contact, just light touch fighting."

This was far from the good chi soaking I came here for. It had been a long time since I'd fought, but I still recalled those times Sifu pushed me to the breaking point. He had perfect control so he never injured me, but I frequently left with bruises and abrasions and very wounded pride. I often cried the whole way home, but I'd never let Sifu see me cry.

I took a deep breath and gathered my energy into my pelvis and solar plexus. From there I could use it to "push" or "defend."

We began lightly sparring using gentle punches, knife hands, back fists and a few kicks. I was feeling the flow of the chi and doing pretty well. In the next second, I was on my ass. Sifu had swept me and let me hit the mat. He usually grabbed me up at the last second. I sat there a little stunned.

"I thought you said no contact." I pouted.

"You were distracted. It may be "no contact" but you need to be fully present. Fight as if your life were on the line always. This is no game, Brava. This is a martial art. If you don't want to do martial arts, go do yoga or ballet."

That stung.

We continued, and I gathered my energy and got back into the flow. Again, he swept behind my knee, but this time he grabbed me up at the last minute and then flung me forward to the mat face first. He let go, and I hit my chin hard. My teeth clacked together.

I was pissed. This was full-out fighting. I jumped up and lunged at him with a face punch. I telegraphed it a mile away, so he simply stepped an inch or so to the left and used my poor balance against me to take me down with a wrist lock. He quickly let me up and scolded me for getting angry.

I recovered my wits and was determined to get a hold of myself. What if the energy got away from me? I couldn't let that happen.

We went on fighting, and I garnered a little more control of my emotions. I never got a strike on him, and he peppered me with light taps to the face and then a wrist lock or take down. Sometimes he stopped me from hitting too hard on the floor and other times he let me fall hard. I was starting to feel angry again and was having trouble reigning it in. I asked for a break, and he answered with a front kick to my solar plexus. He pulled it, but it took my breath all the same.

Why is he doing this to me?

I was struggling to get my breath and trying not to show it when he came at me with a flurry of kicks, punches and strikes that ended in a takedown. I felt tears sting my eyelids. I jumped up and lunged at him with fists flailing like a girl. He grabbed them easily and took me down again. I couldn't stop the tears any longer. I was crying and trying to get my breath at the same time, but it came out in gulps and sobs. Still he showed no mercy. He struck at my ribs and solar plexus until I was hyperventilating. He swept me yet again, and I stayed down on my ass.

He reached out his hand, and I assumed he'd taken mercy on me. When I grabbed it, he flung me around into a choke hold and held me against his chest with his forearm, choking me. I tapped his leg, the universal sign for concession, but he continued to choke me. I tapped again harder. He choked harder. I saw stars forming in front of my eyes. I tapped urgently and struggled. Anger flared in me like a fire fed with gasoline. It erupted. Then came the nausea and telescoping of the room. It was happening, and I had no strength to stop it. I couldn't breathe myself calm.

In the next instant, swords, canes, staffs and other implements of destruction flew off the shelves. I was hardly aware of what was happening. I was barely conscious and only held up by Sifu's arm around my throat. Sifu finally let go of my choke hold. I sunk to the mat on my hands and knees sobbing and gasping with my head hung down like a beaten dog. Finally, fearfully I gaped up at him. He stood in the middle of the room with weapons on the floor all around him. He just stayed like that. I did too. After a few moments I was able to regulate my breath a little.

I rolled from hands and knees to a seat. Still I stared at him. He came and sat in front of me.

"I thought it might be you, Brava, but I had to know."

Honestly, I had no words. A rarity for me, but I had absolutely no words that I could formulate from my brain to my mouth. I just sat and stared.

So did he.

Hours, days, years went by while we sat and stared at each other.

Finally, he said. "Shall I enlighten you?"

I simply nodded.

"You are not alone," he began.

"How many?" I mumbled.

"I don't know them all. I know four."

Four in Atlanta, in Kung Fu? "Where?"

"In the world; that I know of."

For one brief moment, I had begun to feel a sense of relief that I was not as alone as I had felt these many months. But this realization swept any comfort away. I was recovering my wits a little.

"In the whole freaking world, there are only four?"

"That I know of. There are probably more, but I don't know them."

I stared at him.

He stared back.

Finally, I asked. "How did you know?"

"I didn't until today. But I suspected a while ago."

"When?"

"The day you held horse pose when Gene and I fought. I saw what almost happened."

"Are you one too?" I asked him.

"No. I'm a teacher, a guide."

Suddenly it was all too much. I started to cry. I had a million questions, but I couldn't articulate any except one.

"Sifu, can you make it go away?"

"No, Brava. But I can make it easier for you."

"Sometimes I do want it. If you can make it easier, maybe I want the powers after all," I continued. "The others ... who are they?"

"You're the Celtic one, there's an Indian, a Caucasian, a Samoan I think, and some others."

Samoan? That's weird.

I asked. "Who's the Caucasian? Do we know him?"

"It's a she. I know her. You know of her. Remember the Miss Teen USA pageant where the girl totally flubbed her question and the video went viral over the internet?"

"Yea, Miss South Carolina, I think. What about her?"

"It's her," Sifu said.

"What do you mean, it's her?" I asked.

"She's the Caucasian superhero."

"Well, fucking wonderful. I'm in great company."

He just laughed. "Yea, like you two have absolutely nothing in common, right?"

He had a point.

Chapter 40

To get Sporelli off my back, I needed to get Salvatore to go to Italy one way or the other. I'd promised Gene that I wouldn't act alone but I was considering doing it anyway. I hated to break a promise to him, and it scared me even more to think he'd do the same. At least I had superpowers.

I dropped in to Sporelll's store, hoping to run into him. I wanted to meet with him, but I didn't want to go into his office alone, and I didn't want him to know I was coming. I perused the imported delicacies that were too expensive for me to purchase, finally choosing some olive oil. I put it on the counter and noticed that it was the same young lady that had served us in Sporelli's office.

"Hello. I don't know if you remember me, but I'm Brava Falcone, and my nephew and I met with Mr. Sporelli a week ago in his office."

"Yes ma'am, I served you."

"I just came to pick up this olive oil my mom likes. Is Mr. Sporelli in today, by chance, I'd like to give him regards from my mom."

"Certainly, Mrs. Falcone. Right this way."

Shit, I didn't want to go into his office.

"Oh no, dear, I don't want to bother him, and I'd like to look around a moment more. I do so covet those dishes. If he's busy, just give him regards from my mom, Eugenia."

I hoped Sporelli would come out into the showroom so I could pick his brain about the job he wanted me to do, but no way was I going in that office alone. Sure enough, out he came. He was dressed impeccably as always in a tawny brown suit with a silver shirt, royal blue tie and matching pocket hanky. His shoes and belt were light gray suede and his three karat tie pin glittered like the North Star.

We exchanged fake pleasantries.

"Mr. Sporelli, I am considering the task you asked me to do, but I'd like more details."

We walked around the store. It was empty except for the sales girl who kept her distance.

"Brava, just do what you did to your mother's scammers. Whatever that was certainly worked."

I ignored the comment but asked, "Where is Salvatore? How do I even get a meeting with him?"

"We're having a pool party with the entire Sporelli clan and a few close friends this Sunday afternoon after the 11:00 Mass at St. Wolfgang's."

That was the church Mom went to for the big yard sale. Not only the biggest Catholic church in the city but the richest. Figures. I remembered the party with the Malones where I sent Brad, slapping his ass, into the drink. No one caught me that time.

I said to Sporelli, "Assuming I could do something to rattle Salvatore, how could I possibly get him to go to Sicily?"

"You know my son, Antonio, isn't that correct Brava?"

He knows I do. I told him at my house. "Sure, he played with my Louma when they were little."

"Do you know my son's unfortunate choice for an occupation?"

"Yep, Mr. Sporelli. I've actually taken the Ghost Tour, though at the time I did not recognize Boo as your Antonio."

"My brother Sal puts a lot of stock in Boo's abilities. He's very superstitious along with his other more grave faults. He consulted my son last week and I overheard the conversation."

I thought. "Yep, Gene was right. He probably taped it."

"Antonio told him that a big move is coming and instructed him to look for a sign to help him make difficult choices. Antonio said that our dear, departed mother Gabriella, is watching him closely hoping that he will make the noble choice. You, Brava, will be the sign that makes him choose to go to Sicily."

I said nothing. Sporelli continued. "Our mother loved red poppies. They grow ubiquitously in Sicily. I don't care what you do or how you do it, but I'll have some red poppies you can use to convince Salvatore that it is a sign from our mother."

I hate that word "ubiquitous." I don't really understand what it means and it sounds pompous.

"If that's all that's needed, why don't you get Boo to do it? Salvatore already trusts him."

"I've approached my son with this, and he refused."

"So you came to me? What if I refuse?"

"Then I fear something dreadful could happen to your beloved Gene. This city is just not safe for young people."

So the niceties were officially over. I felt sick and nauseous and that dreadful vertigo that happened whenever I used the powers came over me. I knew Dealan was here and I felt glad.

I looked that mafia son of a bitch right in the eye. "Gaetano, you listen to me. I'll do what I can to get that child molesting pig to the fate he deserves in Sicily. But if you so much as touch a hair on Gene's head or anyone else's in my family, then what happened to those scammers will look like a princess birthday party for six-year-old girls. Furthermore, if anything happens to anyone in my family, whether you ordered it or not, I'll come after you. So you better set up some very good protection for every member of my family. Are we clear?"

He looked as shocked as I felt. Those words were not mine. Dealan must have come through me, but it felt good. Sporelli recovered quickly. I guess it was his mafia experience that helped him. He obviously had more mafia experience than I had superpower experience because I was suddenly unnerved. I was losing Dealan's fierceness, and I felt vulnerable. I wasn't about to let him know it, though. I turned on my heel and threw the words over my shoulder. "Get me some fucking poppies for Sunday."

Then in a sweet voice loud enough for the sales clerk, I said "Bye, Bye Mr. Sporelli. It was so nice to see you again, and I'll give Mom your regards. See you Sunday."

Shit, shit, shit what just happened? It took all my composure to walk, not run to my car.

Gene was going to kill me when I told him. I was taking him to the party on Sunday, so I had to tell him.

Gene surprised me again with his reaction. He was angry that I went there alone, but he was more excited that Dealan would show up to protect me.

"See Aunt Brava, I told you she was there to protect you and not just simply for injustice. She'll protect you." He emphasized "you."

"I'm still not sure she is there to help me. She may have just got my ass in trouble. I popped off pretty good to Sporelli."

"As much as I don't like it that you're involved in this, I get the impression that Sporelli won't stop. Not that I think he will after this either, but at least you'll show him not to mess with you. And I suspect if he ever came at you hard, Dealan would show up and help you kick his ass."

I couldn't plan exactly what would happen on Sunday, but I typed some notes "from Sal's mother" begging him to return to their homeland to heal his soul. I didn't know if I'd use them or not, but I wanted to be prepared in some small way.

Sunday turned out to be a beautiful day for a pool party, but I was a nervous wreck. Parties are not my favorite events under the best of circumstances, and these were far from that. Gene and I arrived at 2:30, and the party was in full gear. I wanted to get in and out and with as few people seeing me as possible. I sneaked with Gene to the side of the house where I had a view of everyone, but where I was hidden unless someone looked really hard.

Scanning the group, I located Sporelli talking with the goon that drove him to my house. His wife was with a group of women, a few who I recognized, from when our kids were little. Those women, save for Concetta, treated me like I was lower than dirt. They were super rich, and I always figured their husbands were connected. Now I was sure. Antonio was telling ghost stories to a group of youngsters. Gene spotted Salvatore and pointed him out to me. He was at the bar downing one shot after another of what looked like whiskey. All the better for me, I thought, if he's drunk.

I found a huge plastic vase with about a thousand poppies propped up against the side of the house. I asked Gene to take a few poppies and unobtrusively place them on the bar beside Sal's drink. Gene sauntered over towards the bar like he belonged there. Sal had his head turned toward Boo and Gene scooted the poppies alongside his drink and walked casually back to me. No one took any notice. We watched as Sal turned to take another drink. He saw the poppies and looked around curiously.

The party was pretty raucous at this point and most people were blitzed. As usual, I was doubting Dealan and my powers and worried I couldn't get my emotions high enough, but alas I needn't have worried. Just the tension of the party was enough for some mischief. I raised a little gust of wind under the dress of a woman who was a bitch to me back in the day. Her dress flew up over her face and she let out a little yelp as she struggled to press it back down around her thighs. *Yup that worked.* I was satisfied to notice that she had on granny panties.

I did the same to Sal, though not to raise his dress. I blew a poppy in a gust of wind toward his face. He was getting bleary eyed from the drinks, so his reaction was kinda slow. Then he saw the poppy, and his face blanched and his eyes sorta bugged out. I'd have to really up the ante to scare Sal enough to make him think his dear departed Mama wanted him in Sicily.

Another of the rich bitches that treated me like dirt was floating on a raft sipping some hot pink umbrella drink. She was made up to the nines, dripping in gold jewelry with a gold bathing suit and a gold headband on her fake gold hair. So I gathered some anger and sent a huge wind over the pool causing some mighty waves and tipping her and her umbrella drink into the water. She came up sputtering with raccoon eyes and black mascara streaks running down her cheeks. I enjoyed that. People were looking up toward the sky and scattering toward the house. I tipped over a table loaded with pastries just to be mean.

Gene was laughing and egging me on. "This is so fun, Brava. Raise another dress or two, but pick a hottie this time." He pointed to one of the young women that looked like a stripper. She had on a green halter dress that barely covered her nipples. Her enhanced boobs showed quite a lot of cleavage in the center and they were bulging out under her armpits on the sides. I couldn't help myself at this point. It only took a tiny sideways gust to blow the straps of her dress right off her shoulders. Those babies didn't even jiggle. They just stood at attention, and it didn't faze her one bit for them to be bared. I guess she was used to showing them off.

Gene was giggling like a girl.

Sporelli was herding everyone into the pool house, so he had his back to me. I was getting into it and gestured with my head toward the poppies, lifting them out of the vase and sending them flying toward Salvatore. I had a tornado-like wind fly them in a circle around his head and let them fall at his feet. I sent one of them stem first like a dart up his nose. The red part of the poppy was the only thing sticking out. I found it hilarious and so I did it again with a second poppy. Then I flew one of the notes "from Gabriella" toward him like a paper airplane. It hit him right between the eyes and fluttered to the bar beside his drink. He pulled the poppies out of his nose, and I noticed there were boogers on them. Gene was snorting. Sal took one look at the note and hit the deck; out cold and flat on his face. I think he broke his nose.

"That's it for us, Gene. We're out of here."

We scooted around the side of the house and ran to our car that we'd left down the street. Gene drove while I got a hold of myself. It was lots easier than the time with the scammers.

"Gene, I'm getting good at this. And I loved it!"

"It's a blast for me too Aunt Brava. Have you changed your mind about dropping the principal's pants? We could have some fun."

"I thought you were ridiculous when you suggested it, but I guess I have the same sense of humor as a fifteen-year-old boy. I really got off messing with those bitches. Maybe we can work something out."

I paused, thinking, then said "If I'm going to be a superhero, I'd really like to be a noble one, but the only thing is, I'm just not very noble."

Chapter 41

The next morning I got a call from Gaetano thanking me for taking care of Salvatore.

"He boarded a flight to Sicily this morning."

"Mr. Sporelli, I don't know what you mean. I never made it to your party yesterday. Something came up."

Sporelly sputtered, taken aback but recovered quickly.

"Brava, don't you mess with me. I know there's something about you that you don't want me to know. I will find out."

"Mr. Sporelli if there is something about me as you say, and I'm not saying there is, you had better remember what I said about taking care of my family. Do not dare to threaten me."

I hung up the phone. I pondered the situation with the mafia. Gene was probably right about Sporelli being unwilling to let it go. He wanted to use me, but I hoped I had bought some time. Maybe Sifu could help with that.

Chapter 42

I got a text from Sifu. "Call me when you have a few minutes alone to talk."

Since he'd found out about my powers we'd not had any time alone. I assumed he had spoken with the Association for the Development of Superheroes, or whatever the hell they called their ruling body. At least, I assumed they had a ruling body. So much to learn.

I hoped his text meant we were going to begin training. I needed help. I couldn't get a moment alone until lunchtime and my anxiety was bad so I needed my app. I nearly shoved the last patient out the door and flew out of the office to talk in my car.

He answered on the first ring. "Brava, there's been a situation. The Association called for us to meet Ashely and assist her. A ten-year-old boy was kidnapped by a group called SASH, and we have to save the kid."

"Sifu, I don't know what to do. I've just been winging it. Isn't there someone else who is better at this? We haven't even begun my tr–"

He cut me off. "Brava, there's no time for your insecurity. Get Gene. We need his hacking skills."

"You know about that?"

He sneered. "I know everything." He went back to his real voice. "Brava, let's just say I'm well informed. I'll fill you in more on the way."

"On the way to where, where are we going?"

"Bald Knob, Arkansas."

"Seriously, a kid is in danger and I'm going with Miss South Carolina to Bald Knob Arkansas to rescue him? This sounds bad, Sifu. Who kidnapped him?"

"The Society Against Superheroes. Acronym SASH."

"Oh, my God. There's a society against us? How do they even know we exist? Fuck, fuck, fuck. I have more enemies than the Israelis. I don't want to do this. This is a bad idea, Sifu."

"You may be right, but we're doing it. We think the kid may have powers, and we can't let that be known by this group. You can imagine the danger he's in. Breathe, Brava. Suck it up. We're gonna do this. We leave at eight."

Personal message from A K Robbins

It is for you, my readers, that I write so it would mean a lot if you'd send a short email to introduce yourself. I answer every email personally because you are important to me … but give me a minute to respond please.

I'll email you as soon as the next book in the Brava series is available. My loyal fans will get advance notice and special discounts on upcoming books.

bravafalcone@gmail.com

Follow Brava on Twitter @bravafalcone

Follow Brava on Facebook at https://www.facebook.com/brava.falcone

Checkout my website at www.BravaFalcone.com

Keep in touch with Brava Falcone via twitter @bravafalcone

Also check out her website at bravafalcone.com

Become a loyal fan

Biography of A K Robbins

Every day, I walked the three-mile path along the creeks near my home. And every day I felt my worries and concerns fall away as my senses took in the beauty. But this day I couldn't let go of an incident that bothered me. I kept playing it over and over in my mind, and before I knew it, I had reached the confluence of two creeks. I realized that I had missed the beauty of the morning. At that instant, a great blue heron flew up from out of the creek and circled away. The next moment a Cooper hawk flew, screeching along the creek, and circled behind me. I heard a voice inside my head say "That hawk has a message for you." I followed its continuing calls to a clearing and found him perched on a lone branch high above me. He looked all around in a circle and then down at me and screeched eight, nine, ten times. Then he looked all around again and repeated the screeching eight times, nine times. I felt certain that he was chastising me. Over and over he repeated this as the dew soaked my shoes and chilled my feet. But I stood still as I waited and counted his calls. One hundred and fifty times he screeched before he took one last look down at me and flew away.

It had been a sacred moment, and I understood his lesson. I was to look around and see the big picture so I could follow my destiny and fly.

From that day forward, on every walk, these characters and their stories dropped into my head.

CPSIA information can be obtained at www.ICGtesting.com
Printed in the USA
BVOW04s1534311214

381558BV00012B/348/P